SHADOWS AND NIGHT

Children of Dark
Book One

"The children of the Gods are
blessed, but also cursed."

Brionna Paige McClendon

Brionna Paige McClendon
Visit my website at www.facebook.com/brionnapaigebooks

Printed in the United States of America

First Printing: October 2018

ISBN 9781719944397

"When Darkness Loves the Light, One Shall Always be in Pain."

TABLE OF CONTENTS

PROLOGUE

LONG AGO, it was said that the Goddess of Dark and the God of Light were once lovers. Lovers who shared the world. For when there was light, shadows could sometimes be found. And when there was dark, there was the moon to ignite the night.

But their affair did not last long. For the God of Light; Nicitis, had been caught sharing his body with the Goddess of the Earth; Sybil.

Severina, the Goddess of Dark, cried out in rage and heartache. And when she did, shadows darker than the darkest night poured forth from her mouth and curtained half the world in her darkness – exiling the light from *her* land.

And when the long years passed, their children were enemies. Once their Gods blessed them as they were birthed into this world, they were forever marked as enemies. And so, their Gods feud carried on through them and still through the centuries that passed.

CHAPTER ONE

A BLOOD CONDENTAI

"The beginning of every story is a mystery until the final chapters."

THE NIGHT SEEMED TO BREATHE, and as it exhaled, more shadows cast themselves across the land. Veils of darkness draped over the world – or just this portion of the land. The part of it ruled by the Goddess of Dark; Severina.

A land that only knew eternal darkness. A land where the sun nor the moon never blessed it with their light. A land whose people became the monsters that lurked within the shadows. People who craved blood just as much as they craved the darkness that their Goddess blessed them and this land of Ventaria with.

Eternal night for the children of the Goddess so that they may prowl and hunt until the eternity of darkness claimed their souls and they returned to their Goddess's side and remain there until time itself turned to dust.

Many lives faded with time, bodies growling feeble and aged. Hearts that grew weak and struggled to beat. Lungs that grew shriveled and could hardly hold a breath. Other lives had to be taken by force and if they weren't, then their lives never ended. Seeing the darkness through the ages of eyes that appeared youthful but held wisdom from the centuries.

And Valina, was one of those that had a life of never-ending night. Her crimson eyes seeming youthful but lurking just behind those strange irises was vast pools of knowledge and wisdom. Collected and stored in the vault that she called her mind.

She was one of few, for her kind were not exactly the rarest in the world – but close enough to it. For there were some, not many, who had the power of all the *Condentai.* The Goddess seemed to favor some of her children over others and Valina was one of the favored.

For Valina was a *Blood Condentai.*

A special person with the power to control one's life force; blood. A person who could stop the flow of it in your veins, cause it to erupt your heart, make your eyes weep with crimson. A *Blood Condentai* could even call it forth from your body, rising from it like a veil of mist, and use it as they will it. For blood was at their command and it bowed before them.

And it even kept their seemingly dead heart beating. For all they needed was blood, nothing more and nothing less.

Valina now was on the prowl for that very substance. Her body craving that thick crimson. She was crouched on the edge of a cliff that overlooked the town before her. Her crimson eyes watching the people scurry along the cobblestone street. Picking her prey was easy; if she wasn't in the mood for a fight she would find another *Condentai* or human that wouldn't prove as challenging.

Valina pondered for a moment, testing her mood. And it seemed as though the daggers sheathed at her sides called out to her. And so, she answered their pleas. Her slender, gloved fingers wrapped around the black leather hilts and they hissed as she drew forth the long, obsidian blades. Her gaze traced along the sharp curve and tip of the daggers, tracing along the only sliver of color to be found on her weapons; crimson, which was no surprise.

Valina bowed her head and her grey lids sealed over her eyes. *"Goddess of Dark, hear my prayer, bless me on this night of hunt and many more forward."*

And when her crimson eyes viewed the world before her once more, the beast that had been slumbering within her, had awaken. And it was thirsty for *blood.*

Rising from her crouch, her body took a leap into the air. Down she plummeted, her black cloak swept up by the wind, her hood flying back allowing the length of her silky midnight hair to feel the rush of the air's fingers through her locks. Her leather boots hit the ground, the earth trembling beneath her feet, a thin cloud of dust wafted into the air when she landed.

Her gaze flickered over to her left, her eyes tracing along the cobblestone road that led into the town not too far ahead. But tonight, she would not venture there, no. She turned her attention toward the right, where the vast darkness of forest waited. And there, she would hunt for her prey. With a feral grin, she marched toward those awaiting, crooked hands of the trees, stepping between the aged bodies of them, and set off into the darkness.

———————————————

The shadows seemed to watch Valina as she ventured through the darkness, her eyes allowing her to see perfectly, even in total dark. On light feet she treaded the forest, her pointed ears listening closely to the sounds that disturbed the quiet, to the creatures prowling and waiting in the gathering shadows.

Valina caught sight of one of the forest dwelling creatures. A tarantula. All eight of its crimson eyes stared back at her. The creature was no average sized arachnid. Its body was the size of a small cottage, its eight legs stretching longer than the tallest trees in the forest, its fangs were sharp and coated in poison. The creature made no move toward Valina, the tarantulas of the forest thought of *Blood Condentai* as one of their own. Both of them hunters of blood. Slowly the creature backed into the shadows, allowing them to swallow its body.

Valina smirked at the tarantula. For it was one of the Earth Goddess's children but the ones that crossed over into the land of the Goddess of Dark, well, Severina turned them into something of her own making. As more of a mockery to Sybil, to take something of hers as Sybil had once done to Severina.

Deeper and further she traveled, the blades spinning and dancing within the palms of her hands as she walked.

Then, her feet stilled. The twirling blades had ceased their dance. A smirk quirked at the corners of her lips. Her prey had arrived. Already her mouth seemed to water with eagerness for it knew that soon it would be drowning in blood.

Without looking behind her, she twirled around, her cloak spanning out, and threw one of her obsidian daggers. It flipped head over end through the air. The blade sliced through the wind, aimed at Valina's prey. To any mortal eye, they would not have seen Valina move.

But her prey was no mortal.

A tall, grey skinned man like Valina caught the hilt of the dagger a breath before it met with his exposed chest. His crimson eyes gleamed as a smile curled on his thin lips.

"Ah, my dear Valina, am I your prey for the evening?" His voice was sultry, speaking slow but not too much so. Just enough to radiate with confidence, enough to drive a woman mad.

But Valina was not driven mad. Though his voice was pleasing to the ear, she never fell victim to it. "My prey lately has been too easy; my daggers are crying for a challenge."

The man bowed deeply. His long, silky black hair swept over his shoulder just on one side for the other side of his head was completely shaved – allowing his pointed ear to show. "Always a pleasure challenging you, dear Valina. But I must say, my skills have improved greatly since our blades last met. I hope you can keep up."

Valina knelt into a crouch, the smirk still playing upon her lips. "You always underestimate me, Ventar. Whenever shall you learn?"

"Perhaps when that pretty blade of yours pierces my heart."

"Be careful of what you wish for, Ventar."

And in a blur of movement, Valina was nothing more than a breath of air. She was there and then within a blink, she was not. Her body moving too fast for eyes to track. But, Ventar's could track her. For he was of her kind, a *Blood Condentai.*

He simply side stepped, and she retrieved her dagger from his hand. Her palm heavy with its reassuring weight. Her ears caught the sound of blades hissing from their sheaths. Ventar had reached behind him to withdraw two long, obsidian swords.

"Do you think your daggers can hold up against these, my dear?" He twirled the swords in his hands, his voice and posture radiating with confidence.

Valina's grip tightened on the hilts of her long daggers. "Oh, Ventar, my daggers have never failed me."

She lunged forward. His sword slicing through the air toward her and she dodged to the left. Extending her hand, she swiped the dagger at his exposed side. The sharpened blade kissed his grey skin, a thin line of crimson appearing, tear drops weeping from the wound.

Valina could have ended the fight then, but she preferred to play with her prey.

Raising the blade to her mouth, her tongue flickered out and stole a taste of his blood. At once her mouth was in a frenzy as the sweet liquid met with her taste buds.

Ventar watched with a cocky smile upon his face. "My blood pleases you, does it not? I must say I would not allow anyone else the pleasure of it, my dear Valina."

"Do not take it as a compliment, Ventar. *All* blood pleases me – pleases *us.*"

Ventar said nothing, only approaching her with a predator's movement. His crimson eyes locked with her own. He bent his knees and then lunged. Quickly, Valina tossed up her daggers to meet with his blades. The sounds of them meeting rang out through the dark forest. She felt as he pressed his weight into his swords, but she pushed back with equal strength.

Ventar grinned and when he did, she caught sight of his fangs. "How long do you think you can do this?"

She grinned back, flashing her own sharp teeth. "Forever but I do not feel like wasting my time." She swept out a leg and knocked Ventar's feet from beneath him.

She did not, however, get a chance to leap upon her prey – that would have proven too easy. Ventar thrust his swords toward her as she advanced on him, causing her to leap back. The man was on his feet once more. He did not speak as he dashed forward, brandishing his swords. Her daggers met them once more. Knocking them aside as they tried to strike her. She would not allow her blood to be spilled on this night – or any night.

And when Ventar advanced on her again, she cast a quick glance behind her. Taking a few steps back, she raised her daggers once more to meet with his swords. And when he pushed, she allowed him to push her back. He grinned because he thought he would win, that he would claim her blood. But he was only playing into her trap.

No smile crossed her lips, she did not wish for him to see the deception being played upon him. When her back was pushed against the tree, she allowed the blades of his swords to get dangerously close to her face. Ventar leaned close to her, a victorious smile playing upon his lips, his fangs ready for their claim of blood.

"My dear Valina, you are a strong opponent, but you cannot best me. Now, allow me my drink of blood." He leaned close to her, his mouth lingering above her exposed neck.

It was then that she allowed her smile to show, "Never."

She reared her head back and smashed it against his long, thin nose. A howl escaped him as he staggered back, and she twirled then, sheathing one dagger within the blink of an eye – and ran two steps up the trunk of the aged tree and leapt into the air. Her back arching as she flew and when she landed upon her feet, she was already facing his back.

Ventar had no time to react, to understand that he had been tricked like a child. Her other unsheathed obsidian blade pressed against his exposed neck.

Valina's lips were close to his ear, as she whispered, "You have been bested, Ventar. Now, drop your weapons and allow me my drink."

His swords clattered to the ground as he hung his arms by sides and lowered his knees to the earth. There was no frown to be found upon his face, only a grin. "Never have I been able to best you, my dear. If only we were allowed to control one another's blood, perhaps then I would have a chance."

Blood Condentai could not control one of their own kinds' blood.

"Perhaps not even then." Grabbing a fist full of his silky, midnight hair, she moved his head to the side – exposing his slender neck. Lowering her mouth to his pulsating veins, her fangs grazed his skin. A slight moan escaped Ventar and she knocked him on the head with her free hand, "Do not make this a sexual pleasure for yourself, Ventar."

A chuckle escaped him, but he said nothing more as her fangs pierced his skin, sinking deep, and warm blood flowed into her mouth – sweeping across her tongue as she drank. Her eyes rolled into the back of her head as she became lost within the bloodlust, the hunger. The sweetness enveloped her mind like a silky blanket, the warmness of it coating her soul. She believed that nothing else in the world could taste as sweet as blood, the very thing that kept every living soul alive, herself included.

But, her feeding had to come to an end. Slowly, she removed her fangs from his neck and backed away, releasing her hold on his hair. As he stood, he sheathed his swords and bowed to her.

"Always a pleasure, my dear Valina." And before she could speak, he stood before her and leaned close to her ear, "Perhaps one day I shall win a taste of your blood." And when he moved his head, she felt the wetness of his tongue lick at the corner of her mouth. He dodged the swipe of her dagger. "You had some of my blood on your mouth." He winked.

"Bastard." She hissed.

"The best kind." And then, he vanished into the shadows.

―――――――――――――――

Valina tracked through the forest, wandering through the shadows, and made her way back to where she had started. The cobblestone street soon came into sight. Her black, leather boots padded softly along the stones. The walk was mostly spent in silence for many souls within the town and within the forest were asleep – others waiting patiently in the shadows to strike at their prey.

Many of the shops, homes, and cathedrals she passed were swallowed in darkness, it did not bother her or anyone for the land itself was nothing but darkness, but sometimes lanterns were lit to allow those without the vision of night to see – meaning the humans that lived amongst them.

The grey and black stoned buildings were eerie with silence and Valina liked the silence, it allowed her mind to wander. Some of the black metal street lamps had been left lit, flames crackling and dancing within their glass prisons, swaying to the left and right as the wind brushed against them. The silver metal chains the lanterns hung from creaking in the wind as it rocked on the curled black hook all the lanterns hung from.

Further ahead, past the town and the forest, was a castle that rested at the very top of the highest hill in the land. The castle itself gave anyone who gazed upon it shivers tingling along their spine. Valina was no exception to this. It felt as though an icy, skeletal hand traced its boney fingers along her spine. Her body trembled.

The grey stone loomed above the land, a black metal fence rising high from the ground and wrapping around the grounds of the castle. Crooked, sharp ends pointed into the sky, keeping anyone from daring to scale the fence. But, many tried, and many were left skewered to the pointed ends as a lesson, a warning. As of now, skeletons hung from some and a few fresh bodies hung from others. Sometimes the king would display his enemies' bodies, spies and rebels, for all eyes to see.

Valina dragged her gaze away from the castle. Not many things troubled her, but the sight of the castle was one of the few that did. And she hated more than anything to admit to that. But she was not the only one who lived in fear here, for everyone did.

Soon enough, she found herself facing a four-way split in the cobblestone road. Taking the left road, she wandered down along past the homes that lined the road. A few still having lanterns lit and igniting the path before her – not that she needed it.

Her feet came to a stop before the last home on the street, just close to the edge of the forest. The building was large enough, the grey stone sparkling as if the building were still new though it was as old as she – three hundred. She had built this home with her own hands and it took her many years. Pride always swelled in her chest at the very sight of it.

Opening the silver gate, she walked up the three steps, her eyes glancing at the black lanterns, hanging before her black painted door, and saw flames alive within them. Reaching her gloved hand into her pocket, she retrieved a silver key with a skull crafted at the top and plunged it into the lock. It clicked, and the door opened. Immediately, her nostrils were assaulted with the smell of incense.

Locking the door behind her, Valina set to work removing her cloak and hanging it upon one of the silver hooks on the grey stone wall. Removing her boots, she set them beside the door. Unbuckling the belt that her sheaths filled with daggers hung from, she hooked them on another hook beside her cloak. Finally, she removed her gloves and set them in a silver dish that rested upon a dark wood table on the opposite wall of the hooks.

Before her stretched a dark wooden stair case with black metal railing. On either side of the staircase were doorless doorways to other parts of the house, black painted wood decorated the outer parts of them, dark carvings of decaying flowers and skulls crafted into it. The first floor held the kitchen and living room. Another door just under the staircase led into a bathroom.

As Valina stepped through the doorway that led into the living room, her fingers traced along the carved wood, it took her many months to carve each and every intricate detail. As she leaned her head back, at the top center of the doorway was a carving of her Goddess; Severina. Her long black hair flowing down into the wood, her hands outstretched with shadows twirling from her fingertips.

"And the hunter has returned to its home." She heard a whispered and distant voice speak to her.

Stepping into the living room, she found a short woman standing before an open curtained window. The black silk pushed aside to allow the full view of the darkness to be seen. The woman's back was faced toward Valina as she leaned against the wall, her arms crossed over her plump chest.

"Yes, I have, Ashari." She said to her best friend and occasional lover.

Ashari's white hair fell down her back softly and swept at the floor behind her bare feet. Her dainty, pale hand clutching the dark fabric of the curtain – such a sharp contrast. "It was getting late, the shadows growing deeper, I began to wonder if I should send a spirit to search for you."

Ashari was a *Ghost Condentai* allowing her to speak to the dead and bend their ghostly bodies to her will, sometimes even allowing the dead to speak through her if their own spirits could not speak. Like if something truly tragic happened to them before they died; if their tongue had been cut out, their lips sewed together, acid poured down their throat. Then they could speak through Ashari.

Sometimes, Ashari would go on her own hunts for the ghostly victims, avenging them so that their souls were no longer tied to this world and they can join their Goddess. Other times, if the person deserved death, she allowed them to remain as their own form of torture – to be stuck here with only the *Ghost Condentai* and other spirits to speak too.

"As you can see, I am alright. No need to send a ghostly dog sniffing for me."

Finally, Ashari faced her. Those silver eyes meeting her crimson gaze and a small smile pulled at the woman's plump lips. "I am glad to see you home safely."

"I hope I didn't have you standing there too long."

Ashari moved the curtains back to conceal the windows and made her way to the fireplace. "Not long at all. But, I can see from the way your eyes glow that the feeding was well tonight."

Her mouth watered at the thought of Ventar's blood. "Very well, if I might say."

"And it is safe to assume that your prey was no easy target. I can see the way your hair is mussed and how your heart is still beating faster than normal."

Ashari was an observant woman, sometimes too much so. "I wanted a little bit of challenge tonight."

Valina made her way to the red velveted couch. It was also crafted from dark wood, like the rest of her furniture, the legs curling into rounded points that rested upon the floor. The velvet framed by the wood.

"The hunter seeking its prey." She spoke in her whispered voice. "And the hunter's prey, I am assuming was, Ventar. Am I safe in assuming so?"

Too observant. "Yes."

The fireplace roared to life, flames licking the logs within it. Crackling could be heard as the fire devoured the wood. A warm glow cast itself over the room.

"Two souls attracted to one another, their thirst undeniable, one shall drink and the other shall thirst." Sometimes, Valina wished Ashari wouldn't speak in those haunting riddles. But she had grown used to it over the last hundred years, it was a trait of the *Ghost Condentai.* And sometimes, Valina enjoyed the riddles, just not when they involved Ventar.

Ashari plucked something from the fireplace mantle and moved across the room with fluid grace. "This arrived for you."

Valina took the envelope and tore it open, retrieving the letter within;

My Dearest Valina,

I write to you in hopes that you'll attend my yearly ball. My heart was greatly saddened when your lovely face could not be found within the crowd of dancing bodies. If you chose to arrive this year or not, there shall be a dress sent to you either way. It shall arrive two days after this letter makes it to your gracious hands, just in time for the ball.

Sincerely, Your King Valnar

Though his words were sweet, they were anything but. The king was a mad man that was given too much power. He was another of her kind and she was thankful for that at least. He could not control her mind, body, or organs like the other *Condentai* could.

For many years Valina has tried to keep low, away from his sight, but one can only hide for so long until they are found. And when his eyes found her, he wished for nothing more than to make her his. And she was owned by no man. Her body and mind her own. But the Goddess only knew how long the king could keep hearing no before he took matters into his own hands.

"What are you going to do?" Ashari asked, still standing before her, her silver eyes glancing down at the letter.

Valina stood, Ashari moving aside, and approached the fireplace. With a flick of her wrist, she tossed the letter into the fire and watched as the flames devoured it. "I cannot miss another ball. Last year he was furious that I did not attend." Valina had heard that he had killed three servants in a fit of rage, one of them was a *Blood Condentai* – and her kind were scarce enough and with one of their deaths being on her shoulders. If only she would have attended, they would still be alive. "I do not wish to know what would happen if I did not make an appearance two years in a row."

Ashari said nothing, for there was nothing to say. The woman approached her and placed a tender hand upon Valina's shoulder. For a long while, the women stood there watching the flames.

CHAPTER TWO

A DRESS AND A BALL

"When all of your world is shrouded in darkness, how can you tell which part of it is light?"

THE TWO DAYS came and went in a blur. Valina spending her nights hunting for prey, staying out later than normal, until the shadows were the darkest she had ever seen them, until one of Ashari's ghostly companions tracked her down. Blood filled her body, coating her mind in a moment of peaceful bliss and ignorance. If blood was a drug, then she was addicted. But, she supposed, all *Blood Condentai* were to an extent. They needed it to be alive but as of now, Valina was using it to feel less alive. To distract her mind and herself of the ball that was slowly approaching. She hated how the king made her feel like a coward, how he made her act like that. But, she knew she must act the part or more lives would suffer because of her.

The night of her dress arriving, she did not answer the door when there was a knock upon it. She waited there, standing before it, until she heard the delivery person's feet echo away down the cobblestone road. Only then did she open the door, swipe the grey wrapped box off the top step, and slam the door shut. The grey stone groaned from the force of the door. But she did not care.

The box thudded atop the dark coffee table before her couch and she sat upon it. Her elbows resting on her knees and her chin propped up on her hands. Valina's gaze watched the box and did not stop until she heard the lock click and Ashari entered the home.

The *Ghost Condentai* lingered in the doorway of the living room, her silver eyes resting upon the grey box. "The dress has arrived."

Valina reached toward the box and snatched it from the table. Her fingers tearing into the grey wrapping paper to reveal a white box beneath. Lifting the lid, black fabric spilled out over the box like shadows. She stood, holding the dress up. The midnight fabric flowing down to the floor. A corset was made into the dress and the sleeves would hang low upon her shoulders, leaving her neck and chest exposed. The skirt of the dress was lacey, layers and layers of lace piled atop the other, so they would not reveal too much to the lingering eye.

"I suspect that the king assumed the dress would suit you." Ashari approached then, her delicate fingertips trailing along the fabric. "And I suspect that he would be correct."

Valina snarled but not at her friend, at the king. "The man has a taste for clothing but no taste of emotion, guilt, pity, no feeling. He has no soul."

"Would you like for me to also attend the ball, though I always receive an invitation I never go. Would it ease your mind?"

Valina shook her head and placed a hand upon the woman's cool cheek, "I do not wish for you to be there. For if he put his hands on you, I fear that I shall not be able to hold myself back."

Ashari raised to the tips of her toes and placed a kiss upon Valina's cheek, *"May thy Goddess bless your every step and watch your unguarded back, may she shield thy heart from shattering."*

The dress trailed behind her as she walked, snagging on the cobblestone road, but Valina did not care. Let the stones tear her dress to shreds for when the night was over the dress would be nothing, but scrap fabric thrown into a hungry fire.

Her midnight hair was fashioned in a thick braid that acted as a crown that wrapped around her head. Ashari worked her delicate hands through her long hair. Her cold fingertips barely grazing her scalp as she wove the thick midnight strands together. A few wisps of dark hair framed either side of Valina's face, the wind now tangling with them.

A choker of black velvet with a ruby mounted in its center tied around her throat. The king had made it to where her chest would be vulnerable, but she would not allow her neck to be so. The dress hung low on her shoulders, the sleeves thankfully covered her arms and came to points that rested atop her hands. Valina felt as though the king had a plan in mind, on this evening, and she would not allow him a drink of her blood – not even the smallest droplet.

Soon enough, she found herself before the black fence of the castle. A heavy breath escaped her when no bodies or skeletons could be found hanging from the pointed ends. A crowd of people had already flowed inside the castle, her ears could hear the haunting music of violins singing mournfully out into the darkness. Voices behind her told her that another crowd was on its way and she moved herself into the castle. Her silk flats sounding softly upon the stone stairs as she ascended them. The man checking invitations did not bother asking Valina for hers; he knew she was the guest of honor.

As she found herself inside the grand ballroom, she noticed that many of the men and women wore masks upon their faces. This year was to be a masquerade. To Valina, there was no point in her wearing one to conceal herself from the king's watchful eye. She would be spotted no matter for the dress she wore was of his own choosing.

The room was brightly lit as hundreds of black lanterns hung from the ceiling, flames dancing within them. Silk banners of grey and black looped and hung from the ceiling, dangling just above the heads of the guests. On a small stage in the center of the room was where the music had sounded from. Men and women dressed in black with matching grey masks, played their lovely violins, their faces void of any emotion, their eyes only upon their instruments.

She watched as men and women servants, all dressed in white, carried trays of silver full of wine glasses. And the contents inside the glasses were not wine but blood. Other servants scurried about, not holding a tray and Valina knew why – their white clothes stained with droplets of crimson.

"May I offer a drink, Miss Valina?"

Her crimson gaze found eyes of green, a trait only a human had. The man seemed young though it was hard to tell due to the mask that covered much of his face.

Before her lips could answer, another man approached, "I believe my blood, shall suffice. Am I correct, my dear Valina?"

Valina nearly rolled her eyes but she was grateful that at least Ventar was here and she would not suffer through this night alone. "Thank you but my thirst has dried for the night."

With that being said, the human scurried off to offer another a taste of his blood. He would be doing so until his body could offer no more, until his eyes twinkled with stars and his head met with the cold unforgiving stone as his legs gave out beneath him. Another servant would rush into the room and take his place as others moved him out of sight to rest.

Many of the guests here drank blood but only *Blood Condentai* needed it to survive. The ones of her own kind preferred to sink their fangs into necks and retrieve the blood themselves, the other *Condentai* preferred to drink from glasses.

"I stopped by your house but Ashari told me that you had already left but, in her own words. You know how she is, riddles and questions for everything."

She turned her face away from his and gazed across the room, "Have you come to speak with me only to insult my friend? Or is there another reason you are here?"

Ventar offered his arm to her and without argument, she placed her hand in the crook of his elbow and allowed him to lead her to the furthest corner of the room. "I know you do not enjoy the king, none of us do. I did not wish for you to suffer through this night alone."

Her hand fell from his arm as she crossed her own arms over her chest, she raised a dark brow to him. "You are actually concerned about me? Consider me shocked since you mostly only care for yourself."

Ventar placed a hand over his heart, "My dear, you wound me so. Is it so difficult to believe?"

"Yes."

"A faster reply than I would have hoped for." He sounded hurt, but it was always hard to tell with him, he could act very well.

"There must be another reason that you are here. You know I am fully capable of handling myself."

"There is no doubt about that. But yes, there is another reason."

Valina smirked, "See? Always has be something, a catch."

"Once more, you wound me."

She rolled her eyes, "Why are you truly here?"

"And that, my dear, I cannot say."

She faced him then, her arms by her sides where her daggers should be. Oh, her daggers were still on her, just strapped to her thighs. She learned long ago to never leave her home without a weapon. "What do you mean, Ventar?"

He offered his grey hand to her with a slight bow, "May I have this dance before the king comes and steals you away from me?"

Her gaze flickered down to his awaiting hand. "You shall tell me, Ventar, even if I have to beat the answer out of you." But, she slid her hand into his.

A light chuckle escaped him, "I do not doubt it."

Together, they approached the ballroom floor, going deeper and deeper into the throng of dancing people. Trying as best as they could to conceal themselves from the king, just long enough to have at least one dance before the evening was stolen from her.

Ventar placed one hand on her hip, not too low, and kept a firm hold on her hand as her other rested upon his shoulder. Their feet led them into a slow dance, their steps light, their breathing even. A few times, he would spin her out, her dress fanning out around her like dark shadows, before he spun her back to him.

"Tell me, Ventar, why you are here." She demanded.

"You must guess, my dear."

Her crimson eyes judged him, "It is unlike you to wear something that covers your face. It is something you proudly show off." His dark mask covered his forehead down to the top of his lip.

He spun her out once more and brought her back to him. His lips were close to her ear when he leaned down, "Getting close."

"A ball is something you would hardly attend, especially here since the king...." And it was then that she realized why he had come. Yes, she being part of the reason. But a small part of it. "To rebel." The words whispered traitorously from her lips. To even speak the words marked you a traitor to the king.

Everyone was terrified of the king, even the ones dancing within the room now laughing and seeming happy enough, feared him. She had heard of rebels acting against the king and many of them were mounted on that wicked fence. She even knew a few of the people who had been executed but she never knew until their deaths what they were secretly plotting in the shadows.

"Ventar, you cannot..."

For a moment, his lifeless body flashed before her mind. Mounted for show, the spiked end of the fence protruding from the top of his head. His crimson eyes staring lifelessly at nothingness.

He silenced her lips with his own, just for a moment. As if he knew what had been pictured within her mind. "There are reasons that I am doing this, Valina. And if this night went terribly wrong, then at least I got this chance to dance with such a lovely woman."

And for the first time, in a long time, Valina had found herself flustered. Though she had known Ventar for many years, neither of them ever touched intimately or kissed. She always kept him an arm's reach away from her – the pointed end of her dagger aimed at him.

"Bastard." She snarled but in truth, that was all she could think to say.

Ventar winked, "Only the best kind. Now, my dear, when the screaming begins, I wish for you to flee this place."

"You cannot be serious..."

"Serious about what, Valina?"

Her body had gone stiff at the sound of the king's raspy voice, her face paling. It took all her strength to face the king with a plastered-on smile. He was tall, looming above Valina even though she was quite tall herself. His midnight hair had been delicately combed to one side. A silver crown rested upon his head, the individual points that wrapped around the band of silver were sharpened, the crown itself could be used as a weapon. And as if to prove it to her, Valina's eyes caught sight of a small stain of crimson upon it. The king had his hands in the pockets of his black jacket, crimson trimming running along the cuffs of the sleeves.

"Serious about wishing for another dance. He has two left feet, it seems, a horrid dancer, I find myself offended."

"Always wounding a man, it seems." Ventar did good to act as though nothing were amiss. He grasped her hand and placed a kiss upon it, "Perhaps when next we meet, my dancing will suit you, my dear."

When Ventar dropped her hand and began to disappear into the crowd of dancing people, the king spoke, "There shall be no next dance for you, for she is taken at every ball."

Ventar stopped in his steps, his gaze holding the king's. "My apologies, but I found this lovely woman standing alone with no partner. I could not bear to allow someone of her beauty to be alone on this evening. Perhaps you'll learn that."

Valina had to hold back the smile that twitched at the corner of her lips as she watched the king grow irritated.

The king did not get a chance to retort an answer for Ventar had already vanished into the crowd of people. With a shake of his head, he faced Valina with a grin. "You do look ravishing tonight, my dearest Valina. The dress suits you well, just as I thought it would."

"You are too kind, my king." She hated calling him her king, he was no king of hers, and she would never bow before him.

He extended a gloved hand to her, "May I have the pleasure of a dance?"

No. "You may."

When her hand slid into his, he instantly drew her body close to his. One of his hands riding dangerously low on her back and she held back the snarl that almost escaped her lips. This dance was different from the dance she had with Ventar. This one was not as fluid and graceful but forced and heavy stepped. The king did not spin her out as if he did not wish to risk the chance of someone stealing Valina away – not that anyone would dare. So, he kept her close.

"Why have you covered that beautiful neck of yours?" He asked in a low, raspy voice. "I picked this dress for that very reason, my dear."

"I tend to keep my neck covered." She half snapped without meeting his gaze.

He lowered his face toward the nape of her neck, disgust pooling within the pit of her stomach as she heard him sniff at her scent. "Won't you allow me a drink, my dear? Not even the tiniest drop."

No one ever defied the king but Valina could sometimes get away with it – tempting fate. "No one drinks my blood." Her tone was like stone that was dripping with venom. A warning edge in her voice as if to say, *try it and I shall not care if you are king.*

The king chuckled at that and moved his head away from her neck. The hand that had been resting low on her back came up to stroke her cheek. "One day, your blood shall be mine, my dear."

Before she could reply, chaos erupted through the ballroom. Flames ate away at the silk drappings that hung above the room. Smoke began to fill the air, the haunting music of the violins fading away and screams began to make music of their own. Women and men frantically rushed around as flames had begun to devour dresses and hair. Arms flailed above heads to try and tame the flames only resulting in the fire transferring onto themselves.

When the screaming begins, I ask that you flee this place. Ventar's words echoed around within her head.

Now, she supposed, would be a very good time to flee.

The king released his hold on her as he whipped around to face the flames devouring his castle, thrusting Valina behind him. "Guards! Find the people responsible for this and throw them in the dungeon!"

At once, masked men hurriedly made their way toward the doors where the rebels would have fled but Valina had never seen anyone move toward them until the fire erupted in a blaze. They were still here within the room waiting for the crowd of frightened men and women to make their way toward the doors. Soon enough, they did.

Valina faded into the shadows and followed the terrified crowd out into the night. She was thankful that the ball had ended early and was happy to watch the fire devour the party and its guests but only the ones that deserved to burn, of course.

The dress had been burned and frayed at the ends, smoke still spiraling within the air from the ends. The black lace lay in ashy ruin. As her feet carried her along the street they did not carry her home, instead they led her toward the forest where the shadows waited with open arms and watchful eyes. She allowed her feet to guide her deep into the eternal darkness until she was sure she was utterly alone.

For when she was, her hands set to work tearing the dress from her body. Her nails biting into the fabric, ripping the pretty lace to shreds that fluttered down to the earth. Wisps of black fabric laying all around her. She tore and snarled until nothing remained upon her body. Till the fabric no longer clung to her grey skin.

Finally, that sickening feeling had been rid from the pit of her stomach. She hated many things and the king was number one on the list – anything involving him made her skin crawl. And she had the suspicion that the king knew this and found a sick sort of twisted joy in that – perhaps that was why he always sent dresses for her to wear because he knew she could not turn down the offer from the king. And she absolutely hated the bastard.

Her fingers traced along the hilts of her daggers, the only things left on her body. The leather strappings clinging tightly to her thighs. A smirk found itself upon her lips as she thought of the fire. How the people screamed and danced about. How the lovely decorations were now nothing but ash. And the anger within the king's gaze.

She found great joy in watching the man suffer, for it did not happen as often as it should. One day, she would make him suffer until there was nothing left of him to feel suffering.

"You have an odd habit of being naked in the forest, my dear." A sultry voice spoke from the shadows.

This was not her first time wandering the forest wearing nothing upon her body. For after every ball she attended, she came here, and tore each dress she wore to shreds.

Valina hated how her heart leapt at the sound of Ventar's voice – to know that he had escaped alive. "And you have an odd habit of setting rooms afire."

A chuckle sounded as he stepped forth, his own ball clothes tinged with ashy ruin. "Doing it once makes it into a habit?"

She crossed her arms over her chest, not caring that she was naked – he had found her like this a few times before – after the other balls she attended years ago. "You'll do it again, won't you? The rebels."

All playfulness had left his face then, his crimson gaze turning toward the ever-dark sky. "We shall continue to burn everything, until that castle is nothing but dust upon the wind and the only thing left of the king is the ash from his bones."

There was vengeance within his voice and Valina wondered just what had the king done to Ventar to earn such a hatred? The king did many things, and everyone feared and hated him but Ventar's hatred ran deep.

Just as hers did.

"Why?" She found herself asking, wishing to know the true reason behind Ventar's hatred.

His gaze fell from the sky and landed upon her, his eyes and face hard. Valina had never seen the man so serious before and it worried her. Hatred caused people to do stupid and rash things that led them to their untimely deaths.

"The king has taken from us too long. It is past time that he pays his debt."

She took a step toward him, "But what, Ventar, has he done to *you*." Her gaze never lowered from his, her eyes holding their place.

One moment, he stood a few feet away from her and now he stood so close that she felt the warmth from his body radiating against hers. "My mother was ran through on that damned fence." A growl rumbled within his voice, his crimson eyes burning like a fire had engulfed the inside of his head. "She paid for a crime that she did not commit. Paid with her *life*. He named her a traitor for simply not agreeing with the way he ran this land. A true traitor would have killed their king not disagree with him while remaining loyal." His body began to tremble, "I watched his men drag my mother from our home, kicking and screaming – begging for her life. I watched them run her through on that sharp fence and I heard her screams before the pointed end rammed through her skull and she was silenced forever. They made sure to do it slowly, made sure that she felt every moment of pain while the town watched. My mother was gone."

Valina had never known that that had been his mother. She remembered the day and the screams sometimes still found their way into her dreams, the woman's lifeless eyes staring up at nothing.

She blinked slowly, "That was your mother? I never knew..."

That was also the day that their paths had first crossed.

"Do you remember what you said?" His voice still shook with that the rage that had consumed his mind.

"One day that bastard shall pay for every life he has taken, and I'll gladly be there to watch or perhaps be the one dealing the payment." She repeated those words perfectly – the words that had sealed their friendship and she had never known. Ventar had been standing next to her in the crowd and she saw how his face appeared – sorrow mixed with rage coating his handsome features.

When his grey hand reached for her, she did not back away, remaining perfectly still. His fingertips gently combing through her now freed locks, in her rush to free herself from the fiery ball, the intricate braid had fallen. "There was such a fire in your eyes when you spoke those words, each one a promise of his death, and I decided then that together we could end his reign."

"Ventar, what you speak of is madness. You know we'll be killed. Every attempted assassination on the king has ended in *their* deaths and never his. I do not wish to end up as a decoration upon his fence, Ventar. I cannot."

"His reign is madness, Valina. You know he must be stopped. Everyone knows, and we shall not be alone in this fight, the other rebels will be there seeing that everything burns."

She shook her head, his hand falling from her hair. "I do not know, I shall need time to think. This plan is dangerous and does not only involve our lives but others as well."

Once more his hand reached for her, cupping her cheek as he placed a kiss upon her forehead. His lips brushing against her skin had caused a small fire to kindle within her.

"Take as much time as you need, my dear Valina. For the rebels are gathering in numbers and still forming a plan. We have time, so think on it."

Valina nodded her head.

Her gaze watched as he turned his back to her and approached the shadows that waited. He stopped, just a step away from eternal darkness. And when he spoke, he did not glance over his shoulder.

"I promise upon my life, Valina. That nothing shall happen to yours. I promise that the king shall not have his way with you. I'll place a blade through his heart before he even attempted a thing."

And then, without waiting for her to speak, the shadows devoured him.

CHAPTER THREE

REBELS ON FIRE

"When the body burns, shall the soul burn as well?"

THE KING had demanded the entire town to gather before his castle, guards marching to each and every home escorting people along the cobblestone road. Marching them toward the castle that waited in the shadows atop the hill.

Valina and Ashari stood together, their hands clasped, and fingers entwined, as all eyes watched the line of people step forth from the castle doors. Black sacks draped over their heads, hands and ankles bound in shackles. The exposed skin upon the prisoners' arms and legs were marred with purple and black bruising – some of them had deep wounds that still wept with crimson. Guards marched the line of people toward the fence, toward their deaths.

A lump formed within Valina's throat as her gaze scanned the crowd around her and found no sign of Ventar. Her heart grew heavy as her chest tightened at the horrible thought that had crossed her mind.

Then, a figure stepped forth and stood on the top of the castle steps. The king. Fiery rage then crackled within Valina's veins. Before she wished to slice the king's throat from ear to ear. But now, she wished more than anything to chop his body into pieces, so small that no one could tell it ever belonged to a man. She wanted his body so mangled and horrid that no one could even guess what sort of creature it was that had been mangled so. Her daggers would take their time skinning the flesh from his bones, he would feel every second of agony.

The picture in her mind caused a smirk to play upon her lips.

The king spread his arms wide, the silver crown glistened upon his head from the light of the lanterns that hung from either side of the doors. "My loyal subjects," Valina rolled her eyes, "As you may know, my ball yesterday was ruined. Rebels infiltrated my castle – *my home* – and set fire to the ballroom." He waved his hand toward the line of people before the gates. "And here they are, my guards tracked down any person who appeared suspicious and had them thrown in the dungeons." The crowd was silent. The only sound that found its way into Valina's ears was the king's voice. "They were tortured, beaten, and still they would not speak of other rebels. But do not worry, I shall find them all and all of them shall burn – just like the ones shall today."

Burn. He was going to burn them. Alive. She wandered what would be more painful; being skewered or being eaten alive by flames. Both were painful. Both were horrible. And the sick feeling that dwelled within her stomach, only grew sicklier.

Ashari stood motionless, her silver eyes conveying no emotions. It was if she were a statue given a fleshy appearance. For it did not seem that she even breathed. Valina knew that Ashari would remain behind – after the crowd had dispersed and the bodies left behind to rot – for Ashari would guide their spirits into the afterlife, into the awaiting arms of the Goddess.

No other *Ghost Condentai* dared do what Ashari did after every public execution. And the only reason she was allowed to live was because of Valina. The king knew that if he had her killed then she would hate him more than she did now. But Valina would always hate him and if he dared strike a hand against Ashari then consequences be damned. And Valina would no longer care for her own life as she raced toward the king brandishing her wicked daggers. Perhaps that was the true reason the king never made a move against Ashari – perhaps a part of him feared her. And feared what her rage would make her become, what monster it would turn her into.

"And now, we shall set fire to those who have done so to my home." At the king's gesture, the guards gathered up torches. A single guard carried an open lantern and walked down the line of men who dipped their torches into the licking flames.

Once all the torches had been lit, the men stepped back, and the lone guard resealed the lantern and approached the rebels. One by one he locked their shackles upon the wicked fence. There would be no fleeing – no escape from the devouring flames. His hands tearing the black sacks from the men and women's heads. Gasps had filtered through the crowd. Muffled cries sounding into the air.

And Valina felt a weight lifted from her chest when her eyes did not find Ventar among the prisoners. But some weight remained behind as she gazed upon the rebels who had no hope of surviving.

Many of the rebels were human, one *Mind Condentai* and two *Shadow Condentai* among them.

The *Mind Condentai* stood there motionless. Her face hardened into stone. Her grey eyes blazing with wrath – with hatred. The dark tattoos that inked her bald head had been marred and destroyed from the beatings she took. Blood caked on her pale skin, her thin nose crooked to the side and still weeping. But the woman stood tall, no sign of pain appearing on her strong face. And when their gazes met, Valina felt something brush against her mind.

Bring down the king. A feminine voice spoke into her mind. *Join the rebels, aid us – them. Do not be a coward who hides in the shadows and doing nothing while innocent lives are taken, Valina. Do not allow this to continue, it has gone on long enough.*

And then, the voice was gone. Drifting away, the soft caress around her mind vanishing like the wind. Her crimson eyes blinked at the *Mind Condentai* and the only movement the woman made, was a slight nod of her head. She was right in naming Valina a coward, for that was what she was. Fearing the king, hiding away and doing nothing while others suffered.

One of the *Shadow Condentai* was a tall man, his skin as dark as the night. He too, had been beaten, just as all the rebels had. One leg bent at an awkward angle, but he still held defiance in his wholly black eyes where no white showed in them, just vast pools of shadows. His shoulders were straight, and his strong chin was held high. The long dark hair that fell from his head was tangled and matted. His lips swollen and bleeding, but he still smirked as pride flickered across his gaze.

His dark eyes cast a glance toward the *Mind Condentai* woman beside him. Though she was tall, he was a head taller than her. And the two held gazes for a few breaths and Valina swore she saw love pass between them. A connection that ran deep, down into the souls of their beings.

Valina's gaze drifted back toward the king – giving the lovers some sort of privacy though many other eyes were watching – who wore a twisted smile. A hunger burning within his eyes. Then, with a simple gesture of his hand, the guards stepped forth.

Screams soon filled the silence, shattering it like glass, as the ravenous fire began to devour the rebels. Shackles rattled against the fence as the people tried to free themselves. People within the crowd began to cry out. Names were ripped free from choking throats that held sorrow filled sobs.

Valina's ears began to echo with screams of agony. Singing out like a haunting symphony. Something that would haunt her in her dreams for many nights after. Her hand tightened on Ashari's and the woman remained there motionless, it was as if she had become a ghost herself – fading from the world.

And Valina noticed that the *Mind Condentai* did not scream, did not cry, did not fight against her shackles. She remained there, frozen in place, and allowed the flames to devour her body whole.

Her eyes closed in almost a peaceful acceptance as she waited for her soul to leave the vessel it called home and join the Goddess by her side.

Valina did not know the woman but she had a sense of pride swell within her chest. The woman had been strong until the very end, never allowing the king to break her. She did not grant him that satisfaction. She wished that she had gotten the chance to know the woman personally to, at the very least, learn her name so that she might mourn her properly. The woman's voice still echoed within her mind, speaking of her cowardice. And the way the woman spoke her name as she plucked it from her mind, shall remain forever. A haunting reminder to stop the king, to join the rebels.

The smell of cooking flesh soon filled the air and gags rose within Valina's throat. She had only smelled this once before and it remained as the foulest thing she had ever smelled. Her stomach lurched at the scent, twisting and churning. Those crimson eyes of hers watering. *Wrong.* She thought to herself, *this is wrong.*

Goddess please, hear my prayers, and end this madness. Hear my pleas and allow these souls to suffer no more. Grant them peace. She hoped that Severina had listened as she sent her prayers to the eternal darkness where the Goddess waited.

A woman fell onto her knees ahead of Valina. Her arms stretched toward the sky as she cried out her prayers to the Goddess of Dark. But the Goddess was too late to hear those desperate prayers because soon, the screaming was silenced. The shackles no longer rattling.

The rebels were dead.

And Valina supposed that it was a kindness. The Goddess had listened and made their deaths swift – for it should have taken much longer for the flames to fetch their souls from their bodies. And even the king seemed to notice, his brow creasing and his lips pressing into a thin line. His crimson gaze snapped toward the sky and Valina could have sworn she watched his lips curse the Goddess.

But the crowd still cried their heavy tears with aching hearts. Prayers going to the Goddess to carry their souls, for her to embrace them in the eternity of darkness. For the people did not seem to notice that the Goddess had answered their prayers the best she could, for the Goddess was no longer apart of this world. She was in another, a place of eternal darkness where souls went to rest for all of eternity. And she could only answer prayers as best she could from the other world. All she could do, was make the hearts within their chests stop their beating, she could not guide the souls to her. That was the job of her *Ghost Condentai* children and then, the pathway would be opened to the Goddess.

Many of these people – families – have suffered and would continue to do so until their tears had dried and there was none left to fall from their eyes. Homes would be missing a soul. An empty chair, an empty bed. One plate too many to be found on the dinner table.

And when the king spoke once more, there was the wicked smile to be found upon his face. Valina wished she could slice it off –

slowly with one of her daggers – then she would be the one smiling.

"Let this be a lesson to you all," He gestured to the charred bodies with dark smoke rising from them. "All of you who wish to rebel against your king shall meet this fate. No lives shall be spared."

Then, his crimson gaze had found Valina's in the crowd. His smile widened. Her eyes narrowed, her lips pressed into a thin line.

Bastard.

The word was brandished within her own crimson eyes. The king only let out a small chuckle as he turned on his heel and retreated into the castle. Then the guards began to unlock the shackles and proceeded to run the lifeless bodies of the rebels through on the fence – leaving them as decoration for all eyes to see.

The people watched as their loved ones were skewered upon that damned fence. Valina clenched her free hand into a fist by her side as her gaze watched the poor souls be left there, the sharp ends protruding from the tops of their skulls.

One day I shall burn that damned fence and castle to the ground.

And it was then that she had decided.

A few more choked sobs sounded into the air, a few more whispered, broken names being said like a prayer. One by one, the crowd dispersed. Leaving with one less member of their family, one less person from their lives.

Ashari stepped forward, her hand falling from Valina's as her silver eyes viewed the bodies. The woman knelt onto her knees and her arms spread wide. Her white hair pooled around her like milky water.

"May thy souls come forth – come to me. Allow me to see, allow me to speak. Do not fret and do not hide, for I am here. Allow me to aid, allow me to ease. Come forth and thy shall find the Goddess."

It was always a strange and haunting experience to watch Ashari perform this ritual. Her voice was distant, almost vacant, as if her own soul was leaving her. Those silver eyes staring into nothingness. Ashari's body seeming as though it were fading from view – taking on an almost ghostly form. Her white hair gliding along a ghostly wind. A chill brushed along Valina's spine and she knew that the spirits of the rebels had come forth.

Ashari lowered her arms and her gaze flickered back and forth, taking in the sight of the rebels before her. She rose onto her feet once more and moved forward, her arm outstretched, and seemed to place two fingers against the air – against one of the rebels' foreheads. A soft wind brushed through Ashari's hair, and from where Valina stood she could see the *Ghost Conedentai's* silver eyes begin to glow.

"The Goddess awaits, go now and join her in the sleep of eternal darkness. Your pain has ended, and you are free. May thy find peace in the Goddess's arms. Until our souls meet again."

Ashari continued to the other rebels and one by one, that ghostly chill began to disappear as the spirits vanished, going to meet their Goddess in that eternity of darkness.

Many ghosts required the deaths of the people whose hands had killed them. But the rebels knew that the king would not be killed so easily, so, they took their passage to that eternal dark. And there they would remain, waiting to hear prayers speaking of the king's death. And only then, would they peacefully rest.

Though the Goddess was a powerful being, there was only so much she could do from the eternal darkness. She was *Condentai* of all things; blood, mind, ghost, shadow, organ, body, and death. And when she once walked this world, she controlled all. Her power never ending, just like the night that shrouded this world. But when her and the other Gods left this world behind, their grasp upon it weakened. And so, to their children they gifted them portions of their powers. A special connection between child and God.

And when it came to the *Ghost Condentai* the Goddess relied on them to send her the souls that were tormented. For Severina could only retrieve those that were not stuck upon this earth from a bloody death. Only those who had slipped into eternal darkness in their sleep or those who had accidentally slipped from a cliff or drowned in a river. Only those who were not shackled to this world by blood, only those, the Goddess herself could reach out to and bring them with her. And that was where the *Ghost Condentai* came in, righting the wrongs that had been done to those that did not deserve those sorts of deaths. Only they could free them, shatter their shackles, and send them along that eternal path.

Valina approached Ashari and placed a gentle hand upon her cool shoulder, "Come let us go home."

Ashari leaned into Valina and together, they walked the silent cobblestone street, leaving the castle far behind them.

Valina knew when Ashari needed space, to be alone with her thoughts. So, she wandered into the darkness, her boots softly echoing into the quiet night. No souls were found lurking within the shadows. All homes were shrouded in silence as the towns people mourned the loss of their people. Families praying together for the lost souls, friends and lovers crying into the hands that covered their faces. Hearts were aching and shattering on this eternal night. And Valina's was one of them. Her mind could not shake the voice of the *Mind Condentai*.

Do not be a coward who hides in the shadows.

If she had not been a coward, could she have saved the rebels? Started an uprising right there with the gathered towns people? She wondered just how many of them would have stood and fought and then she wondered how many would remain behind, their fear plaguing them as the fear had plagued her.

Valina soon found herself standing before one of the seven cathedrals within the town. This particular one praised her kind – the *Blood Condentai*. The stone was black, the night seeming to devour the building. The arched, stained glass windows were crimson with a dark outlining of the Goddess of Dark and other depictions of *Blood Condentai*.

Severina could be found in every cathedral within the town, for she was *Condentai* of all, mother to all. But every depiction differed from the last. In this cathedral, she appeared as grey skinned as Valina. Long fangs protruding from her mouth, blood dripping from plump lips. Pointed ears appearing beneath long midnight locks. In other cathedrals she shared the traits of the other *Condentai*. Appearing as a different woman in each. No one knew what she truly looked like, only the souls that had met her after they passed. Which left her remaining children behind with their imaginations.

The cathedral though, was a grand sight to be seen. The height of it gracefully reached to the eternal dark sky, as if it were reaching up for the Goddess. Two tall spires rose from the cathedral, beautiful and haunting. And on either side of the building were towers – where the priests and priestess resided. Flying Buttresses extended from the sides of the building and the towers, the arches curved as they met the earth. They aided in spreading the weight of the towers, spires, and other high rises from the cathedral so that it may not crumble in upon itself. And they also added an eye catching decorative to the building.

Valina's boots softly ascended the stairs that led up to the tall, arched doorway. The doors were crafted from the darkest of wood. A depiction of the Goddess carved into it. Her hands stretched out on either side, palms up and shadows rising like smoke from her hands. As Valina pushed open the doors, the Goddess split in two down the middle. Before her, the nave stretched out long. The dark wooden floors were polished and the light from the lanterns that hung low – in a row down the middle of the high arched ceiling – danced upon them.

Rows and rows of wooden, red velvet cushioned benches lined along the side aisles as she walked down the center of the nave. Pillars rose at the beginning of every aisle before a bench, stretching toward the ceiling and aiding it to stand. Carvings could be found etched into the stone pillars, many of which were carved by Valina's own hands. Her fingertips brushed against them as she passed them. Toward the end of the room, there was a rise within the wooden floor, like a small stage. Three rows of steps that were softened with a crimson rug, led up to it.

There, Valina found The Fountain of Offering. Humans came and went here, praising and worshipping the *Blood Condentai* as if they were Gods themselves. And there, they offered their blood. The Priests and Priestesses extracting it with a knife or fangs, human and other of Valina's kind lived and worked here within these hauntingly beautiful walls. Other humans offered their blood to Severina but *Blood Condentai* could still drink it, for the offering was there for them to dampen their thirst if their hunts did not go well or they simply wished for a night to rest. And tonight, Valina wished for a night of rest. No fighting, for she found her soul and heart were too heavy.

Behind the fountain, could be found the chancel. Another set of stairs led up to a higher rise within the floor, a decorative railing attached to either side of the staircase, the crimson rug continuing up it. There, the Priests and Priestesses could be found singing their prayers to the Goddess and to the *Blood Condentai.* Their voices beautiful but chilling. Ghostly and haunting as they echoed throughout the quiet cathedral, reverberating within Valina's bones.

Many nights, Valina found herself here. Sitting upon a velvet bench and listening to the songs that sang from their lips. It soothed her soul when it ached. On nights her mind wandered across her family. The family that now stood by the Goddess's side. All except one who was nowhere to be found because she did not wish to be found; Valina's mother. After her father had been named a traitor to the crown, the king had him burned along with other members of her family who were suspected.

Valina was only a child then. Before King Valnar claimed that silver crown as his. For it was the king before, his father, who had her family burned. Her aunts, grandparents, cousins. All of them devoured by those wicked flames. The king's wicked cackles echoing within her nightmares partnered with her families screams of agony. Her mother and her were forced to watch. A child made to watch her entire family die, the first time she had smelled cooked flesh, and she retched upon the earth as tears burned her cheeks. She remembered crying out for her father, begging the king to stop. But it only caused him to laugh more.

That was also the day that Valina had first seen the king's son, Valnar. They were the same age. Both children forced to watch something that no child should. The boy stood there, no laughter upon his face, no sign of wickedness to be found. And when their eyes met, it was pity and sorrow that Valina had found within those crimson eyes.

And she often caught herself thinking back to that day and wondering what had happened to that boy to make him into something so wicked, like his father before him. She thought of what could have been between them – friendship or love – if it hadn't of been for his father. On that day, they were on opposite sides of that cruel fence, and to this day, they still found themselves on those opposing sides.

The echoing sounds of footsteps broke Valina free of her thoughts. The steps became quiet once they reached her bench. The velvet cushion sank down as another person joined her. She did not gaze upon the man that now sat beside her.

"Today was not easy." Ventar said, his gaze following Valina's toward The Fountain of Offering.

"No, watching people burn is rather easy. I find myself enjoying the sight of it." She snapped though she did not mean too. Her anger was toward the king, not Ventar. But he knew that. He always did.

"I'm close with many of the rebels. And today, I had to watch my friends burn. Their screams shall never leave me. I had disappointed them. I was supposed to protect them. But I failed them."

It was then that Valina cast a glance at Ventar. His eyes still focused ahead, his mouth pressed into a thin line, a vein in his neck throbbing. His shoulders slumped heavily. "You did not fail them, Ventar. They joined the rebels knowing the risk. They fought for this land and these people."

A heavy sigh escaped him as he shook his head. "We all joined knowing the risk, pledging our lives to this cause. But, it never gets easier seeing your friends die. Watching them being killed off one by one and there's nothing you can do but watch."

"I understand."

It was Ventar's turn to cast a glance at her. "You were friends with the rebels who burned today?"

Slightly, Valina shook her head. "I watched my own family burn." Her gaze was focused upon the fountain, needing to keep her attention on something. The blood spurted and pooled in the bottom level of the fountain.

"I never knew." His voice was softly spoken, as if he did not wish to speak too loudly and cause more damage to an already damaged heart.

"I was a child. My family accused of treason. The king before Valnar forced my mother and I to watch them all burn."

And when she finally revealed to Ventar the secret that plagued her heart and past, she felt the tightness within her chest, slowly begin to loosen and unwind.

Her ears listened to the sound of a snarl ripple from Ventar. "The day that bastard died was one of the best and worst days. And soon, that bastard son of his shall burn. Slowly. So, he knows what true pain feels like."

Silence draped over them like a wool blanket. Muffling even their quiet breathing. Both of them staring ahead, losing themselves to the thoughts that plagued the darkness of their minds.

"What was her name. The *Mind Condentai.*"

"Mellena." He spoke. "A close friend of mine."

Valina cast her gaze down upon her hands, staring into the empty palms of them. Where her blades normally rested on nights like these – nights of hunt. But not on this night. "She named me a coward. And she is right in doing so."

"You are no coward, Valina."

Finally, her gaze met with his, a fierce look afire in her crimson eyes. "I am. A coward hides in fear. And that is what I did – what I *do.* I should have helped burn that damned castle to the ground, but I was a coward and fled. I should have fought for those rebels today, but I allowed fear to plague me."

"Valina..."

She shook her head. "Not anymore. I shall not stand by and watch a moment – a second – longer as innocent people die. Starting now, I'm a rebel. And I will fight. No more fear. No more hiding." She spoke with confidence, with a burning passion, a promise. The shadows shall no longer be her hiding place.

A smile caressed Ventar's lips, his eyes softening. "You are the bravest person I know, my dear Valina."

"Then you don't know many people." She wasn't truly brave, not yet. But one day, she shall be.

His hand reached for her and she remained perfectly still. The soft brush of his fingertips trailed across the skin of her cheek. His hand cupped her face and she leaned into the warmth of his palm. Valina would be lying to herself if the thought never crossed her mind of having Ventar as more than a friend. He was handsome and soft when he wished to be. Though teasing her seemed to be his favorite pastime and she found that she liked that. His personality matched well with hers, there was no denying it.

Ventar inched closer to Valina, their lips a breath away from one another. Their crimson eyes locked and soon the space was filled. Lips meeting in soft kisses before mouths began to devour each other. His hand slid to the back of her head, grabbing a fistful of her hair as the craving of her drove his mind into a frenzy. A groan found its way into her throat as he gently tugged on her hair. Valina nipped at his bottom lip, her fangs piercing skin and drawing forth his blood. A moan escaped him.

Her tongue flickered out and tasted the blood coating her lips. Sweetness and warmth erupted through her mouth, while it was still buzzing from the frenzy of the kiss. Ventar's mouth covered hers once more and Valina's hands found themselves tangling within his hair as she dragged him down upon the bench. The weight of his body pressing against hers, the warmth from him pooling upon her, wrapping around her being.

His hands braced on either side of her head and she dared to allow her own to slip beneath his grey tunic. Her fingertips traveling along the muscles carved into his stomach and chest. A warm ache began to tingle between her thighs as their kiss deepened. His tongue swept into her mouth, tasting her as she tasted him. Both of them lost to the bliss of the moment, forgetting about the day, forgetting about those screams, the smell of the burned bodies. For now, it was only them. And they needed this small distraction for the road ahead was only going to become bloodier.

Valina's fingers traced along the silver buckle of his belt, slightly tugging upon it. Ventar laughed against her lips as his eyes fluttered open once more, "My dear Valina, though I would love more than anything to bed you, I do not think doing so in a cathedral would prove appropriate."

Her fangs nipped at his bottom lip, tugging on that soft skin. "Since when did begin to care about being appropriate?"

Ventar leaned down, his mouth lingering before her neck. His lips tracing along it, the warmth of his breath igniting her skin. "Another night, and you shall be mine, my dear."

"Perhaps I won't be in the mood then." But, she would be.

His gaze found hers once more, "I know how to set a mood, Valina."

Her heart thundered at the thought. When she rose up, her lips met with his briefly once more. "Don't keep me waiting too long."

Ventar lifted his body from hers and offered his hand, "I would not dream of it, my dear."

And when she placed her hand in his, he led her away from the cathedral, and walked her home through the darkness.

CHAPTER FOUR

A MEETING OF REBELS

"When rebels stand and fight, will peace find its way into the night?"

ASHARI STOOD before the end of Valina's dark, wooden fourposter bed. The midnight curtains tied back, allowing wandering eyes to see Valina's naked form hidden beneath the sheets. Ashari's silver eyes watched the rise and fall of Valina's chest as deep breaths escaped and entered the slumbering woman. Her body was wrapped in silky, crimson sheets, her midnight hair tangling and spanning across her dark pillows. A groan escaped her as she shifted and lay on her side, her dark brows began to crease together. Her plump lips beginning to set in a frown. A noise sounded from Valina's throat, a choked sob. And it was then, that a lone tear escaped her closed eye and rolled down her cheek.

On light feet, Ashari approached the side of Valina's bed and came to rest upon it. Her pale hand reaching toward the nightmare tormented woman. Gently, it came to rest upon her cheek, her thumb stroking the lone tear away.

"My hunter, it is time to wake." Her voice was soft and gentle, calling Valina forth from her nightmares.

Slowly, those crimson eyes awakened and stared back at Ashari. Valina did not speak, only leaning into Ashari's palm, her hand coming up and resting against it – breathing in her scent. "It always feels as though I'm reliving that day, that I'm that scared little girl again." Valina's voice was barely a whisper.

"I know. But that day has come and passed. The spirits of your family are at peace by the Goddess's side."

Valina simply nodded her head.

"The hunter returned home late from the darkness. Was your hunt well? Or was there trouble within the shadows?"

Valina moved Ashari's hand away from her face and held it before her, her other hand allowing her fingers to trace over the lines in Ashari's palm. "I know that you wish to be alone after your ritual, so I visited the Cathedral of the *Blood Condentai.* Ventar found me there."

Ashari raised a white brow, a hint of a smirk twitching at the corner of her lip. "Oh, so the hunter had become the hunted. What did he wish to speak of?"

"The rebels." She said, "I told him I would join their cause. After yesterday, I decided it was time for me to stop being a coward."

Those haunting eyes slowly blinked as they gazed upon the naked woman laying upon the bed. "You were never a coward. But a person who has suffered through something great and many souls never glimpse that sort of agony or feel it."

"Do you think I'm a fool? For joining them, knowing it could very well end my life."

"No, I do not think you a fool. Your soul has always been a brave one, dear friend. But I do wonder if the rebels could find themselves in need of a *Ghost Condentai.* Do you think they would have a use for me?"

Valina's hand stilled its tracing, her gaze meeting with the woman's before her. "You wish to join?"

She smiled, "I do."

Valina nodded her head, "I shall tell Ventar when I see him later."

"And speaking of our other hunter, what else did the two of you speak of? You were gone for a long while."

Heat crept into the skin of Valina's cheeks, her lips aching at the thought of the kiss that was shared between them on the bench. "I would have allowed him to devour me in that cathedral."

Ashari tilted her head back as a laugh escaped her, "Oh dear, whatever would the Priest and Priestesses have thought? Perhaps their souls would have been too terrified to interfere."

"He promised another night. And the waiting had better be worth it."

Ashari lifted a hand to her forehead, "It seems as though my love making has failed in satisfying you, whatever shall I do?"

Valina smiled as she sat up, leaning toward the *Ghost Condentai.* "We immortals keep many lovers, you of all people should know that." She leaned close and her lips met with Ashari's – cold and sweet. "And your love making has never been a disappointment."

Ashari's hand gently lay atop Valina's. "Be safe, my hunter."

"Always." She winked.

Once Valina had dressed herself in clothes that were darker than the shadows themselves, she ventured out into the eternal night. The wind bitterly nipped at the flesh upon her cheeks. Soon, the effects of winter would be creeping into their part of the world. Though no light ventured here, the seasons of the Earth always lingered. And though Severina was powerful she could not halt all of Sybil's creations.

Winter was Valina's favorite season, the snow and the ice were beautiful as they coated this haunted land. Bringing some sort of light into their dark world. The cold against her flesh was lovely and miserable all at once. She loved how she could return home from being nearly frozen and huddle before the fire wrapped in the thickest blanket she could find. Oftentimes Ashari would join her by the fire, leaned into one another.

Traveling through the cold shadows, Valina made her way back to the cathedral. Once more, the massive structure loomed above her. As she ascended the stairs, Valina felt as though she felt eyes watching her every move, but she did not dare glance back. Forcing the doors open, voices drifted out into the night. A haunting song singing from the lips of worshippers. Valina entered the cathedral.

As she walked down the nave and found herself a seat upon one of the many benches, she watched the scene before her. A human woman stood before The Fountain of Offering. A Priest standing to the left side of her and a Priestess standing on the right. Their crimson cloaks flowed down to the floor, their hoods covering half their faces. The Priest continued to sing while the Priestess withdrew a long, thin dagger from one of her billowy sleeves. The silver blade glinted in the light from the fire that danced within the lanterns above.

The Priestess lay a gentle hand upon the back of the woman's head and she bowed over the lip of the fountain. Other voices carried through the air from the chancel – all of their faces were veiled in crimson hoods. As the song came closer to its climax, the Priestess raised the wicked dagger into the air and stilled like a statue. Waiting. And then, when the voices rose high and goosebumps swelled along Valina's skin – the Priestess drug the dagger across the woman's neck. But not too deeply, just enough to draw forth droplets of blood. The human made no whimper of pain, not a single sound had escaped her throat when the blade kissed her delicate skin. And Valina wondered just how often the woman sacrificed her blood to that fountain.

The Priestess led the woman to a far wall where a basin of water sat upon a wooden table. The Priestess lowered her hood to reveal skin as grey as Valina's and crimson eyes that were soft paired with a smile that was gentle.

"You did well. The Goddess and the *Blood Condentai* thank you for your offering, for your sacrifice. May thy be blessed on this eternal night."

The human did not speak, only gazing upon the Priestess with admiration. The crimson cloaked woman reached for a cloth and dipped it into the basin and began to clean the human's wound.

Beside Valina, the bench groaned as another took a seat upon its velvet cushion. Neither *Condentai* cast a glance at the other.

"The king has guards wandering the roads." Ventar said. "Do you think you were followed?"

"I felt eyes watching me." She said. "Is it safe to meet with the rebels tonight?"

A chuckle escaped the man. "It is never truly safe. Tonight, just means we'll have to be more careful than before."

Valina nodded her head. "Ashari wishes to know if the rebels find themselves in need of a *Ghost Condentai.*"

"Ah, now the spirit whisperer wishes to join us. Of course, there is always room for more."

"Shall we go then?" Valina did not wait for an answer as she rose to her feet, her hands resting upon the hilts of her daggers.

Ventar stood, "We shall."

Together, they stepped out into the darkness.

The pair found themselves standing before a tavern. The wooden sign swinging within the cold breeze. *Tavern of Ventaria* – the words had been burned into the wood, the rusted chains it hung from groaning with each thrust of the wind. Laughter and music could be heard coming from within. Flames flickered and cast a golden glow from the windows, dousing the road in their light. A few men staggered out, humans, chuckling and clinging to one another trying not to fall upon their faces.

Valina cast a sideward glance at Ventar. "I would not think this to be a place of meeting."

He offered his hand to her with a smile, "Thinking of something more profound? A fortress of unbreakable walls?"

She rolled her eyes but placed her hand within his and allowed the man to guide her toward the door. Ventar placed a gloved hand upon it and shoved it open. The smell and cloud of pipe smoke assaulted her first, her nose wrinkling at the scent.

Then came the voices. Many laughing others shouting in rage claiming a cheat in a game of cards. Glasses clinked upon the wooden counter as men and women downed their drinks in bets. There was a small stage in the far corner of the tavern. Three people stood upon it, each one holding a different instrument. One *Mind Condentai* man held a guitar, a *Shadow Condentai* woman playing the strings upon a violin, and a human man blowing horribly into a harmonica. A shout sounded from the bar as a human woman planted her fist into a man's face whose hand had wandered into a place that it should not have wandered.

"Such a lovely place." Sarcasm dripped within Valina's voice.

Ventar leaned down and she felt the brush of his lips trace along the curve of her pointed ear. "It shall grow on you, my dear."

Placing his hand upon her lower back, he led her toward the bar. A short woman stood behind it, cleaning a glass with a rag that didn't appear all too clean. Her grey hair was woven into a long, thick braid that swept down past her hips. When the woman faced the pair, Valina found herself in awe of the woman. Her skin was so pale it caused her to look sickly, as if she had already died and was brought back to life. Shadows of hollowness haunted the underneath of her eyes. Those ghostly, milky appearing eyes that stared upon them as if they could see down into their very souls. The woman's cheeks were sunken in, but it did not take away from her beauty.

The woman was one of the rarest of the *Condentai*; a *Dead Condentai*. A person who could summon the dead, reanimate corpses to the wielders desire. They could raise an army of the dead if they wished it. They were immortal creatures like Valina, Ashari, and the *Shadow Condentai.*

Ventar leaned against the counter, his voice kept low to a whisper. "I'll have two shots of freedom and three shots of death."

The woman cast her milky eyes toward Valina. "And she'll have the same." Ventar said.

The *Dead Condentai* met gazes with a man that sat upon a stool beside Ventar. The woman nodded her head so subtly that Valina almost thought the woman hadn't inclined her head at all. The man was human, but he rose from his stool. He did not speak a word to the pair. Ventar's hand was still upon Valina's back and he urged her forth, to follow the man.

The patrons within the tavern paid no attention as the trio drifted through the shadows. The man led them toward a hallway on the other side of the bar. There were four doors to be found; a back exit, two separate restrooms, and a broom closet. The human turned the knob on the broom closet door and waved for the two to follow him. Once they were inside, the door closed behind them and a lantern was lit. The room was a cramped space. Slender shelves were nailed upon the walls holding a small variety of cleaning supplies and other oddities. Brooms, mops, and buckets lining against the walls.

The man bent down and grabbed the edge of the raggedy, purple rug that covered the wooden floor. Moving the rug aside revealed a small door within the floorboards. The man lowered his fist toward it and knocked five times. Each knock was spaced by heart beats. The first knock sounded and two heartbeats past. The second and three passed, and so on and so on.

For a moment, there was only an answering silence. Until a lock clicking sounded and the door swung open. A young human girl, appearing to be in her teens beamed up at the trio. Her brown hair was cropped short to frame her oval face, her thin lips painted crimson, and her bright blue eyes twinkled up at them.

"Ventar, always a pleasure." The young girl's gaze drifted toward Valina. Admiration flickered within those lovely eyes. "And a newcomer. Also, a pleasure. Welcome to the rebels, I'm Lillian. Come, come!"

Ventar was the first down the narrow flight of groaning stairs. Valina placed her booted foot atop the first stair and it let out a moan as she placed her weight upon it. Down and down she went. Ventar and Lillian waiting at the bottom. The *Blood Condentai* held out his gloved hand to her as she reached the bottom stairs. Above them, the small door slammed shut and the muffled sound of the rug drug across the wooden floor.

Valina glanced upon the gloved hand but did not place her own within his palm. She stood beside him and waited for Lillian to speak. Ventar kept a solid face, not letting any hint that Valina rejecting his offered hand bothered him in the slightest.

"This way, you'll get to meet the others!" The human girl was energetic and seemed as though she did not belong in this dark part of the world. As if she were placed here by mistake and her true home was the light side. But, everyone who lived here had a shadow within them. And Valina wondered what Lillian's shadow was.

Ahead there was a doorway within the left side of the underground wall. The pair followed the young girl through it and found themselves within another cramped room. Lillian skipped toward the door and reached her hand into a pocket within her grey dress, withdrawing a rusted silver key. Slipping it into the lock, the door was opened to reveal a rather large room filled with people.

And when the trio entered, all talk was silenced as every pair of eyes turned their attention toward the new arrival. A group of four men and one woman stood hunched over a table, their hands pressed against it. All of their gazes glared toward Valina. But she did not cower – instead she held her back straighter and her chin higher.

The eldest man of the group – which Valina supposed were the leaders of the rebellion – pushed himself off the table and approached them. Lillian moved aside with a bow of her head and drifted into the shadows of the room.

The man was a *Shadow Condentai* and she noted the grey-white scars that marred his midnight skin. Both sides of his head had been shaved and single, long braid ran down the center of his head and snaked over his shoulder. His grey tunic had no sleeves, seeming to be torn at the seams, revealing muscled arms with scars dancing along them. This man has seen many battles. More than Valina could ever imagine. Upon one of his eyes was a black patch and stark scar peaked from behind the fabric, raising slightly above his brow and reaching toward the middle of his cheek. His nose was crooked to the side – broken and never fixed.

His wholly black eye drifted from Valina's head, down to her toes, and finally meeting with her crimson eyes. "What have you lost that brings you to us?" His voice was husky and rasped. "What has caused you to risk your life to end the king?" His eyes narrowed, "What has brought you to your death, girl?"

Valina was no mere girl and she would not be talked down to like she was a child with no brain within her pretty head. She was a woman – strong and fierce.

Holding his gaze, she answered, "The deaths of my family. As a child I was forced to watch them all burn. The deaths of those rebels yesterday where I was once again forced to watch others burn. I made a vow to end the king's reign – even if it costs my life. And I am no child and I shall not be talked to as if I am useless. I am a *Blood Condentai.* I am Valina Veshanr. And I shall avenge my family and every innocent who has lost their life to the hand of the king."

A gasp sounded within the room at the sound of Valina's tone – at the challenge within her words. A dare to name her a child again. The man stood before her, two heads taller, and she did not stand down.

Then, a smile cracked upon his hardened face, his dark eye gleaming. Uncrossing his arms, he placed a warm, massive hand upon her shoulder. "You have your father's spirit."

At the mention of her father, her heart swelled and ached. His screams broke through her mind. His body being devoured by those flames. But she shook the thoughts and suppressed them as she always had, sealing them away.

"You knew my father?" She asked.

He nodded his head and crossed his arms once more. "When you stepped into this room, I had a feeling. And when you spoke your last name, I knew." A heavy, saddened sigh escaped the man. "Your father was like a brother. And he shall be greatly missed – *is*."

Valina felt those traitorous tears begin to claw at the backs of her eyes but she willed them away.

"My name is, Shandal Shandoral. Welcome to the rebellion. Come, allow me to introduce you to everyone."

It took an hour to formally introduce Valina to every member. Ventar never once leaving her side, a steady support though she did not need it, but she was happy he was there. Many of the members were human, all of them ranging in age – teenagers to elders. And there was at least one of every *Condentai* to be found within the room, except there were no *Ghost Condentai* to be found. But Valina and Ventar remained the only two of their kind. It seemed as though the others of their few numbers preferred the safety the shadows offered to their already scarce kind.

There were three *Mind Condentai*, two female and one male. And she felt the brush of them within her mind as they plucked through her thoughts. Valina was not bothered by this – for she had nothing to hide. She would not betray these people, they had already suffered enough. But after tonight, she would not be so forgiving, she did like to keep some sense of privacy.

Two *Body Condentai* – both male. There were many of this type of *Condentai*, they were not as rare as some of the others. They were mortals like humans. And their power over bodies could be quite terrifying. Rendering you unable to have control over your own limbs. They could force you to slice open your own throat and dance naked within the streets. Their skin was a shade darker than Valina's grey skin. Their eyes, wholly white. And though these two men had shaved heads, the others of their kind had locks of light grey. They were tall and muscular people.

There were four of the *Organ Condentai* – two females and two males. And she suspected that they were some of the more valued members of the rebellion. Able to repair any injured organs or stop them dead. Like the *Body Condentai* they too were mortal. Their skin was dark like the *Shadow Condentai*, their hair crimson, their eyes a burning orange. The women choose to fashion their hair into long braids that swept toward the ground, silver clasps and beads threaded throughout the woven braids. The men kept their hair short, combed neatly to the side with a single braid in their hair.

Five *Shadow Condentai* – Shandal, two women, and two more men. One of the women was Shandal's wife, married for nearly a hundred years. And the other woman was their daughter, a young and beautiful woman and twin to one of the other men.

Then, there was only one *Dead Condentai* to be found within the room. A lone man who was stood in the darkest corner of the room. He shared those same milky eyes as the woman above within the bar – just as all *Dead Condentai* shared that trait. His grey hair was cut short, wisps of it sweeping into those ghostly eyes of his. The shadows beneath them were more purple than grey like the woman's above had been. And his cheeks were sunken in as well, his skin sickly and pale. But no matter their appearance, they were a *Condentai* to be feared.

"And this here, is Diaval. One of our newest members." Shandal then gestured his hand toward the woman beside him, "And this is Valina, our other newest member."

Diaval's gaze flickered up from the floor and met with Valina's. Her skin prickled as the heaviness of his eyes weighed upon her. Slowly, he removed himself from the wall and approached the *Blood Condentai.* With a gentle and slow movement, he caught Valina's hand and placed a kiss upon it. The man's lips were bitterly cold.

"A pleasure," His voice was that of a haunting whisper. And when he turned his face up to gaze upon her once more, the golden light from the lanterns cast over his face. And Valina found that he was quite handsome. Though his features were sharp and others sunken in, she found him hauntingly beautiful.

Valina said nothing, only nodding her head as he dropped her hand. The *Dead Condentai* stalked back into the shadows.

As the trio walked away, Shandal spoke in a lowered tone, "I think you found yourself an admirer, Valina."

She cast a sideways glance toward the man with a questioning brow raised.

"He has never once spoke to a newcomer so directly, let alone kissing their hand."

Valina found herself casting a glance back over her shoulder and found milky eyes watching them go. Their gazes held for a heartbeat before he cast his down to the floor.

Shandal led them toward the table where the leaders were gathered. Which, Valina learned where his family. His wife, daughter, son, and the other *Shadow Condentai* was his cousin. Shandal began the rebels many years before he married his wife and then she became the second in command. Before her, though, Valina's father had held that position. Shandal gave her bits and pieces of information to fill her in on the rebels and the secret life her father kept hidden.

Shandal's wife, Shadari, approached Valina and took both of her hands within hers. "Welcome to the rebels, my dear. And I am truly sorry for the loss you have suffered. But we shall avenge all those who have been lost. That is why we formed – to avenge and to protect." Her smile was sweet and gentle, like that of a mother's.

But Valina's own mother had left her many years ago. Never to return. Leaving a young girl all alone in this dark world. To fend and protect herself. If her mother was teaching her a lesson, it was one of the cruelest; *you shall always be alone.* That there is only you who can guard your own back. And Valina supposed the lesson did teach her, caused her to strengthen her mind and body. But alone? Valina knew she was not. She never would be.

Valina nodded and said nothing. The other leaders all greeted her in almost the same way; welcome and sorry for your loss. She knew they meant well, for everyone within this room has lost something, someone, to the hands of the king.

They gathered around the table where a map and bits of other parchment were scattered. Letters and plans – an outlay of the castle both inside and out. A map of the land of Ventaria. Little silver figurines were scattered across the map, positioned. They represented each of the rebels. Shandal pulled open a drawer on the side of the table and withdrew another figurine.

"For our newcomer." He placed Valina's figurine upon the map where the tavern was roughly sketched along with other figurines.

She eyed the tiny piece of silver. "Perhaps you'll be adding another to the map as well."

Shandal raised a brow, "Is there another wishing to join our cause?"

She nodded, "Ashari, a close friend. She wonders if the rebels find themselves in need of a *Ghost Condentai*."

The man raised his brows, a smile upon his face, as he reached his hand back into the drawer and placed another figurine next to Valina's. "We shall be eagerly awaiting her arrival."

The loud sound of someone clearing their throat echoed through the room, drawing all attention. "Now, that introductions are over, may we please proceed with our plans?" The *Shadow Condentai* that was cousin to Shandal, glared up at Valina from the map, his jaw tense.

Valina matched the man's glare from across the table.

"Shadanar." Shandal growled.

The man's gaze fell from Valina's and returned the map, a growl escaping him.

Shandal shook his head. "Our next plan of action is always the same when we lose people. Track down the guards who played a role in their deaths and kill them. An eye for an eye, as always."

Grim expressions cast themselves over the faces of the leaders, Ventar included.

"An eye for an eye." They all spoke at once.

Valina remembered the face of the man who had set her father's body afire – her family's bodies afire. He was her first kill, her first slaughter. There was no mercy shown. Her daggers sliced into his flesh, skinning him alive. His screams still rang within her ears to this day, finding themselves woven into her nightmares.

She remembered how warm his blood felt against her skin as it sprayed from the wounds. Like a crimson rain. "My name is Valina Veshanr. You burned my family." She repeated those words with each stab of her daggers. She wanted the man to know who she was, what he had done, and what shall become of him.

And what became of him was a bloody pile of severed limbs.

Valina supposed it marked her a monster for what she had done to the man. That she felt no guilt nor remorse. She had smiled like a serpent upon the mangled body before her bloody boots. But still she felt that his death was not enough. Her crimson gaze drifted toward the castle and the only the death that would be enough would be the king's. But his death had come and not by her hands. He had died when she reached the age of one hundred and fifty and his son ascended the throne at the same age as she – still claiming his seat upon the throne to this day.

"Tonight, we shall send out a handful of rebels to take care of the guards. They'll be easy targets as they prowl the roads." Shandal said.

"Groups of two. No one goes alone. We shall not risk more deaths of our people." Shadanar added.

"Agreed." Shadari nodded her head.

Ventar stepped closer to the table, laying his hand atop the map. "I volunteer."

Shandal met his gaze with a nod, "Take Valina with you."

Shadanar snarled and stood straight, shoulders back. "You already trust this woman? Allowing her to meet us is one thing, but allowing her to see our maps, plans, and going out on missions is another. It is too soon. This is wrong."

Valina stepped forth to speak, but Shandal silenced her with a raised hand. Sealing her lips, she nodded her head, showing respect for the leader of the rebellion.

Shandal lay both his hands flat atop the table and matched Shadanar's glare. "Valina's father was a valued member of this rebellion. This woman was forced to watch him and her family burn. So, yes, I am allowing her to see what we plan to do because she shall be just as valued as every member here is." His voice lowered to a warning, "If you have a problem with my authority, you may always challenge me for the position if you think me unfit." His hand moved to rest upon the hilt of a dagger strapped to his side.

Shadanar bared his teeth, a growl escaping him, and he stalked away from the table into the shadows.

A sigh escaped Shandal as he shook his head, his dark gaze meeting with Valina's. "I must apologize about him. As you know, each of us has lost something. But he has lost more than must."

Valina nodded her head. She understood his resentment toward her, but she would prove that resentment wrong.

Many groups disappeared into the night, Lillian was among them. The young girl had changed from her simple dress to dark leathered clothes that clung to every dip and curve of her lithe body. Swords strapped across her back and daggers clasped within her dainty hands.

Ventar and Valina were some of the last to leave and as they approached the door that led toward the stairs, she felt a heavy gaze upon her. Stopping in her tracks at the doorway, she glanced beside her to find Diaval lingering within the darkness. The man did not move but his voice whispered into the air.

"Safe hunting, Valina Veshanr."

"And to you." With an incline of her head, she stepped through the doorway.

Ventar waited for her at the bottom of the stairs, and they ascended above, to begin their hunt.

CHAPTER FIVE

A NIGHT OF BLOOD

"When the hunters begin their prowl, their prey try to hide, but not even the shadows can save them."

V ALINA'S DAGGERS weighed within the palms of her grey hands. They seemed to call out, crying for a taste of blood, pleading to bite into flesh. Soon. She thought, soon, the daggers would feast just as she would. The guards were just below them, a few who had played a role in the deaths of the rebels. Their chat filtered into the air, drifting to the pair's listening ears.

And what was heard, caused a snarl to ripple from Valina's lips. The one taller guard spoke of Mellena, the *Mind Condentai.* Saying what a waste it was to burn a perfectly good body when the king could have had her as a personal whore. The grip upon her daggers tightened as the men chuckled.

Oh, how she would enjoy this slaughter.

"Goddess of Dark, hear my prayer, bless me on this night of hunt and many more forward." The prayer was spoken within her mind, but

her lips moved in silence, sending her unspoken words forth into the air.

Ventar glanced at her and with a nod of his head, the two ascended from the rooftop. Their boots sounding lightly upon the cobblestone road. The guards' backs were faced to them, unaware of the predators that were lurking just behind them within the shadows. On light, silent feet, the pair crept up to the men.

Ventar reached around and lay his obsidian sword upon one of the men's necks. The sharpened blade cutting deep into his flesh. His arms flailed and grasped at the sword trying desperately to break free. But the blade did not budge, Ventar showing no sign of struggle. The blade bit into the man's pale fingers, slicing deep to the bone. Crimson soaked the blade and spurted to the ground. A whimper of pain gasped from the man's lips as blood began to pool at the corners of his mouth.

The guard's partner bellowed, his hand reaching for the sword strapped to his side, but it never unsheathed it. With a flick of her wrist, Valina sent one of her daggers twirling through the air. Head over end it spun until it found its mark upon the center of the man's hand. A shocked cry escaped him as he beheld the wicked blade that had burrowed deep into his flesh.

Before the man could extract the dagger from his hand, his body stilled, his brown eyes growing wide. A wicked grin crossed Valina's lips as she commanded the blood within him. It no longer ran like rivers through his veins, his heartbeat slowly coming to a halt. The blood began to crawl toward the surface, his pale skin taking on a red hue. His body would now only know pain until his death as the blood stilled and halted within him.

With slow, predator-like steps, she approached the man. Their faces were close. She wished for the man to see who the cause of his untimely end would be. For him to look her in the eyes and *know.*

Her lips curled like serpents, her voice taking on a pur as she spoke. "Where is your king now?" She stalked around him. "There shall be no one to save you from the monsters." She flashed her sharp fangs at the man once she stood before his face once more. Fury burning like a blaze within his eyes. "And now, you die. This is for Mellena. For all the rebels you have slaughtered."

His brown eyes widened as crimson tears began to weep from them, staining his pale skin as they trickled down. The man's mouth gaped open, but no wail escaped him. His skin changing, a dark hue of red rising and rising. Until, a veil of mist burst forth from his flesh. With a lifeless groan, the man toppled over onto the cobblestone, leaving behind a crimson cloud in the shape of a human body standing where he once stood. His eyes were wide as they stared upon the eternal night sky. His skin a deathly pale color.

"There is no peace in the afterlife for you, no Goddess there with her arms open in welcome. She shall look upon you and cast you into an eternity of darkness that is not of peace – but a place where agony lurks, where screams shall always sound. And that shall be your resting place."

The Priest and Priestess in every Cathedral preached about the two eternal darks. The one of serenity, where the Goddess bares her arms in welcome. And the other that is a prison of agony, where you shall forever be tormented.

And Valina always caught her mind drifting, thinking of which dark the Goddess shall cast her in. Perhaps the agony of eternity would be waiting for her – she was no innocent.

But then again, no one within this dark land truly was.

A gurgling sound caused Valina's gaze to break away from the lifeless body of the guard. Ventar had drug his sword across the guard's throat that he still held, the blade digging deep to the bone and crimson spurted and rained through the air. The sight of it caused Valina's mouth to water. The body of the guard Ventar held thudded to the ground before his feet. Flicking his sword, some of the blood coating it splattered upon the cobblestone.

Valina knelt, her crimson eyes staring upon the lifeless bodies before her. Reaching a grey hand out, she dipped her fingers into the pool of blood spilling from the guards' bodies. Her forefinger and thumb rubbing the dark liquid together.

"I do not feel a single thread of guilt for taking these lives." Her voice was whispered but was not weak. Strength sounded within her words. "And I suppose that marks me a monster, for enjoying the deaths we brought upon these men." Her gaze drifted toward the sky, seeming to search for the Goddess. "And I suppose that I do not care. These men were monsters. These deaths were welled deserved. It takes a monster to kill a monster."

Footsteps sounded behind her as Ventar approached closer. "We are all monsters, in our own ways."

And, he was right.

Valina did not rise from her crouch, instead, her gaze had fallen back toward the blood that had pooled upon the ground. Her mouth had begun to water, crying out for that sweet nectar of life. Casting a glance over her shoulder, her eyes met with Ventar's. "No sense in wasting it."

When her crimson eyes beheld the thick liquid once more, it stirred and rippled. And slowly, it drifted into the air. A crimson river streaming into the wind, dancing along the currents. The stream split into two, one of them sailing over Valina's head toward the *Condentai* just behind her. She did not glance back to see if he had accepted the blood offering.

Valina's lips parted, allowing the stream of blood entrance into her mouth. It rippled like gentle waves within the air as it made its way toward her. And when the crimson touched her tongue, her mind had exploded in a frenzy as she drank her fill. Her eyes began to roll into the back of her head as her lids closed over them. She allowed herself to be lost to the feeding, to the drug of the blood.

For a moment, all the pain within her heart had faded, all the memories of hurt where gone. For a moment, she was only a woman, a *Blood Condentai*, enjoying the prize of her hunt. But, all moments faded and came to an end. When the last drop of blood rolled down her throat, all the pain and memories came rushing back.

The grey skin covering her eyes, pulled back, allowing her to gaze upon the bodies once more. Rising to her feet, she pulled the hood of her cloak over her head. "I suppose we return to the rebels?"

Ventar pulled his hood on as well, "We do."

The rebels returned to the room beneath the tavern. Groups of two going in one at a time with several minutes spacing between the next group following in after. Everyone was gathered before the table, many of them were coated in blood, some of theirs and some of their prey. No lives were lost, a handful of them were injured. No one would be praying to the Goddess on this night, mourning souls that had been lost.

Lillian was one of the few who had been injured, her left arm marred with a gash that tore through the leather fabric of her clothing, slicing from the shoulder down to the elbow. But the human girl did not show any sign of pain upon her face as crimson wept from her wound. There was a victorious spark within her blue gaze, a smirk quirking at the corner of her thin lips. Blood was splattered across her right cheek but Valina guessed it was not the girl's blood.

The few who were seriously injured were taken care of by the elder humans who could no longer see battle but still proved their use to the rebels. They worked stitching deep wounds that burrowed down to the bone in arms and legs. *Organ Condentai* were no help when it came to flesh wounds, only wounds of the organs and nothing more. Not one rebel made a cry or whimper of pain as the needles and thread sewed through their skin, lacing it together once more.

Though there were a few *Condentai* to be found, the humans outnumbered them. They had no powers to rely on as her kind did. What they lacked in power, they made up for in strength and determination. And being skilled with a blade, helped as well.

Ventar and Valina were near the doorway, leaning against the wall, allowing the rebellion to talk about how each hunt had went. Noting how many guards were killed, how many of their own had been injured.

Eventually, Shandal waved the pair over as the other rebels had drifted away into the shadows, disappearing for the night. "And, how was your hunt?" There was tiredness within his voice, his shoulders slumped with a heavy weight. His gaze seeming drained of any life.

"We found two guards, both are now dead." Ventar spoke.

Shandal nodded his head and slashed two tally marks upon the parchment before him with a stick of coal. Valina's gaze wandered across the long list of tally marks, each one marking a sign of death for the king's guards.

"Are either of you needing medical attention?" His wholly black eye never ventured away from that parchment, his gaze gliding across each and every dark mark.

"We are well." Ventar said, casting a worried glance upon the leader before him.

Shandal nodded his head. "Good. Both of you are free to go, I have plans to make and go over before our next meeting."

His wife, Shadari, approached. Her gaze gentle with concern as she placed a delicate hand upon his arm. Finally, his gaze drifted away from those marks and stared upon the woman before him. "My love, it is time to rest. It has been a long night for us all. Work on the plans tomorrow."

With one last glance upon the parchment, a heavy sigh escaped him as he nodded his head. "Tomorrow."

With a grunted farewell, the couple drifted away into the shadows. As Ventar and Valina made their way toward the doorway, she heard a low voice whispering from the darkness. Glancing toward a corner on the other side of the room, she found Lillian sitting upon a wooden chair, cleaning her daggers with a rag that was stained in blood.

The young girl's eyes were closed as she whispered, almost quietly singing, *"Goddess of Earth, Goddess of Night, bless my life from this night on. Bless my blades for each and every hunt. Bless my soul for when one day, it shall meet its end."*

Her voice was subtle, a little rasp drug behind every word. Each syllable sung delicately and light. Lillian's face appeared even more youthful, even with the blood upon her cheek and her short brown hair tangled and mussed.

She appeared like any young girl, innocent. Someone who has never seen bloodshed, has never felt a heart shatter. But there was also something dark lingering within her, haunting some of the tones within her voice as she sang. Lillian was not just any young girl; she has seen something truly gut wrenching and now her blades are stained with blood as she quested for vengeance, to fill a void within herself that may never be truly filled.

When the young girl's blue eyes viewed the room before her once more, she found Valina standing a few feet away, her crimson eyes staring curiously upon her. "You pray to Sybil and to Severina?" The *Blood Condentai* asked.

A soft smile crossed Lillian's lips. "I do. I think it only right to do so, to pay respect to one Goddess who created me and another who watches over me."

Though Severina hated many – almost all – of Sybil's creations; she did not appear to hate the humans. There was a softness within the Goddess of Dark's heart for them, frail beings with lives that did not last long compared to some of her own children. For some of even Severina's were not eternal as Valina and others but their lives still extended those of humans. Humans who were not given any sort of power to protect them, leaving them almost defenseless except for their will, their determination, and strong minds.

"I know many *Condentai* look down upon us – the king included – as if we are nothing but the dirt on the bottom of their boots. As though our lives are worthless, as though we are weak." Lillian transformed from the young, energetic girl that Valina had first met, into a woman with a heart of steel. "But we are not weak, and I shall not be seen as so."

Valina accused herself for sometimes thinking of humans as weak beings but they were so much more than that, so much more than she ever gave them credit for.

"I shall not lie to you when I say that I once thought the same." Lillian's steel blue gaze met with hers. "But I know that I thought wrong. You are not weak, Lillian."

To Valina's surprise, a wide smile appeared on Lillian's lips, the youthfulness returning to her face. "I'm glad you have changed your view on us." But her smile faltered as she added, "But I must admit that I once only thought of your kind as monsters." Her gaze flickered across Valina's face as she rose from the wooden chair, "But I know not all of your kind are."

But the woman before Valina had no idea of the monstrous things that Valina has done and still plan on doing. Knowing nothing of the blood thirsty beast lurking just beneath her flesh.

As Lillian walked away, she said over her shoulder, *"May thy Goddess watch over you."* Before she disappeared into the shadows.

Before Valina herself vanished for the night, she cast a glance around the room, her crimson eyes searching for the lone *Dead Condentai.* But Diaval was nowhere to be found, at least to the wandering eye. As she turned and made her exit, the man took a step forth from the shadows, his milky eyes still lingering upon the doorway.

The walk was silent, save for the gentle wind that whispered into their ears. Ventar kept a steady pace beside Valina, ensuring that she made it home safely – even though she could defend herself quite well. But Valina saw no point in arguing, Ventar would have followed her anyways just to be sure. And in truth, she appreciated his steady presence.

When they finally stood before the little fence around her house, he grasped her hand and placed a kiss upon her bare skin. "Goodnight, my dear Valina." His voice purred her name like a sweet sin.

Ventar turned his back upon Valina and began to walk along the cobblestone road before she called out to him, "And when is the night that I was promised going to happen, Ventar?"

He stopped within his tracks and within a blink, he stood before the woman, his body almost pressed against her own. A wicked grin curling upon his thin lips. One of his arms struck out and wrapped itself around her waist, drawing her body closer, pressing their chests together until their hearts could beat against one another. His other hand cupped her cheek, tilting her head at the perfect angle as he lowered his. Their lips met in burning passion. Her body engulfed by it, by the feeling of his smooth lips against her own.

The way his mouth devoured hers, his tongue gliding across her teeth, pleading for entrance. And so, she allowed it. His tongue tangled with hers, dancing between their lips. Panted, hungry breaths began to escape them. Ventar's fingers that now rested upon her hip, dug hungrily into her skin, a growl rumbling within his chest. She felt it vibrate against her own.

As she pressed her body more into his, she felt his bulge rub against her and a warmth ignited between her thighs. Her hands reached around his neck, her fingers tangling within his midnight locks as she deepened their kiss. Both of Ventar's hands now greedily dug into her hips, tugging on her shirt. A moan threatened to escape from Valina's mouth as Ventar took her bottom lip between his teeth – careful not to draw blood – and tugged.

As she went to return to the kiss, Ventar placed a finger over her lips. Her eyes fluttered open once more to find him grinning down at her. "That, my dear, is only a taste of what you'll be having in the coming nights."

Heat flared within Valina's face, *"Bastard."* She growled, her body aching for him, the warmth still lingering between her thighs.

He winked a crimson eye at her before vanishing, "Only the best kind." His voice whispered through the silence.

Ashari was seated upon the couch, a fire crackling within the fireplace, and the curtains ajar. Her silver eyes staring out into the darkness that lurked just beyond the glass. When the sound of the door opening, and closing met with her ears, her gaze drifted to the doorway to find Valina lingering within it.

"The hunter returns from the shadows, though not visible, the hunter's hands weep with blood." Slowly, she blinked. "I assume your night was well?"

A sigh escaped Valina as she approached the window and closed the curtains, concealing them from wandering eyes that might be lurking. She slumped on the couch beside Ashari, kicking her feet up onto the table. "Most of the rebels approve of me, save for one. He shall be fun to deal with."

Ashari nodded her head, "The ghosts whispered to me. Telling me of your slaughter."

Valina rolled her eyes. Many times, has Ashari sent her ghostly dogs out sniffing for her, watching her every move, and reporting back to the *Ghost Condentai*. But Valina knew she only did so because she cared.

"I killed a guard and Ventar the other. I'm sure your ghosts told you that already, though."

A cold hand rested atop of Valina's. Silver eyes gazing down upon them. "They tell me of what they see but they cannot tell me of what you feel, my friend."

"I feel the same after every hunt; no remorse. Those I kill deserved it. I do not kill without meaning."

Once more Ashari nodded her head. "And did the rebels find themselves in need of a *Ghost Condentai?*"

"The leader said he'll be eagerly awaiting your arrival."

Ashari's face was alight, a smile appearing upon her pale pink lips. "May I join you when next you go?"

Valina couldn't help but smile at Ashari's eagerness. Giving a light squeeze to the *Ghost Condentai's* hand, she said, "Of course."

"And now, may I ask, was that Ventar's voice that I heard outside?" A little grin found itself upon Ashari's lips, one of her brows raised.

A scoff escaped Valina as her eyes rolled, "Yes."

"And when shall this promised night happen, might I ask?"

"He refuses to tell me, and the damned bastard made we want to fuck him right there on the street. He said it was a taste of what's to come." That warm ache began to throb between her thighs once more when she thought of the hungry way Ventar had devoured her lips.

A chuckle sounded from Ashari as she moved her hand to cover her lips. "This man is going to drive you insane, I do believe."

And it was moments like these that caused Valina to forget Ashari's strange ways. The way she spoke as if she was not truly here in body, as if her spirit had wandered far away.

"I'll gut that bastard." Valina growled as she rose from the couch and marched toward the doorway.

Then, the *Ghost Condentai's* voice whispered after her into the hallway. "Sleep well my hunter, for dreams may bring to life what lays dormant within our deepest aches." Her voice had drifted away, monotone with no emotion.

Valina cast a glance toward the doorway over her shoulder but found no Ashari standing there. Silence settled over the home save for the crackling of the fire. With a sigh, Valina continued up the stairs to her bedroom. Ready to lay her body to rest.

CHAPTER SIX

LIGHT IN THE DARK

"When light finds its way into the darkness, where shall the shadows hide?"

THE NIGHT had begun peacefully. Ashari and Valina venturing out into the town market, shopping for clothing and candied treats. Perhaps a few new decorations for their shared home. Humans and *Condentai* bustled along the cobblestone road, lanterns igniting the night in a warm glow. Merchants lined their carts along the sides of the road before the shops, bakeries, and homes. Many of the owners weren't pleased, of course, but there wasn't much they could do.

A cart stood out to Valina. A small cart with glass-like shelves lining atop it with little figurines scattered along them. Approaching the cart, the merchant smiled sweetly to Valina. An elder human woman. She sat peacefully upon her wooden chair, a purple cushion beneath her. Her grey hair was woven into a crown, the braid wrapping around her head. She wore a dark blue, simple dress, and a grey scarf swung over her shoulders. Her green eyes drifted up from the ground and a smile appeared on the elder's face.

"Welcome, *Blood Condentai.* Have my trinkets caught your eye?" Her voice was hoarse but still coated with gentleness.

Valina approached the cart closer. Many of the figurines were crafted from wood – something Valina loved to do in her spare time – but others were made from glass. They were carved into the shapes of varying animals, others seemed to be men and women in robes, and there were many carvings of the Goddess of Earth and the Goddess of Dark. And as her eyes wandered, she found one figurine of a man. But not just any man.

The God of Light; Nicitis.

She cast a glance over at the elder woman. And those green eyes fell upon that lone glass figure. "You are not the first to gaze upon it with questioning eyes, *Condentai.*"

"Why only one?" She asked.

The elder woman eyed the figure, "I pray to all three. Though we are in the land of dark, there is still light to be found here. If not from the sun, then it comes from those that surround us. Light within a child's laughter, within a lover's embrace, within a mother's tenderness, within a father's protectiveness. For you see, there is light all around us. And I have been waiting to see which person would be attracted toward that light."

Valina had never once thought of that, in all her years. Never once considered what people did or the smallest pleasures in life were *light.* And she thought that perhaps, she wasn't all dark, that there could be light found within her, as well. If only she searched deep enough.

Her gaze drifted over to the other Goddess figurines. "I'll take it and one each of the Goddesses, please."

The elder woman nodded her head with a smile. Leaning on her wooden cane, she slowly rose from her chair and approached the cart. Bending down, she opened one of the small doors and retrieved a cloth bag and few pieces of stray fabric. Her aged hands set to work delicately wrapping the glass figures in the cloth and placing them within the bag.

"May thy Gods watch over you, *Condentai.*"

As the woman handed over the bag, she bowed her head. Taking the bag from her hands, Valina reached into the cloth coin bag that hung by her side. "How much do I owe you?"

"Nothing."

Valina blinked. "Ten gold Ventra."

The figures were not worth more than a few copper or silver Ventra. But to Valina, they were worth much more. Many people did not appreciate the long hours that was spent in creating something. Forming something with your hands born from your soul. And it seemed as though only those who had an appreciation for the arts, understood that.

"I cannot take it." The elder woman shook her head and returned to her seat. A heavy breath of exhaustion escaping her.

Reaching into her coin bag, Valina placed ten gold Ventra upon the cart, close enough for the woman to grab. "Many do not appreciate the work that goes into something such as this, but I do.

Take this as a gift, an offering, for your work. Take it and return home. Rest and create."

Those green eyes of the elder woman's met with Valina's. A glaze covering them as tears began to swell. "Thank you."

Valina nodded her head and stepped away from the cart, "May thy Gods watch over you."

When Valina returned to Ashari's side, she found a smile upon the woman's face. "A hunter whose heart is pure." Her voice was haunting, "Always a soft spot for the arts."

Casting a glance over her shoulder she watched as a young boy helped the elder woman pack up her trinkets with care before shutting down the cart for the day and returning home.

Returning her attention to the *Ghost Condentai*, she noticed the cloth bag that hung from her ghostly hand. "I see you have found something of interest."

"Black curtains with silver embroidery and depictions of spirits. I thought they would look lovely in my room."

Ashari always collected trinkets that related to her kind. There were many glass figurines within her room, a few of Severina but mostly of spirits. Some of them had hands covering their weeping faces, others had their mouths opened in an eternal scream. A few paintings were scattered along the walls. Many of them depicting *Ghost Condentai* performing their ritual, releasing ghosts to their Goddess.

The pair continued their walk along through the market. Sweet scents wafted into the air, drifting toward their noses. The smell of caramel caused Valina's mouth to water. Though her kind could survive on blood alone, she often indulged herself in some of the smaller pleasures; sometimes over indulging when it came to the sweets.

A giggle sounded beside her, "Hungry, my hunter?"

With a smile, Valina grasped Ashari's hand, entwining their fingers, and approached one of the candy merchants. A human man was shouting about candied apples. And since the sun did not reach their dark half of the world, the king allowed strict trade from the light side. Though they offered fruits, plants (even though they did not last long without the sun), and vegetables. The dark side could only offer handmade crafts; clothes, blankets, tapestries, figurines. There was not much else to offer.

The man eyed the pair approaching his cart. A wide smile spreading across his middle-aged face. "Ah, welcome! Have my treats led you here?"

Ashari answered, "My friend here loves treats."

The man clapped his hands together, "Good! Good! My most popular treat for today has been my candied apples! Perhaps those are what drew you here?"

Valina nodded her head but her gaze was not upon the man but upon the candied apples before her on the cart. Some were only glazed in caramel while others had nuts, raisins, or chocolate bits sprinkled atop them.

They approached the cart and grabbed two of the apples, one sprinkled with nuts, the other was only caramel. "For two beautiful ladies, these are for you." The man's brown eyes were kind, his smile sweet, just like his treats.

"Allow us to pay." Valina was already reaching into her pouch when the man shoved the apples her way.

"No, please accept them." His gaze moved to peer over Valina's shoulder. "I saw what you did for my mother. And I thank you. So, accept these as a token of my gratitude. Please."

When Valina glanced back, she saw the elder woman and young boy heading away from the market. The young boy pushed the cart, the woman's chair resting atop it, and Valina guessed that her trinkets were hidden away behind the little doors. And it appeared to her that the young boy was this merchant's son. Sharing almost the same face.

Taking the apples from his hands, she bowed her head, "Thank you, and may thy Gods bless you."

"They already have, through you, *Condentai.* You made my mother's day and perhaps the rest of her life, however long that may be." He bowed low at the waist, "Gods bless you, friend."

The pair strolled along, Ashari nibbling on the caramel apple and Valina taking large bites from hers – she had chosen the one with the nuts. Her mouth crackled as the sweet caramel met with her tongue. She closed her eyes, savoring the treat.

"Nothing in life compares to sweets." Valina muttered with a mouthful of apple.

Ashari raised a brow, "Nothing? Love-making included?"

Valina glanced at the apple, considering, "They are a close tie."

Ashari giggled and took another nibble from her apple. They continued along, the night seeming to go along perfectly. As if for a moment, there was peace. That the king did not exist, those bodies upon that damned fence had vanished, that the rebels had not burned days before. But of course, the reality of their world always had to come tumbling back – rolling in like a thundering storm.

Guards stormed the streets, pouring in from all corners. Their voices shouting together, "The king has requested every soul present at his castle – *now.*"

Ashari and Valina cast warry glances at one another before falling into step with the crowd of towns people, heading toward the castle.

The charred bodies of the rebels were still skewered upon that wicked fence. Crows of shadow had come and plucked the burnt eyes out of the peoples' sockets, their mouths opened in eternal agony.

Before the castle doors, stood the mad king himself. A grin upon his face, but something was different – a gleam within his eyes that suggested this event was something that would never be forgotten. Valina felt a stone weigh within her stomach, her gut twisting.

She felt a light brush against her hand and cold fingers entwining with her own. Ashari held her gaze for a moment, nodding her head slightly. The pair turned their eyes back to the castle.

The king stretched his arms out, "My loyal subjects. Today, I have a true treat for us all. For an enemy has stumbled into our darkened land."

The stone began to burn like an inferno within the pit of her stomach. No. It couldn't be. Utter silence – that was almost deafening to the ears – had draped over the crowd of gathered towns people. All eyes were upon the king.

His lips pulled back to reveal his grin, his fangs flashing. "Today, you have the pleasure of watching with your own eyes the death of our enemy."

He took a step aside as two guards filtered through the castle doors. And just behind them was a person chained with a sack tossed over their head. Their shoulders were held back, head straight, and they did not fumble with their steps. Two more guards followed behind them. The gathered group approached the fence and the two guards behind them, forced the person down onto their knees. A grunt of pain had escaped from the person – man, as the grunt was more on the masculine side.

The king descended the stairs, his hands held behind his back, as he approached the fence. "My guards caught this *thing* lurking not too far from my castle. Perhaps he was fool enough to think he could slaughter me in my sleep. Perhaps he sought to slaughter us all – signal his friends – but that shall not be happening, not to us anyways. For the slaughter shall be upon him."

The king reached out with his gloved hand and tore the sack away from the man's head. Long hair of gold spilled out over his white tunic. His skin was a soft shade of brown and Valina wondered just how beautiful he may be bathed beneath the sun's golden glow, how his skin might glow along with it. His jawline was sharp, his cheekbones carved perfectly. The man glanced up at the king with those blue eyes of his, one of them blooming with purple. Those full lips of his pressed into a thin line. Valina noticed the split in his bottom lip, the blood that was caked onto his chin.

A gasp had escaped from the crowd, hands reaching to cover gaping mouths, eyes wide open as they viewed the man. A child of Light. Son of the God Nicitis. Their born enemy.

None of these people – Valina included – have ever seen with their own eyes a child of light. They have never stepped foot inside their land. And the trades were met at the line dividing their worlds. The king and his guards the only ones to lay eyes upon those of the light.

Valina did not find herself surprised when hisses found their way into her ears, as many of the people began to chant; *burn, burn, burn!* Once before, when she was young, Valina shared the same hatred. For everyone that was born within the dark world, was raised to hate those of the light. But as Valina grew older and gained a mind of her own, she began to think differently. Her views changing as her body did. Though their Gods were enemies it did not mean that they had to be.

Her crimson eyes watched as the king grabbed a fistful of the man's beautiful hair and forced his head back. A snarl rippled across Valina's lips.

The king knelt low, a smile still upon his face, as he said, "Are you ready to burn, child of Nicitis? Are you ready to return to your makers side?"

The man held the king's gaze, defiance written within it, "I shall not be burning today."

The king's brow furrowed as he released his hold on the man's hair. Taking a step back, he nodded to his guards. Each one of them holding an unlit torch. But before the fire could ignite them, the golden-haired man did something that shocked every soul watching.

A burst of blinding, golden light ignited their dark world. Shrieks and hisses sounded through the air. And from Valina's own lips was a cry of pain, as her eyes had never been a witness to a light so bright in all her three hundred years. Her hand and Ashari's hand had drifted apart from one another as both women raised their arms to shield their eyes. A strong gust of wind blew their way, sweeping Valina's cloak along its current, tugging her hood back and unleashing her midnight locks.

And when the wind had settled, and the light had vanished, Valina dared a glance. All around her were scattered groups of frightened people. Mothers huddled over their small, crying children. Men standing before their families, ready to guard them with their lives. And when Valina glanced toward the castle, she saw an empty spot where the man was once knelt on his knees. And she noticed that not one soul had been harmed from that blast of light.

The king stood where he had been when the light ignited, his crimson eyes ravenous, the veins within his neck throbbing. *"FIND HIM!"* His voice roared and echoed across the land. *"FIND HIM AND BURN THE BASTARD!"*

At once, his guards scrambled to their feet and rushed off in all directions in search for the missing child of Nicitis. Valina found herself hoping that he was never found.

When Valina glanced toward the castle again, she found the king's gaze staring back. His crimson eyes were afire with flames that danced within his irises. And she fought back the smirk that began to form.

"A light has been found within the darkness." Ashari's eyes lingered ahead, upon the empty spot beside the raging king.

The cathedral of the *Ghost Condentai* loomed above Valina and Ashari. The pair standing before the steps that led inside. All seven cathedrals were crafted the exact same. The only differences between them were the artworks within the stained-glass windows and symbols of the Goddess upon the doors. The windows here depicted haunting images of Ashari's kind. Casting them as if they were wayward spirits themselves. Their skin made to look as though it could be seen through. And the Goddess was no exception to this in their depiction of her. Her long hair as white as the skin they created for her. Her eyes silver and all-seeing. And from the palms of her out stretched hands were souls returning to their maker.

Ashari approached the step and began to take them, appearing as if her feet were not meeting with the ground, as if spirits had lifted her upon ghostly hands and gently glided her toward the doors. When she stood before them, she glanced over her pale, exposed shoulder. Her white dress spilled out around her like a milky pool.

The sleeves long and flowing by her sides. Those silver eyes meeting with crimson ones.

"Are you not to join me within the cathedral, dear friend?"

Valina lingered at the bottom stair, her arms crossed over her chest. "No. Other *Condentai* are not so much welcomed within there or any other Cathedral. I shall remain here, as you pray."

"The hunter fears the ghosts lingering within the walls." Her voice had taken on that monotone sound, her gaze drifting away.

Valina has once before entered the cathedral of the *Ghost Condentai*. And it felt as though eyes were watching from every corner, a ghostly breath always cold against your ear. And the *Condentai* within were not as welcoming to visitors not of their kind. They were more of a secluded kind, preferring to be with their own or the spirits of the deceased.

Ashari offered a dainty hand, "Come. I shall not take long, my hunter."

Valina's gaze lingered upon her hand for a moment, and with a sigh, she marched up the stairs, and placed her hand within Ashari's. A sweet smile tugged at the *Ghost Condentai's* lips as she led Valina inside the haunted cathedral.

The inside had the exact same layout as all the cathedrals. But instead of crimson velvet cushioned benches, they were silver cushioned. There was no Fountain of Offering to be found within, only an altar holding the place of where it would have resided. An altar that featured a large, grey stone carving of Severina. Candles circled it upon tall, black stands.

The first set of candle stands reached high above Severina's head and the rest following lowered in height all the way down to her knees where her legs were crossed over one another. The flames flickered against a ghostly wind in time with each other. A golden glow surrounded the Goddess of Dark where shadows should have been devouring her. But Valina made no comment. Upon the next level of the altar, just below the stone carving, a long thin table sat. White candles were lined from one end to the other and a wooden bowl was sat just in the center, grey smoke curling from it. Valina had caught the scent of sage burning as soon as they entered.

Ashari took a step upon the silver carpet that trailed from the doors all the way toward the altar. "I shall not be long." She whispered to the air.

As Ashari approached the altar, Valina cast a glance around her. Some *Ghost Condentai* were scattered, many sitting upon the benches, others praying before the stone Goddess, some lingering within the corners, watching from the shadows. But for a moment, all silver eyes were upon her – their gazes heavy with judgement. Valina ignored them and took a seat upon the bench closest to the door and waited for her friend to finish her prayers.

Once the *Ghost Condentai* realized Valina was not leaving anytime soon, they returned their gazes ahead or closed their eyes as they prayed. Ahead at the altar, Ashari was knelt before the statue along with two other women. They were upon their knees, heads bent downward, and hands clasped before them.

Within the haunting silence of the cathedral, Valina's ears could hear their whispered prayers. And she watched as their bodies began to fade into the air just like they did when they performed their ritual. A hint of them still lingered here – within the world of the living. Another part of them drifting to the world of the dead, greeting the wandering spirits. The spirits who had yet to decide if they were ready to leave this world behind them.

The women's long, white hair began to stir along a ghostly wind. Rising and rippling behind them. A cold chill crept toward Valina then, beginning at the base of her spine and working upward. As if the skeletal hand of death traced its bony fingers along her spine. She suppressed the shiver. A chilling air whispered past her ear – perhaps it was a wandering spirit wishing to speak but she could not hear them. Only feeling their unvoiced words. She felt gazes upon her, but it was not the gazes of the *Condentai* within the room. But gazes of the dead.

And this was why Valina did not much like to come to the cathedral of the *Ghost Condentai.* The dead always lingered here. Always watching and always listening.

While Valina waited, her mind had begun to wander. Journeying back to that strange man – that beautiful man. A man that was the child of Nicitis, a man who was supposed to be her enemy. And though Valina knew that they were marked as enemies from birth, she believed that he was no enemy. For an enemy would have slaughtered the king and everyone watching, but his light had damaged nothing but the chains holding him.

Why had he come to their dark side of the world? A child of light finding themselves within the dark and shadows that lurked.

Continuing to wander deeper into her thoughts, they drifted toward his appearance. To that brown skin she wished to reach and trail her fingers against. To that golden hair that flowed like silk, wanting to comb her slender fingers through it. She had never once seen hair so golden before – the humans' hair within this land were dull and dark.

"Is the hunter prepared to leave?" Ashari's gentle voice shattered through Valina's drifting thoughts.

She blinked up at the ghostly woman standing before her. "If you are, Ashari."

When the *Ghost Condentai* nodded her head, Valina rose from the bench. As they approached the doors, she asked, "If you do not mind me asking, what did you pray for?"

Ashari stood before the doors, her silver gaze lingering upon the carving of the Goddess upon them. "The son of Nicitis. I prayed that he finds his way home safely."

"You hold no hatred toward our natural enemy?"

Ashari slowly blinked. "No." She answered, "Two Gods whom are at war with one another pass the hatred onto their children. But, do the children truly wish for it?"

Valina stared upon the carving, "No."

Without another word whispered between them, the pair left the cathedral and the spirits lingering within it, behind.

CHAPTER SEVEN

A PROMISED NIGHT

*"A night of promise soon begins, but shall something stir
within the darkness while bodies are at work?"*

VALINA WAS awakened from her slumber by a knock upon her door – which she was thankful for. Screams and cries of pure agony rattled through her dreams, turning them into nightmares of her own making. From her deepest aches that scarred her soul. Her family was before her once more, her own body small and frail. Bodies caught afire, flames eating hungrily at flesh, devouring souls.

A cold sweat had damped her skin, her breathing heavy, her heart thrashing about within her chest. Ashari lingered before the doorway, the dark wood door ajar. Within her ghostly hands was a damp washcloth. She approached the bed with a gentle smile and seated herself upon the edge. Without speaking, she began to press the washcloth against Valina's forehead.

"The terrors of the night disturb your dreams." She whispered.

Valina closed her eyes as Ashari patted her face, the damp rag cool against her raging skin. "I am beginning to think they may never leave me."

Ashari lowered the washcloth and held Valina's gaze, "In time, all hurt fades. All aches within the soul heal." Ashari placed a cool hand against Valina's chest, "And all shattered hearts mend their pieces."

Valina grasped Ashari's hand and moved it aside, moving closer to the *Ghost Condentai.* Cupping the woman's face between her hands, she placed her lips against hers. Ashari's lips were always cool but always sweet. After a few moments, Valina pulled away, and gazed into those silver eyes.

"I love you."

Ashari smiled, her eyes softening. "And I love you, my hunter."

"And now, may I ask why I was awakened?"

Ashari giggled, "Another hunter has come knocking for you."

Valina raised a brow, "And what does he want?"

Ashari rose from the bed and approached the door, "Dress and see for yourself." Silver eyes scanned Valina's naked form beneath the sheet, except for her top half which was exposed for all eyes to see. "Or perhaps don't."

Valina dressed herself in a nice fitted, black long-sleeved shirt and slipped into some black trousers. The wood floor was cool against her bare, grey feet. She padded down the stairs and stopped at the bottom of them. Her crimson eyes took in the sight of grinning *Blood Condentai* that stood before the door.

"Hello, my dear Valina."

Crossing her arms over her chest, she raised a brow. "And what brings you to my home?"

Ashari had vanished back up the stairs, leaving the two alone. Ventar approached the doorway that led into the living room. His crimson eyes admiring the carving within the dark wood. His hand traced along some of the carvings.

"You do wonderful work, a true artist." Admiration coated his voice. "When shall you grace my home with your work?"

Valina stood beside him then but her eyes were upon the carving of the Goddess above the doorway. "When shall I get the night that I was promised? A woman can only wait so long, Ventar."

Ventar turned his crimson gaze upon her, his grin returning. "And that, my dear, is why I have come."

A thrill rushed along Valina's spine, warmth blossoming between her thighs at the thoughts that had transpired within her mind. "And do you wish to bed me here or have you planned something else?"

Ventar leaned down, brushing aside her sleep mussed, midnight hair from her long ear. His breath warm against her skin, "I have something special planned, my dear."

"Allow me to slip my boots on."

Ventar nodded his head and approached the door while she tugged her boots on as quickly as she could. As any gentlemen would do, Ventar opened the door for her and bowed. "My lady."

With a roll of her eyes and a fire raging between her thighs, she stepped out into the night with Ventar just behind her.

Their walk would be a long one for Ventar resided on the other side of the town, his home lingering on the edge of the wicked forest. Though they could travel faster, Valina did not wish to indulge in Ventar's ego, so they kept a steady pace while her heart thundered within her chest.

"Is there no meeting with the rebels?" Valina asked.

"There is always a meeting, my dear. But I figured both of us could use a break from the madness, just for a night."

Madness was all she knew. Most of her life tainted in it. Her family burned. The king and his wicked intentions with her. The blood that coated *her* hands. She wondered if she would ever truly know peace.

"And what do you think about the child of Nicitis that escaped yesterday?" She found herself questioning.

For a moment, Ventar remained silent. Valina cast a glance toward the man walking beside her and found his face set in stone. His brows furrowed, his eyes focused ahead.

Finally, he spoke, "I truly do not know what to think of the man. I shall admit that when I first saw him, I felt nothing but hatred for he is supposed to be our enemy. But, I do not believe that he is." He continued, "Of course I did not think that until after he had escaped. When I looked around and realized that not a single soul had been harmed from his power. Though I did curse him for not killing the king right then and there."

A breath of relief escaped Valina's lips. She did not hold much hope of Ventar changing his mind, but he too had noticed that the man did not harm anyone when he had the chance to do so. But the other towns people would not have seen that, the hatred blinding them.

"I think he would make a wonderful asset to the rebels." Valina spoke.

Ventar nodded his head. "Assuming he hasn't already returned home and assuming that he wishes to also murder our lovely king." He turned his crimson gaze upon her, "Why do you think he was here within our lands?"

Valina wished she knew the answer, her mind questioning the same. She kept her gaze ahead of them, as if she could see past the darkness, past the wicked forest, and catch a glimpse of that land of light. "I truly have no idea."

"Let us not focus on those matters for now, they are worries for another time – not tonight." A sultry tone coated his voice. Before, the tone and sound of it did not affect her but now she found it alluring.

A smirk tugged at the corners of her lips. "Tonight, there shall be only one thing upon our minds."

"If you can even think straight, my dear." Ventar leaned down and purred into Valina's ear, igniting her body with a fire that torched her soul.

"We'll see who shall be keeping their mind by the end of the night."

Ventar chuckled, "Always wishing for a challenge, my dear."

Valina flashed her fangs, "Always."

———————————————

Ventar and Valina found themselves on the outskirts of the town. The forest lingering close by, the shadows seeming to watch them, the creatures of the forest hiding and waiting for their prey.

They stood before his home, it was modest and small. The dark stone blending in with the night so wandering eyes from a distance would not be able to see it. There was nothing surrounding his home, no fence – nothing. Just the forest behind it. Ventar approached the wooden door, slipped his hand into a trouser pocket, and slid the key inside the lock. Opening the door, he stepped aside, allowing Valina first entrance into his home.

And once the door was closed and locked, there was not a single word spoken between the pair. They stood within the entry hallway, their gazes never breaking. And then, they pounced. Two predators claiming each other as prey. Hands clawed hungrily at skin. Another pair of hands tangled within midnight hair.

A moan escaped Valina as Ventar forced her against the wall, never breaking their kiss. His hands freed themselves of her hips and gripped her thighs, wrapping her legs around him. Deeper her fingers dug into his locks. Tighter her legs gripped him, forcing their pulsating bodies closer. His tongue was warm within her mouth, exploring until her tongue met with his in a dance.

An angry growl sounded from Valina as Ventar had broken their kiss, shattering the spell that had captivated her body. "Why did you stop?"

She leaned toward him to continue but he only placed a finger against her lips. "Though I could fuck you against this wall right now, I did say that I had something special planned, my dear."

"And what is it?" Impatience clawed at her.

Ventar kept his hold on her as he removed her from the wall. "You shall see."

As they rounded a corner, a stairway came into sight. And Valina's gaze caught sight of crimson petals showering the floor leading up the stairs. Though flowers could not grow in their dark land, the light side brought them in as part of their trade. Of course, each trade was always overseen by the king and several armed guards.

"I did not know you had such a romantic side to you, Ventar."

"There is much you do not know about me yet, my dear." He began to ascend the stairs, crushing the petals beneath his boots. "But tonight, there shall be a few things you'll learn."

Heat flared within her body at the promise lingering within his words. When they reached the second floor of his home, they were faced with a narrow hall stretching out to the left and right beside them. Following the crimson petals to the left, he lingered before the first door which was cracked open a tad. Warm light slithered through the small crack. Pushing the door open, Valina's eyes took in the sight of the room before her.

A four-poster bed was pushed toward the center of the wall a few feet from them. Crimson curtains draped on either side, brushing against the wooden floor. Petals were scattered about the room and spread across the grey sheet of the bed. Candles could be found casting a golden glow about the room. Some were placed along the floor, others upon the nightstands on either side of the bed. Incense that smelled of vanilla, drifted toward the pair.

Ventar approached the bed, "I know how much you love sweets, I assumed the incense would please you."

It did. "So thoughtful." Valina purred into his ear, her teeth nipping at the flesh.

"You'll soon see how thoughtful I can be."

Ventar lay her down upon the bed, the silky petals all around her and beneath her. "How long have you thought about bedding me, Ventar?"

He leaned over her, their faces dangerously close. Their gazes locked. "For a long time, my dear."

Valina leaned up and took his bottom lip between her teeth. A growl rumbled within Ventar's chest. Releasing his lips, she looked into his eyes, "The time for waiting is over."

"That it is, my Valina." His voice had taken on a deeper tone, as if the beast lurking within had come out to play. The way her name rumbled from his lips, churned something wicked deep within her, awakening her own beast.

His mouth had claimed hers. Their lips crashing against one another. Warmth erupted through Valina's body, beginning at her head and working its way down to her toes. Animalistic sounds escaped the pair as they devoured one another. Ventar's mouth left hers and began to trail down her body. His lips grazing the skin of her neck, causing her toes to curl within her boots. His fangs gently nipped at her flesh, drawing forth a moan from her.

As he lowered down to her breasts, Valina worked on tugging off her long-sleeved shirt but Ventar had another idea in mind. The shirt was torn from her body within the blink of an eye and lay shredded upon the floor.

"You owe me another." Valina said, not at all angry with the shirt. The action had turned her on even more, wishing he would shred every piece of clothing from her body.

And Ventar did just that, as if he could read her mind. He tugged her boots off and they thudded against the wood. Off her pants came, being tossed onto the floor as if they were nothing – and for now they were. The belt that her daggers were hooked to clattered onto the floor. Now, her body was laid bare before him. A feast for his eyes. And feast, they did. They glowed with a hunger she had never seen before within his gaze. But then, there was this longing that lingered there as he stared upon her. As if he had waited his whole life for this moment – for her. All these years and he would finally claim her as his.

"Is the hunter going to claim his prey, or continue staring?" Valina propped herself up on her elbows and spread her legs. Her fingers venturing down low, touching herself before him.

A grin spread across his lips as he knelt onto his knees at the end of the bed. Valina inched closer to him, her legs opening more. "My dear, you shall stop a heart in a man's chest one day."

"Then I hope today is not that day, it would ruin the fun."

He gripped her legs and tugged her closer, his mouth lingering dangerously close to the inside of her thighs. She could feel his warm breath against her. A flare ignited at the place between her thighs, heat rushing through her body as she felt his breath against her, knowing how close his mouth was.

"Not today, my dear. I've waited to long for this to die now."

Impatience snapped in her voice as her body raged in fire, "Then stop talking."

There was no more speaking, only a chuckle from him before his mouth had begun to devour her. Her breath caught in her throat as her hands gripped the grey sheets, crushing the petals that littered the bed within her palms. Ventar's tongue worked gracefully against her, her hips moving against it. One of her hands unclasped the sheet and reached for his head, tangling her fingers within his silky, midnight hair. Moans had begun to escape her lips, filling the silence. While he devoured her, Ventar moved one of his hands, and she felt as his thumb began to rub against her clit. Her back arched and her fingers dug deeper into his hair, her other hand clenching the sheet tighter.

Her body was on fire. Her mind engulfed by pleasure, her thoughts were a whirlwind – nothing making sense. She wanted more. She wanted to feel him inside of her, not just his tongue.

"Ventar..." His name escaped her lips in a hungry, hot breath.

She glanced down to find his crimson eyes watching her with a predator's gaze. "Too much for you, my dear?"

She snarled at the cockiness in his tone. "Not enough."

He raised a dark brow but stood. Crawling onto the bed, he leaned over her, his face lingering just above her own. Down he lowered more, toward her neck. Those soft lips of his grazing her skin, driving her mind into a frenzy. His warm breath traced along her ear as he whispered, "Tell me what you want, Valina. Voice your desires."

"I want you to fuck me, Ventar." A growl escaped her.

A grin curled at his lips, "Your wish is my command."

Ventar worked on unfastening his trousers. And when they fell, her eyes dared to glance. The warm ache of desire turned into a raging inferno as her eyes stared at the size of him. Then his shirt fluttered to the floor, revealing his muscular body that Valina admired. Her eyes tracing along every inch, every curve of that muscle.

She tasted blood in her mouth when her teeth bit too hard upon her bottom lip. "Are you going to continue to stand there and stare or are you going to make sweet, sweet love to me?"

Ventar chuckled as he climbed onto the bed once more, "Sweet and ravenous love, my dear."

And when he leaned over, she felt the tip of him of brush against her. Another moan whispered from her wetted lips, a panted breath of desire. Ventar spread her legs, grasped his cock, and with a thrust, he had filled her. Her eyes were wide as a loud moan echoed within the room. Valina had lovers before but none compared to the size of Ventar. She had never felt such pleasure before from that first thrust – until now.

"Do you wish for me to take it slow?"

Valina's lips curled into a snarl, "No. I want you to *take me.*"

His lips brushed against hers before he gazed into her eyes, "I hope you are prepared for the beast that you've awakened."

Valina's nails dug into his back, drawing forth a rumbling growl from him. "And I hope that you are prepared for mine."

Words were no longer spoken between the pair, for they had been lost and replaced with the sounds of moans and growls and gasping breaths. Ventar thrust himself into Valina repeatedly, drawing forth such pleasure from her body that she felt she would burst. Her skin felt as though it were on fire as the passion scorched through her.

Ventar's body was atop her own, his face buried within the nape of her neck, his lips kissing her skin. One of her hands clawed at his back while the other tangled within his hair. Repeatedly he pounded inside of her. And each time, it brought a louder and louder moan from her mouth.

And before he could thrust himself inside her again, she stopped him. His head lifted from her neck – and she was sure there would be marks left when morning came – and confusion was found upon his face. "Tired already, my dear?"

She placed her hand upon his chest and leaned up from the bed, "Not even close." Her voice purred as she flipped him upon his back with such speed that he had no time to react as Valina straddled him. Her face lowered down to his, their lips a breath away from one another. "Now, it's my turn."

Valina felt his hardened cock rubbing against her clit, her own wetness coating it. Her hand grasped him, and she fully sat upon him; his cock filled her once more, that pleasure returning and erupting within her being. Then, her hips set to work – moving against him. Fast and faster her heart thundered as she moved against him. Ventar's hands gripped her thighs, the veins in his arms rippling to the surface. She braced her hands against his chest, her nails seeping into his skin and drawing forth that sweet crimson. Leaning down, her tongue swept across the fresh wounds. Ventar did not complain, did not speak, as she drank her fill.

Her mouth was buzzing as the blood danced across her tongue. She felt Ventar's hand brush against her cheek and her eyes opened to find his crimson ones staring back. Cupping her cheek, he led her down to him and their lips met. His blood still coating her mouth.

Blood Condentai normally shared blood during sex – adding to the pleasure of the moment – awakening the beasts lurking within them.

Valina broke free of the kiss and straightened herself, Ventar watching her every move with those predator eyes. She glanced down upon her arm. Holding it up to her mouth, her fangs grazed her skin. She thought it only fair that Ventar had a taste of her blood since she had drunk of his. This would be her first time ever allowing anyone a taste of her blood. No lovers before were ever granted that pleasure. Though she had tasted them, she had never once felt guilty in doing so. If they did not wish for her to drink, they would have protested, but they did not, allowing her to drink her fill.

As she was ready to bite down, a hand gripped her wrist, and pulled it away from her mouth. "No." Ventar's voice was rasped.

Valina cocked her head with a brow raised, "No?"

He lowered her arm down to her side. And when he released his grip upon it, his fingertips trailed across her skin in a loving, gentle gesture. "This would be your first time sharing your blood, am I correct?"

"Yes. Do you wish to not be the first drinker of my blood?"

A soft smile appeared on his lips, "Though it would be the greatest honor, my dear. Do not do so just because you drank of my blood. Wait until you are ready to give it."

Within her chest, she felt something flutter. As if a butterfly had long ago been locked away within the cage she called her heart and gently beat its wings as it began to awaken from its eternal slumber.

Her hand reached for him, her fingertips brushing against his cheek. "A true romantic you are, Ventar."

His hand formed over her own, "Only for you, my Valina."

And there it was again, that flutter, as he called her *his*.

"Now, enough with the sweet talk, may we continue fucking like animals?"

And that gleam returned to Ventar's eyes as the beast clawed its way to the surface. "We may, how would you like us to continue?"

Valina glanced toward the other side of the room, her eyes lingering upon the wall. "I want you to fuck me against that wall."

"Your wish is my command."

Ventar gripped Valina's hips as he rose from the bed, her legs wrapping themselves around him. Within a second, he had her against the wall, and they continued where they had left off. The wood behind her back groaned as he pounded her against it.

The pair continued on like this for many hours, allowing time to slip away from them, allowing their minds to forget the horrors that surrounded them and plagued their minds – tainting their souls. They lost themselves within one another. The pleasure burning away their pain – for now.

And while the hunters tore into one another, a light was lurking within the shadows of the forest. A plan stirring within his mind – a plan of revenge.

CHAPTER EIGHT

LIGHT MEETS DARK

"When enemies meet, shall blood be spilled?"

WHEN VALINA awoke she found herself wrapped in silky sheets, her head resting upon a chest marred by scratches. A grin curled upon her lips as the memory of the night before, came flooding back. Peering upon Ventar's sleeping face, caused something within her chest to flutter – that caged butterfly flapping its stiff wings. His heartbeat echoed within her ears and for a moment, she lay there enjoying the rhythmic beat.

With a heavy sigh, Valina began to free herself from the sleeping hunter's arms. The bed shifted slightly as she quickly moved from it. A grunt of annoyance escaped her as she searched the floor for her clothes, only to find them shredded and littering the ground. Snatching her boots and belt – which thankfully hadn't been torn – she quickly made her way toward the door. Casting a glance over her shoulder, she found Ventar still deep within his slumber.

Something snagged in her chest as she wished to rejoin him. But, she looked away and entered the hall.

When she stood before the door, she slid her feet into her boots and fastened the belt around her waist. The sheaths her daggers were held in brushed against the bare skin of her thighs. Her gaze drifted toward the wall as she eyed one of the three cloaks that was hanging upon silver hooks. Taking the oldest appearing one, she draped it across her shoulders and pulled the hood over her head.

Then, she opened the door and the found the night waiting for her.

The hunter began to stir from his slumber, fading away from his dreams. Dreams of a beautiful woman wrapped within his arms as they made love. His hand reached for that beautiful woman, but it felt no silky skin, only the bed sheet. When his crimson eyes viewed the world once more, he found his bed empty of an extra body, but still found that the sheet was warm. The beautiful hunter had snuck away into the shadows, leaving her prey alone within the bed, his heart yearning for her.

His hand clutched the sheet, "My Valina." He whispered to the silence.

The chilling wind nipped at Valina's bare skin. A shudder rushing along her spine. But the chill did not bother her – no matter how much her body shivered. She had always loved the colder days of the year, when the winter from the land of light drifted toward the dark.

As she walked along through the shadows, the silence welcomed her. The predators lingering within the forest watching with their bloodthirsty eyes. But none dared challenge her for they knew of the monster that she could become. And none of them felt like being skinned on this night.

But there was one who lurked, one whose eyes were watching Valina's every silent move. He took a step forth from the shadows and the other predators watching turned their gazes upon him. Still, none had made their move. He was foreign to them, something entirely new. His scent unlike anyone's within this side of the world. And they were curious as to how the *Blood Condentai* who prowled the night, would react to the newcomer. So, they watched.

The man of light approached the woman of dark – thinking that she had not heard his footsteps, but the hunter heard for he was not light upon his feet.

Still she walked along, tricking the man into thinking that she had not heard him. Changing her course, she approached the forest, the trees waiting in the shadows, and she entered that darkness. The man followed close behind.

Deeper and deeper she led him, where the cluster of trees grew thicker and the shadows poured from every corner. The forest had become a maze and Valina quickened her pace, the cloak snagging upon crooked branches. The man lost his footing many times, his eyes not used to this sort of darkness. And when he finally found it within himself to summon upon his light, he found that he was alone within a cluster of trees. Ungodly screeches sounded from retreating shadows as the monsters of dark ran away from the light.

The golden glow emanating from his hand chased away the shadows and possibly the woman he sought. Or so he thought. Valina lurked just above him, crouching upon a branch, her crimson eyes watching him.

He was just as beautiful as he was the last time she saw him. His wave of golden hair falling down the length of his back, his brown skin smooth. And she wondered if it felt silky to the touch. She watched as his blue eyes searched for her. That golden light igniting their dark world in a light that was banned from this land. A light that this land had not seen in centuries.

Her hand raised to shield her eyes from it, tears swelling as the brightness burned them. Thankfully, he dimmed that damned light. The monster within her wanted to slice his hand off just to extinguish that glow. But she silenced the beast and readied herself to leap. Wrapping her hands around the hilts of her daggers, she drew them forth. Then, she pounced. The wind lifting her cloak as she fell, her hood falling from her head. A quiet thud sounded as she landed upon the earth. The man whirled around but she was faster. Within an instant, she had him backed against a tree, one dagger against his throat and the other pressed against his side.

"Why are you following me, son of Nicitis?" A snarl crept into her voice – her nose crinkled as she revealed her fangs to the man.

The man showed no signs of fear, only gazing upon her curiously with those beautiful eyes. Seeming to take in every feature of her face and she found herself doing the same to him. "I remember you." His voice was deep, "You were one of the few who did not hiss burn amongst the crowd."

She pressed the blade against his throat, not enough to draw blood. "You should never follow a monster into the shadows."

"Mark me a fool then."

"Why did you follow me?" She asked again, a snarl rippling across her lips.

He cocked his head to the side, those eyes still upon her. "I believe you can aid me."

"And what do you think I could aid you in?"

He took in a breath, "I wish to bring down the king."

She blinked. The blade lowering slightly from his throat. Her brow raised, "You wish to murder our king?"

His blue eyes narrowed, "I know you wish the same. I saw the look in your eyes."

Her blade pressed against his throat once more, "But why do *you* wish to kill him?"

His shoulders squared as he straightened himself, their gazes locking, and she found something like a promise of death afire within those eyes of his. "Because he has been killing my people."

Silence settled around them, even the predators of the night halted their breathing for a moment.

"He has sent assassins into our land, murdering innocents – children even." A vein within his neck throbbed at that. "Striking people down during trades if they dared to look him in the eyes. My brother was one of the many that he slaughtered. And I seek revenge for his death, for all those who died by his doing."

Valina felt his pain then – having lost her family by the hands of the king. The dagger lowered from the man's throat and she took a step back. Sheathing her weapons, she spoke, "I shall aid you."

His brows raised, his mouth slightly open. "Why?"

Her crimson gaze drifted toward the ever-dark sky, a heavy sigh escaping her. "Because, I too, have lost family by the king's doing. I share your pain and vengeance."

The man lingered before the tree, unsure if he should approach the mysterious woman before him. "You trust me so easily?"

Her crimson gaze snapped back to him, "I never spoke words of trust, I said I would aid you. Trust, that is something you would have to earn, child of Nicitis."

He nodded his head, "Fair enough, child of Severina."

The hood concealed her face once more as she pulled it over her head, "Valina." She spoke her name.

"Luzell."

Her body began to disappear into the reaching shadows. "Until next time, Luzell."

Luzell took an advancing step toward her then, one hand reaching out into the shadows. "And when shall this next time be?"

The shadows halted, as did she, "Three nights from now, here."

And then, she was gone. Leaving behind the son of Nicitis in the eternal darkness. She did not know how he would survive within their land, but she knew he would find a way.

Afterall, he made it this far.

When Valina returned to her home, she kicked off her boots and they thudded against the ground. The cloak fell from her shoulders and fluttered down upon the wooden floor. Unclasping her belt, she set it upon the table before the door and made her way into the living room, where she knew she would find the *Ghost Condentai.*

Ashari stood before the window, the curtains open wide. Her white hair had been woven into one thick braid that swept down to her ankles. Her grey nightgown pooling upon the wooden floor, the sleeves long and billowy.

"The hunter has returned from the shadows." Her voice echoed through the room. "And she has found a light within the darkness of our world."

Valina leaned against the doorframe, her arms crossed over her exposed chest. "I assume you had your ghost friends searching for me then."

Pale hands drew the curtains over the window, concealing the two from the watching eyes of the night. When Ashari faced her, those silver eyes took in Valina's naked form. "It seems as though much has happened, my hunter."

Valina inclined her head to the couch and the two approached, sitting themselves upon it. "Which would you like to hear first?"

"Let's begin with the man of light, then we shall discuss your ravenous night with the hunter." A glimmer of mischief twinkled in those silver eyes.

Valina chuckled. "How much did your ghostly companions tell you?"

The glimmer vanished, her face settling into emotionlessness. "They only caught a glimpse of you two, they fled when the man summoned upon his light. The creatures of the dark fear that light."

Valina leaned back on the couch, kicking her feet up onto the table before them. "He wishes to murder the king."

Ashari turned her attention back to Valina then, "Don't we all wish the same?"

"The king has been sending assassins into the land of light, killing children even." Her hands curled into fists at the thought of such young, innocent lives being stolen from this world. She was a monster, but her monstrosity halted at certain things – never would she kill a child. "He's also been killing people during trades just for looking him in the eye. Luzell's brother was one of the many killed by our gracious king."

Ashari sat there, her eyes staring ahead, seeming to lose herself within her own head. "Valnar shall reap everything that he has given, all shall come back tenfold, and his death shall be something that is never forgotten in the many years to come."

Valina often forgot that a monster also resided within Ashari. It did not make itself known often but when it did, Valina was reminded of how monstrous even the kindest of people could become.

She placed a grey hand atop of Ashari's pale one that had formed into a fist. Silver eyes flickered down to gaze upon their hands, and her own slowly unfurled from the fist.

"Now, would you like to discuss about your passionate night with Ventar?"

A smile crept upon Valina's lips. Her body flushed at the memories. "It was indeed a night of promise."

Ashari laughed, "And did the promise continue when you woke?"

The smile had faded away from Valina's face then as guilt had begun to surface within her, clawing at her seams. Her had fell away from Ashari's. "It did not."

Ashari raised a ghostly brow, "You left before he awoke?"

Valina nodded her head. Not knowing what to say or how to voice the feelings that were stirring within her.

"Do you regret what occurred between the two of you?"

"No. It was a distraction that both of us needed and nothing more." That was a lie – she knew it.

"You call it a distraction, but you fear allowing him to get too close. Tell me, my hunter, why do you fear it?"

Valina quickly rose from the couch, not wishing to speak more on this subject. "Later, I shall be joining the rebels once more, you are free to come if you wish it."

Ashari folded her hands into her lap and delicately nodded her head, "I shall join you."

Steam filtered through the room, thickening and dampening the air that breathed into her lungs. Wisps of steam curled from the water's surface that surrounded Valina's naked form. She sat there in the tub, her knees pulled toward her chest and her arms wrapped around them. Her mind had wandered far from the world, digging deeper and deeper into her memories. Her family flashed before her eyes – memories of happier times, before flames had devoured them. Then came that day, where she cried out to the king, to the Goddess to save her family while her young ears were filled with their screams. While the smell of burning flesh drifted toward her nose. Something prickled within her eyes, burning and clawing wishing to be freed. And here within the solitude of her bathroom, she allowed those tears to fall. They burned their way down her cheeks, causing the water to ripple as they fell into the tub.

A sigh escaped Valina's lips as she began to draw herself out of those memories, tucking them away until she was ready to torment herself once more. Since that day and the day of her mother leaving, she did not allow many to grow close to her out of fear of two things; the king would take them away or they would disappear. Both were much in the same. The only person she felt safe allowing in was Ashari, and she figured the king only spares her life because he does not see her as a threat lover wise. If only he knew.

But, Ventar. That was another matter. He was already a rebel – Valina now claiming that title as well – and that marked him a dead man if the king found out. But if he were to see them together in that way, Valina did not wish to know what would happen to him. So, she would have to keep Ventar at a distance, just far enough that if she reached for him, only her fingertips would graze him.

A knocking upon the door shattered her thoughts. "Valina, the king has arrived and wishes to speak with you."

Her stomach sank into the deepest pits of her being. "I shall be out in a moment."

She heard the soft footfalls of Ashari's feet as she walked away.

Valina climbed out of the tub, dried her body and wrapped a silky, black robe around herself. She tugged at the knot of hair atop her head and allowed her midnight locks to fall past her shoulders and down to her hips – concealing her neck from the hungry eyes of the king, concealing the marks that Ventar had left behind.

When she stood atop the stairs, she found the king standing before the door, Ashari lingered within the doorway that led into the living room. Silver eyes met with hers and with a slight nod of her head, Ashari vanished into the room – leaving Valina alone with the king.

He stood there, a cocky smile upon that damned handsome face. His midnight hair slicked back but no crown was found resting atop his wicked head. There was a glint within his crimson eyes as they devoured Valina's form within the robe.

Valina made her way down the stairs and halted at the last step, remaining there. "And what has brought our king to my home?"

His eyes took one last, ravenous glance upon her form before returning to meet her gaze. "You always look lovely, my Valina. Still a shame that you refuse to have your neck bare before me but that shall change in time."

Her nails bit into the wood of the staircase railing. "I bare my neck for none." Though she had bared it freely to Ventar, but the king certainly did not need to know that. "Now, why are you here?"

The king held his hands behind his back as he approached the stairs, standing a breath away from Valina. She had to force herself to remain in place as she locked gazes with him. "As you know, our enemy escaped from me and I am now on the hunt for him."

Her chest tightened.

"I have some of my best men looking for him, but I would like to also have one of the best women hunting for him as well."

She hated that pride had swelled in her chest at his compliment. Having your monstrosity recognized as a skilled trait that was sought after, was something that one should not be proud of. But in their land, it was. Her ears could hear her daggers practically singing out for her. But they would not be used against Luzell.

"And what shall you have me do, my king?"

The king smiled, his fangs flashing. "My Valina, you know what I would wish for you to do." He took a step closer, "I wish for you to skin him, just like you did to that guard who burned your family." His voice purred almost every word to her, his smile never fading. "I want you to make that man suffer and then bring me his head as a trophy."

Her skin crawled. Her mind screaming out cursed words to the king – words that would have her head spiked on his damned fence. Her fist shook by her side, her nails digging deeper into the wood of the railing. How dare he speak of her family.

How. Dare. He.

"Perhaps he has already returned to his side of the world. Such a shame I cannot fulfill your request, *my king.*" A hiss escaped her lips.

He only raised a brow to her, but the smile still remained. "And when he returns, my dear, you shall be the one to bring me his head."

She dipped her head stiffly to him, "Is there anything else you need or was that all?"

His crimson eyes flickered over her body, seeming to undress her within his mind. "There is always something I need from you, but I shall have it in time." When he turned his back upon her, she had half a mind to snap his neck.

He approached the doorway that led into the living room. Valina cast a glance in there and found no sign of the *Ghost Condentai.*

Where the hell did Ashari disappear too? She thought, not recalling ever seeing the woman leave the room.

The king traced a grey finger along the carvings within the wooden doorframe. And for a moment, his crimson eyes softened – that wickedness vanishing. As if another person had taken over, another soul dwelling somewhere within the man. And Valina was reminded of the young boy that he once was, before his father ever corrupted him, a young boy who gazed upon her with such sadness that it had broken her child heart even more. But that boy was gone, just as the girl was. Both of them different and changed. But both had not changed for the better.

"Whenever shall you grace my castle with your beautiful carvings, my Valina?"

She drew the robe around her body tighter. "When you pay just like everyone else."

A grin spread across his lips, a chuckle escaping him. The king faced her and dipped his head, "I bid a goodnight, my dear."

"Goodnight, my king."

As he stood before the opened door, he said over his shoulder, "I do hope I shall be seeing you at my birthday ball this year. You haven't attended in quite some time."

"We shall see."

His crimson eyes glanced at her briefly over his shoulder before he stepped out in the night.

For a long moment, she remained at the last stair on the staircase, her hand still gripping the railing. She waited until she was sure he could no longer hear her. Her hand loosened, stiff, and her shoulders relaxed as she let out a breath.

Soft footsteps found their way into her ears and she glanced over at the kitchen doorway to find Ashari standing there, with a cup held between her hands – steam rising from its contents. She approached Valina and extended the porcelain, white cup to her with a smile. "Contraceptive tea, for your ravenous night with the hunter."

Valina's head fell back as laughter escaped her.

CHAPTER NINE

A LONE PETAL

"When death seeks comfort with a shadow, something stirs within them both."

ASHARI AND Valina wandered out into the night, silence draping around them like a thick cloak. The pair kept close to the darkest shadows, their eyes watching for spying gazes. Hurriedly, they made their way toward the *Tavern of Ventaria.*

Ashari cast weary eyes upon the place and Valina remembered how she first felt gazing upon this tavern. Placing a light hand upon the *Ghost Condentai's* shoulder, she said with a smile, "It'll grow on you." Just as Ventar had told her.

Together, they entered the tavern. And just like the first time, the smoke assaulted them. Ashari wrinkled her nose at the scent, her brows creasing together. Voices were loud and carried through the bar, laughter and yelling could be heard coming from all sides of the room. The same band that played during her first arrival, could be seen once more playing the same tune.

"The music is rather... lovely." Ashari said, not even bothering trying to put a smile on for show.

Valina laughed and took the woman's hand within her own and led her toward the bar. Her eyes fell upon the back of the bartender, the woman's grey hair woven in that same long braid, washing a glass with that still dirty appearing rag. Approaching the counter, Valina tapped her knuckles upon it – drawing the *Dead Condentai's* attention. The woman faced the pair, the woman's milky eyes lingered upon Valina for a moment, recognizing her, and they drifted toward Ashari, where they remained.

Keeping her voice low, she repeated the words that Ventar spoke, "We'll have two shots of freedom and three shots of death."

The woman's milky eyes drifted toward the same human man. His dark eyes met briefly with hers and the woman subtly inclined her head. As the man rose from the chair, he ran a hand through his mousy brown hair. He brushed past the pair and they took that as an invitation to follow, otherwise they'd be left behind at the bar.

They wove through the crowd, making their way into the shadows and into the hallway he led her before. Once he opened the broom closet door, they hurriedly entered and closed the door behind them.

Ashari cast a quick glance about the room, a brow raised. Valina smiled and winked a crimson eye at her puzzled friend. The human man knelt down and removed the raggedy rug that concealed the little door. His fist knocked five times upon the wooden floorboards, once again, each knock spaced by heart beats.

While they waited for an answer, Ashari leaned over and whispered, "And where is the other hunter to be found?"

Her chest tightened at the mention of Ventar. "Perhaps he awaits below."

Suddenly, the small door swung open and Lillian's beaming face looked up at them. "Valina, welcome back!" Her twinkling blue eyes darted over to Ashari, and her smile widened, "And another newcomer! Come, come!"

Valina took the first step down the narrow flight of stairs. When she didn't hear the sound of light footsteps following behind her, she cast a glance back to find Ashari before the man. She bowed her head, her white hair sweeping over her shoulders to curtain her face. *"May thy Goddess bless your every step and watch your unguarded back; may she shield thy heart from shattering."*

The man stared at her with those dark eyes of his, his hand nervously running through his hair. "T-Thank you." His voice was deeper than Valina thought it would be.

Ashari smiled before facing the stairs. Nothing was spoken between the two but Valina offered a grey hand to the woman. Ashari placed her cold one into Valina's and together, they descended into the darkness – the door closed above them but this time, it was not slammed.

Lillian skipped ahead of them, energetic as ever. "This way!" She wandered through the narrow doorway with Valina and Ashari trailing close behind her. They stood within a cramped, empty room much like the broom closet once more. Lillian fished into her pocket of her dress and withdrew the rusted, silver key, sliding it into the lock of the door before them. And once that door was opened, Valina took in the sight of the large room and the table where the leaders of the rebellion where gathered.

Everyone within the room cast a glance toward their small group. Their eyes stilled on Valina for a moment, recognizing her, before they drifted toward the newcomer. Ashari did not cower beneath their heavy gazes, instead she stared right back.

Valina approached the table, and stood before it, Ashari to her right. "Hello again, Shandal. I have brought the *Ghost Condentai* that I told you about."

His wholly black eye drifted toward Ashari. Shandal removed himself from the table and approached the woman, Valina taking a step aside. He crossed his muscular arms over his chest. "What have you lost that brings you to us?" He began to speak the very words he spoke to Valina and she guessed he questioned every newcomer the same. "What has caused you to risk your life to end the king?" He narrowed his eye, "What has brought you to your death, girl?"

For a long moment, Ashari only stared back with those silver eyes of hers, slowly blinking. Her head delicately cocked to the side, "The spirits speak to me." She began to say in her monotone voice. "They whisper of your aches that bind your soul."

Shandal seemed to flitch at her words and Valina wondered just what pain bound him. What pain caused him to form the rebellion and become its leader?

"We all suffer aches." Her hand drifted toward her chest, resting atop her heart. "Mine have brought me here so none shall suffer what I have suffered." The room grew hauntingly silent, all gazes were upon the ghostly woman. "My sister was raped by three of the king's guards and I was forced to watch." Valina felt something within her dark heart crack. "And when they were finished with her, they forced her to watch as they took their turns with me." And Valina's heart shattered within her chest – turning into dust. In all the years she has known her, Ashari never once spoke of such pain and she understood why. "They killed her before my eyes and beat me almost to the point of death and left me naked within a dark alley with my sister's body beside me, thinking I would be dead soon."

Valina did not think, her body moving for her. She stood beside her friend and grasped one of her hands, squeezing gently. Ashari offered a soft smile before meeting Shandal's black eye once more.

"If they assumed I was to live, they assumed that they would have broken my spirit, that I would kill myself from the heartache they had caused me. But they were wrong. I found strength within myself to live and to live for my sister as well." Ashari's eyes narrowed, and for the first time, Valina witnessed hatred afire within her gaze. "When I found those men again, I made sure they paid for what they had done. For the life they took, for my body that they had abused. Their screams still echo within my dreams, their blood still warm upon my hands. And some nights I feel as though their spirits lurk over my shoulders for I never granted them a safe passage to the Goddess or the prison of eternal dark." Ashari turned her head to glance over her shoulder but none stood behind her as she spoke, "They shall forever be trapped here.

Where none can save them, where none can see or speak to them. This is their prison."

Shandal remained where he stood, his black eye wide, lips unspeaking. And it was Shadari who spoke and approached Ashari, brushing past her husband to wrap the *Ghost Condentai* in an embrace. Valina saw tears staining the woman's black cheeks, glistening within her dark eyes. "Welcome to the rebels, my dear." Her voice shook, choking on her sobs. "You are not the first to come to us with this story and it breaks my heart every time my ears listen to it." Valina still kept ahold on Ashari's hand, refusing to let go. "We formed this rebellion to avenge and to protect, and that is what we continue to do." The woman leaned back, her hands cupping either side of Ashari's face, her silver eyes wide with tears lining within them. "Welcome, my dear. Welcome."

"Thank you." Ashari's voice was that of a whisper.

"And now we accept any person who waltzes in here with a tragic tale? This woman could have conjured the story up within her pretty little head and she is really a spy for the king, here to end all of our lives, to risk everything that we have built and accomplished here!"

Shadanar's dark gaze met with Valina's. A snarl that was animalistic rippled from her lips, her fangs bared as she stared down the man that dared speak to Ashari in that way. Her daggers cried out at her sides and her hands wrapped around the hilts, drawing them forth. "Just as you trusted this blood whore, which I still think is a mistake."

But as Valina took a step to approach him, Shandal beat her to it. He stood before his cousin, a blade against the man's throat. Fury ablaze within his dark eye. "Do not dare speak that way to her or any of our members. We do not mock those who have suffered. Their pain is real, their stories are real. And if you do not approve of who *I* accept, then you are free to leave and never return."

Shadanar's lips moved to speak, but no words escaped him as a ghostly chill crept into the room. Valina glanced to her side to find Ashari moving toward the man. A wind caused her hair to float around her, her dress rippling along a haunting breeze. Her body almost fading from view, her silver eyes beginning to glow.

"Those whose souls ache the greatest, wish upon others the pain that was inflicted upon them – their hearts that may never mend, their souls that forever may remain fractured. They unleash the burning aches within them, hoping that it shall ease their burdens that weigh so heavily upon their shoulders if they unleash it upon another. But it only worsens the ache, never truly facing it. And forever shall they remain in that churning darkness within them. Forever shall they wish upon others the misery that has tainted their life."

Ashari stood before Shadanar, Shandal backing away, her silver eyes gazing deep into his as if she could see into the spirit caged within his body. "I heard them," She spoke gently, "Your family whispered to me. They wished for me to seek you and tell you one final message; *Do not allow our deaths to coat your heart in hatred. We do not ask you to forget us, but to remember the happier times, not our deaths. We wish for you the best that life has to offer."* She reached a hand toward the *Shadow Condentai* that gazed upon her with wide eyes and she placed her hand above his heart, *"Tell my father that I love him and that my death – our deaths – are not his fault. Tell him to live for us all."*

A lone tear escaped his dark eye and his lips finally gave voice to words, "Shandalla." He crooked, "My beautiful daughter." Tears spilled down the man's cheeks. "She did not deserve what happened to her. None of them did."

Ashari offered a gentle smile, the ghostly wind fading away and the room warming once more. "They are at peace now. And it is time for you to do the same."

"Thank you and I apologize, for the foul things I said." Shadanar cast a glance toward Valina, "And to you. My daughter would be ashamed of the way I've been acting." A sigh escaped him as he hung his head. "I have allowed hatred to disease me. No longer." Shadanar's dark gaze lifted, he nodded his head toward Shandal and the rest of us, then he turned his back upon the watching room, and vanished through the doorway.

For a long moment, not a single soul uttered a word, no one moved, as all gazes lingered upon the doorway that Shadanar had stepped through.

It was Shandal who broke the silence as he approached Ashari, placing a hand upon her shoulder. "I think you gave my cousin the push he needed to move on and accept and I thank you, *Ghost Condentai.*"

"Ashari." She spoke, "You may call me Ashari."

Shandal offered a smile, "Shandal."

"You never cease to amaze me." Valina said as she walked toward the pair.

"It is not only my duty as a *Ghost Condentai* to free the spirits trapped within this world, but also to free those living that have ghosts lingering within them."

"Come, allow us to talk." Shandal led them toward the leaders table.

Valina cast a glance about the room, searching for crimson eyes watching her. And sure enough, she found a crimson gaze staring back. Ventar lingered within the darkest shadows of the furthest corner in the room. Neither hunter made a move toward the other, instead, their gazes broke free of each other.

The group gathered around the table. Shandal pulled open a drawer and drew forth a little silver figurine and placed it next to Valina's upon the map. "For our newest member." He said. "Now, let us discuss our plan on this night." His dark eye fell upon Ashari, "For you, if you do not mind, we have lost many of our members and there are no others of your kind amongst us. Would you do the honors of searching for their ghosts and releasing them to the Goddess?"

Her silver eyes watched him closely, "There are many within this room as we speak, wishing for freedom to join our Goddess." She bowed her head, "I shall set them free."

"Thank you." Shandal said. His gaze drifted toward Valina, "Tonight, we observe. No killing unless necessary. Watch and listen, see if the king is plotting."

Valina wished for nothing more than to skin all of the king's guards alive but she was not the leader here and she did not wish to risk these people's lives or their trust. She inclined her head to the man.

Light footsteps approached the table and all eyes turned to gaze upon the *Dead Condentai* that approached. His grey hair swept into his milky eyes that were fixed upon Valina, they did not drift to glance upon the other members surrounding the table. "Valina Veshanr, may I join you on tonight's hunt?"

She blinked at the strange but handsome man. "You may, Diaval."

A small smile seemed to quirk at the corner of his lips, an awkward sort of movement as if he did not smile often.

Shandal grunted, drawing forth everyone's attention. "An eye for an eye." He said, the others repeating those words. Valina guessed they were the rebels' parting words of luck, a strange phrase but she supposed it made sense.

As the rebels filtered out into the night, Diaval and Valina followed in their footsteps. As Valina passed through the doorway, she glanced over to find Ventar watching her.

"Safe hunting, Valina." He spoke in an almost dismissive tone, but there was a longing lingering within his tone, the want and need for her haunting his crimson eyes.

She inclined her head, putting on an act as though what happened between them was only sex and nothing more. Though that was far from the truth. "And to you, Ventar."

Then the *Blood* and the *Dead Condentai* ventured into the shadows.

Two creatures of the night lingered upon the blackened shingles of a roof. They were crouched low, Valina having her daggers ready within her hands. The blades sang to her, whispering to her listening ears. Pleading for a taste of blood, but not on this night. Only if it were necessary. It was almost as if she could feel the daggers disappointment.

Below them were three drunken guards outside another one of the taverns located within the town – *Tavern of the King* – Valina rolled her eyes at the name. This one placed closer to the castle thus it was more frequently visited by the king's guards. The building itself was beautiful, the inside even more so. The stone it was crafted from was a light shade of grey. Two windows were beside the double doors that were crafted from the darkest wood and polished. A single lantern mounted above the doors and a lone flame dancing within the black metal frame that held it captive behind glass.

Laughter echoed from below them and Valina cast her eyes back down upon the guards. "The women are looking good tonight." One of the heavier set guards remarked as he ran a hand through his amber hair.

"Saw the blue-eyed beauty eyeing you, Hansel." A guard with his head shaved, slapped the amber haired man on the back with a grin.

"Perhaps I shall have some fun tonight." Hansel chuckled.

"Then what are you waiting for, take her up to the rooms and fuck her pretty brains out." The third guard with long brown hair kept woven in a braid shouted, shoving his friend back toward the doors.

Hansel staggered through the doors, his voice shouting for the woman of blue eyes – Amalia. Below, his friends laugh.

It seemed as though an hour had passed and nothing of importance slipped from the guards' throats. They only spoke of bedding women and drinking their lives away. It appeared to Valina that these guards were low in ranking within the king's guard.

Finally, the two staggered into the bar, off to drink themselves into a drunken stupor. Valina rolled her eyes, a breath of annoyance escaping her lips. A wasted night.

"It appears as though our hunt was not very pleasing." Diaval spoke in hushed whisper in case there were listening ears.

Valina sheathed her daggers. "Appears so." She cast a glance toward him, his milky eyes gazing straight ahead toward the castle. "Why did you wish to join me?"

For a moment, he did not answer. His brows began to furrow as he took his bottom lip between his teeth, her eyes watching the movement. "You intrigue me." He finally spoke, his lips moving subtly.

She raised a brow, "From what I hear, not many intrigue you."

A small smile tugged at the corner of his lips. "I suppose Shandal told you of that."

"You suppose correctly."

His gaze finally drifted toward her, her breath hitching within her throat as his eyes found hers, looking into her. Her own eyes took in his striking features, though his cheeks were sunken in, his cheekbones and jaw were sculpted well and sharp. His nose not too long and not too slender. The man's lips were thin but appeared smooth and she found herself wishing to know what they felt like against her own.

Diaval caught her lingering eyes and a light blush crept into his cheeks, causing Valina to smile. "When I saw you waltz into the room, you radiated such strength with each step. Your eyes sharpened like steel, but I could see something lurking behind that steel, a darkness and a deep wanting. I found myself compelled to you, wishing to know just what haunted your mind, encasing your heart." Then, his milky gaze drifted toward her lips, "Wishing to know just what your soul was craving."

Valina's eyes broke away from the heaviness of his gaze, her throat tightening, and she cursed herself for being so foolish. Feeling as though she were a little girl once more, before her family burned, batting her young lashes at the boys her age wondering which one she would like to marry – or should she say which *ones.*

"Perhaps one day, you shall know."

Beside her, the shingles shifted as Diaval rose onto his feet, offering his pale hand to her with a smile, "I shall be awaiting that day."

Her crimson eyes fell upon his hand and she slid her own into his palm. He helped her to her feet and for a moment, they remained where they were as if their boots had been nailed down to the roof. Diaval's hand still clutching Valina's gently, their gazes unmoving and locked. The world seemed to still around them.

Diaval's gaze flickered down to Valina's plump lips. Her body told her to take a step closer to him, to invite him in. But she remembered the night she had just spent with Ventar and found it unfair to all three of them if she so soon made a move upon another man. Another night, but not tonight.

"I'm sure the rebels are waiting for our return." Her voice shattered the silence, breaking the spell of Diaval's gaze.

He blinked, "Allow us to return."

The pair leapt down from the roof, their small journey spent in silence.

Once they had returned, their bodies were encased in a haunting chill. Their skin prickling as they entered the room. Their gazes falling upon the *Ghost Condentai* that sat upon the floor in the center of the room. Her silver eyes vacant, staring ahead. Ashari's white hair stirred upon a ghostly breeze. Her body faded from view, half still lingering within this world. No one disturbed her, many not even gazing upon her. Valina wondered just how long her friend had been at this. Wondered just how many rebels' souls she had freed and how many still lingered here.

Diaval and Valina walked around Ashari, careful not to disturb her, and approached the table. Shandal and Shadari remained the only ones at the table, the other leaders vanished for night. Diaval approached Shandal and told him of their actionless night, reporting the details of the drunken bastards at the other tavern.

The leader nodded his head to the pair, dismissing them for the night.

Diaval caught Valina's hand and placed another cold kiss upon her grey skin. His milky eyes slid up to meet with hers, "Goodnight, Valina Veshanr."

"Goodnight, Diaval."

The *Dead Condentai* gave her a small smile, bowed his head, and disappeared into the shadows.

Ashari rose from the ground, her eyes slowly blinking as she left behind of the realm of spirits. "Many more still cry to me, many more still linger here within this room." Valina noticed the tiredness within Ashari's gaze. Having to do that ritual for so long had to have drained almost all of her energy. "I shall free their crying souls another night. For now, I must rest."

Valina nodded her head and followed Ashari toward the door but stopped within her tracks. Her gaze had fallen upon a lone, crimson petal upon the floor. She peered around the room but found no sign of the other *Blood Condentai.* Kneeling down, her fingers plucked the silky petal from the ground. The vanilla scent still lingered upon it – along with Ventar's.

Gently, Valina tucked the petal into one of the inside pockets of her cloak and stepped through the doorway.

When the creatures of the night returned to their home, Valina watched Ashari ascend the staircase, her pale hand trailing up the wooden railing, her white hair sweeping behind her.

"You never told me." Valina's voice was so hushed that no mortal ear would have ever heard her whispered words.

Ashari halted in her steps, her back still facing the *Blood Condentai* who lingered by the door. "I never wished to place that burden upon you."

"It would never have been a burden, Ashari. I am here so that you may not carry such things alone, that you may share them with me if the weight becomes too much to bear."

Ashari peered over her a shoulder, a ghost of a smile upon her lips and a sadness that ran deep into her soul lingered within her silver eyes. "Thank you, my friend."

CHAPTER TEN

A NOBLE SACRIFICE

"When a person sacrifices themselves to save others, the people never forget that act of kindness."

T HE TOWN was once more gathered before the wicked fence surrounding the castle. Guards had pounded their fists upon every door within the town, every home, and every shop. And marching the people toward the king and whatever cruelty he was showcasing on this night.

The chilly air draped over Valina's shoulders like a winter blanket. Her breath foggy within the air before her. Her crimson gaze was locked upon the king who stood upon the stairs before the doors leading into the castle. That damned, cocky smile upon his face. That ravenous hunger lurking within his gaze. Ashari and Valina found themselves further back within the crowd this time, the people shoving themselves in front of the pair. Valina barred her fangs, hissing at those who shoved Ashari. They gazed upon her in fear, their bodies beginning to slightly tremble at the sight of the snarling *Blood Condentai.* It caused a smile to form upon her lips.

The king took a graceful step aside as guards marched forth, leading the poor victims of the king's wicked intent. There were four people gathered in a line before the fence and they were forced down upon their knees. Grunts escaping them as their bones met hard with the earth. From where Valina stood, the prisoners seemed short, small. But the distance between them was enough to distort size. She hoped that the feeling deep within her gut was wrong. But something clawed at her mind saying that it wasn't.

"Today, my loyal subjects, I have another treat for your eyes to feast upon." He took a leisure step down the stairs, his arms spread wide. "Here we have more traitors to the crown," He swept his hand through the air with disgust as he gestured at the line of people.

Valina felt her stomach drop. A soft brush of skin swept over her hand as another's entwined their fingers with her own. She met Ashari's silver eyes, worry was to be found within the *Ghost Condentai's* eyes. They turned their attentions back toward the king where she found that his gaze was upon her, spotting her so easily within the crowd of people. She did not bother hiding her disgust and hatred, barring her fangs for his eyes to see. But, he only chuckled.

With a nod of his head, the guards tore away the dark sacks that hid away the identity of the prisoners. Shrieks and cries echoed through the crowd. Valina blinked. Her mind trying to process the sight before her. They were children. *Children.*

Beside her, a woman cried out, "That's my niece! Please no!" The human woman fell onto her knees, hands clutched over her chest. She bowed her head, her brown hair curtaining her crying eyes.

"Today I bring to you the deaths of the rebels that could be. Children that could follow in their parents' footsteps." The king held his hands behind his back, "I orphaned them after I murdered their parents, but it only seems fit that I end the cycle of rebels starting with the youngest soon to be members."

An *Organ Condentai* man leapt forth from the crowd, his dark hands wrapping around the bars of the fence. "I'll stop your heart dead in your chest before you harm these children! I'll make you pay for -"

The man's screaming threats had been cut off. The king keeping his narrowed eyes upon him as a veil of red mist escaped the man's body. He fell to the ground, only a cloud of blood left behind where he once stood before the fence.

Valina knew what was to happen after the king killed those who dared come forth and voice their darkest desires to the king. Guards would search the town for the person's family and murder them all, search for the person's friends and slaughter them.

The king's gaze slid toward the children, annoyance was written upon his face. "Kill them." He barked the order.

Valina's daggers called out, and she listened to their pleas, to the plea within her heart, to the pleas of the crying children. Her hand jerked free of Ashari's, and both hands wrapped around the hilts of her wicked daggers. Ashari made no move to stop her, but to aid her. Together. They would go together.

As the blades began to lift from their sheaths, a cloaked figure approached the fence. The guards halted their torch lighting. The king glared upon the person before him.

Slowly, the person lowered their hood. Valina caught sight of midnight hair, one side of the man's head was shaved. Her heart hammered within her chest, her breath caught within her throat.

No.

Ventar spread his arms wide, "If you want to kill a true traitor to the crown, then here I am. Burn me."

Valina found her voice once more, a cry breaking free from her tightened throat, *"Ventar!"* She cried his name into the chilly air, echoing within the night. She cried his name as a lover would as they watched their lover meet their end.

And she could have sworn she saw him flinch.

As she moved to leap forth, strong arms had wrapped around her body. Animalist snarls escaped her mouth. She wanted to claw at the man's eyes who held her captive, but her arms were pinned by her sides. Valina craned her neck to peer at the bastard who dared lay his hands on her, but her anger began to simmer out as she stared into one wholly black eye, the other covered by a patch.

"Shandal." She spoke the leader of the rebellions name, "We have to stop him!"

But Shandal only shook his head.

The king's laughter drew her attention forth. "I knew this tactic would draw one of you traitors forth, the others seeming to be too much of cowards." His crimson gaze slid up and down Ventar's form, a wicked smile curling at the corners of his lips, "I shall enjoy watching you die, Ventar."

Guards wove their way through the crowd, ready to take Ventar prisoner. The *Blood Condentai* merely laughed, "If you can catch me, my king."

Just as a guard leapt forth to claim Ventar, he spun out of reach and dashed into the crowd of people. The guards chased close behind him, shoving people to the ground that stood in their way. The guards were fast but *Blood Condentai* were faster.

She turned her head just in time to see Ventar sprinting past them. The world had slowed around them. And as their gazes locked, Valina could have sworn she saw regret within his crimson eyes. His lips began to move as he mouthed the words; *my Valina.*

Then, he was gone. Followed by the guards. Which, Valina noticed that some of the guards were *Body* and *Mind Condentai* but neither of them was using their powers upon Ventar.

Valina's gaze flickered up to Shandal, a questioning brow raised.

The *Shadow Condentai* leaned down and whispered into her ear, "Our new inside people." He spoke.

The king ordered to have the children released and thrown back out into the crowd. Valina found herself taken back by this, the king showing mercy, sparring lives. She did not allow herself to think too much on that, did not fool herself into thinking that there was just the smallest bit of good hiding away inside that wicked man. Anytime the king did something, it was for him and no one else. Every action, every word, served his purpose. Freeing the children would spark belief in some of these people for their king once more, bowing before his feet.

Valina knew how he worked, and she refused to ever bow.

Valina sat alone within her room. Stripped of all her clothes. The bed sheets wrapping around her. Thoughts had driven sleep away long ago, worry tightening her chest. The king had ordered everyone to return home as he sent his guards searching the land for the fleeing *Blood Condentai.* The people were to remain within their homes until Ventar was found.

"Goddess of Dark, hear my prayer, may I ask that Ventar never be found. May I ask that he hides within the darkest of shadows, safe from the king's sight."

Laying in her bed, Valina could not sleep. Her mind thinking of all the horrible ways the king could have Ventar killed. An image of his body spiked on the king's fence flashed within her mind. His eyes wide but unseeing -the life taken from him, *stolen from him.*

The covers flew off her body as she leapt off her bed. She would not sit here and wonder, she would go search for the man. She did not care if the king found her wandering in the darkness, ignoring his order. He would not kill her – that she knew – but he could do other things to her that would make her wish for death.

Slipping into her darkest clothes, she wandered on silent feet into the hallway. Glancing toward her left at the end of the hall, she found Ashari's door closed. Quickly, she prowled down the stairs, and flew out the front door. As she stood on the first step, she gazed around her. Not a single soul could be found or heard wandering the cobblestone road. An eerie silence curtaining itself over the town. Grasping her hood, she lowered it over her head, concealing her face. Then, she began her hunt for Ventar.

There was no sign of him. The *Blood Condentai* had trekked through the shadows, through the forest, and alleyways between shops and homes. But there was no sign of the man that she hunted for. Not even the smallest trace of his scent found its way into her nose.

Fear had claimed her then. Panic rising within, clawing inside her. Her mind swarming with a thousand thoughts. A buzzing sounding within her ears.

She shook her head, forcing those thoughts and feelings away. There was one more place she could look. His home. She prayed that the guards hadn't been there yet, though it was a foolish thought. Foolish to hold on to hope in this dark land. Foolish to allow herself to allow another within her heart.

Valina smelled it before she ever saw it. The scent of smoke burned through the air. *No.* Her feet traveled faster, almost as if she were floating above the ground. The air thickened with a grey haze. *No.*

Then, the sight was before her. Her feet had halted, rooted to the ground as she stared wide-eyed at Ventar's home. Flames had devoured it, the roof already caved in. The smoke rising from the house was thick and dark, mixing with the shadows nearby. Ravenous, red and orange flames flickered and danced as they burned their way through his home.

Watching the flames caused those horrible memories to resurface. Screams began to ring within her ears. Her hands clasped over them as she shook her head. Her family was there, burning. Agony rattled through the air. Burning flesh assaulted her.

"No! Make it stop!" A snarl sounded from her, but tears swelled within her eyes, clawing behind them as they pled to be freed.

She forced her crimson eyes open and found the king and his guards standing away from the home, watching it burn. Hatred raged inside her, an inferno scorching through her veins. The daggers by her sides called out and she listened. Drawing them forth, she launched herself toward the king.

She would skin him alive, slowly, making sure that he felt every bit of pain. She would severe each of his limbs from his body and toss them into that raging fire. Her body and blades would be coated in the king's blood. Then, she would take his head and spike it on his own damned fence. The picture within her mind was gruesome but beautiful. A wicked, feral grin crossed her lips as the thoughts pleased her. The beast was out to play.

The king was just a few strides away. His death coming so close.

One of her daggers raised into the air, ready to plant it into the king's back. But one of the guards caught sight of her and Valina cursed herself as she locked gazes with the *Body Condentai.* The guard raised his hand and her own stilled within the air, unmoving. Her feet became frozen. Every part of her body immobilized.

My soul be damned. She was furious at herself for being reckless. She should have taken the guards down first but there were too many. Now, she would pay the price of her foolishness.

The king slowly turned to face her, and his wicked smile could be found, causing her blood to boil. "Ah, my dear Valina." His voice purred her name.

"I'm not your dear." A snarl rippled from her lips. She was surprised that the *Body Condentai* allowed her use of her mouth because she would soon be cursing them all.

A chuckle escaped him as he faced the burning home once more, sweeping his arm toward it. "Come to watch your dear friend burn, my dear?"

She blinked, and her gaze slid toward Ventar's house. "No."

"One of my guards found him returning to his home after a long night of running." The king turned toward her, and his hand reached for her face, his finger tracing down her cheek. "But I knew he couldn't run forever."

"Fuck. You." A growl rumbled behind each word, a threat lingering within them. She would have the king's head.

But his smile only widened as he took a step closer to her, his hand brushing aside her hair, exposing her neck. She wanted to thrash her body, to move, to escape. But none of her limbs would answer her calls. The king lowered his face into the nape of her neck, his warm breath tracing along her skin that had begun to crawl. He took a sharp inhale, taking in her scent. His lips just a breath away from her skin.

"Get the fuck off me." She tried to will her arm, to stab the king in his damned face. A frustrated snarl echoed around them. She hated this. Hated the king. And hated herself.

Hated herself for allowing Ventar into her damned, dead heart. Hated herself for not being able to save him. Hated herself for not being able to save her family all those years ago. And now, she was failing them all over again. So close she had come to killing the king, but so far.

She would mourn for Ventar when she was locked away within her room, safe from questioning and judging eyes. That is if she left here alive. But, for now, she would burn with hatred. She would picture the king dying a hundred different ways by her blades. Picture herself coated in his blood as she made it rain from his body.

"One day, you shall be mine, my Valina."

"I shall never be yours."

The king stole one last sniff of her scent, his lips lingering upon her neck, before he took a step back. His hand still caressed her cheek. "One day." He turned his attention toward the man that held her body prisoner. "Free her once we are far enough away but I trust that she won't do anything so foolish again," His crimson eyes met with hers, "Unless you would also like to lose another friend. The *Ghost Condentai* Ashari has been troublesome as of late." The corner of his lips quirked up, "I shall leave that up to you."

"*Bastard.*" She snarled.

"Until next time, my dear."

Valina watched as the king vanished into the eternal night, his guards following close behind him – all except the *Body Condentai.* He stayed just far enough away to give himself a running chance once he freed her. Watching the man hurriedly make his way toward the king, only encouraged the beast within Valina. Running always made hunting more fun. But she suppressed the howling need to give chase. The king would not take another person from her. His day would come, and she would be there to watch or be the one reaping his soul.

The short journey home was silent, Valina numb to the world around her. Her body no longer felt like hers, she was just a mindless husk trapped within a vessel. The feet moving but she gave them no command to do so, she was allowing her body to move on its own, trusting that it would safely return her home.

And once she stepped foot through the door, Ashari greeted her. The woman standing before her, her silver eyes meeting with hers. A word did not utter from the *Ghost Condentai's* pale lips.

"He's dead." Valina found her voice but it did not sound like hers. A choked sob sounding within her throat. "Ventar is dead." She gave voice to the thoughts that had swarmed her mind. Gave voice to the fear that had come to be.

A lone tear escaped her eye and rolled down her cheek. Ashari gently swiped her finger and wiped the tear away. "The spirits told me of what happened," She spoke in a gentle, whispered voice. "They told me of a home eaten by flames and a *Blood Condentai* losing control of her body."

"I'll kill him." Tears poured from her eyes, streaming down her cheeks in warm rivers. "I'll kill them all."

Ashari wrapped her arms around Valina and she fell into the embrace, her knees buckling beneath her. Ashari kept a firm hold on the broken *Blood Condentai* as they lowered to the floor together. Valina cried her sorrows into Ashari's shoulder, cried out her pain, her heartache. She cried until there was nothing left to cry.

Ashari did not utter a word of complaint. She allowed her friend to cry, to feel what she never allowed herself to feel. One of her hands gently combed through Valina's midnight hair, soothing her, while the other rubbed circles on her back.

The pair remained by the door, knelt on their knees, wrapped in each other's embraces, for a long while.

After one last, shuddering sob, Valina moved her head from Ashari's shoulder. The woman's dress was wetted with tears and snot.

"Do not worry of that." Ashari spoke, "That can be cleaned." Her cool hand gently cupped Valina's wet cheek. "I worry of you, my hunter."

"I'll keep him where I keep my family." Her hand raised to her chest and that caged butterfly weakly flapped its wings.

"And there is where I keep my sister." She said, placing her other hand upon Valina's with a sad smile. "Here, they are always with you."

"Thank you, Ashari."

The *Ghost Condentai* placed both hands on either side of Valina's head, leaned forward, and placed a kiss upon her brow. *"May thy Goddess mend and protect thy heart."*

Alone within her room, Valina was curled on her side, her body twisted in the crimson sheets. Silent tears wetted her pillow. And clutched within her grey hand was the lone, dying petal. The scent of vanilla and Ventar barely clinging onto it. Lifting the petal to her nose, she breathed in those fading scents.

Her dreams were the worse they had ever been. Nightmares bursting through her mind. Flames devouring her thoughts. Screams echoed around. Bodies afire flashed before her eyes. Then faces appeared. Each member of her family and one by one they burst into flames. Ventar's face arrived last. And she felt her heart darken, another crack forming as he too, set aflame.

CHAPTER ELEVEN

THREE NIGHTS HAVE PASSED

"When light welcomes the dark, shall the dark welcome the light?"

THE TIME HAD COME. The three nights have come to pass. It was time to once again meet with the child of Nicitis; Luzell.

Valina stirred from her sleep, the nightmares finally setting her free, for now. Tossing the sheets from her body, she leapt from her bed and entered her bathroom. She found a new fire within herself. A new-found determination. As the embers of her old vengeance sizzled out, a new one began to kindle. Having the child of light join them could be their downfall or their rising.

As she stood before the grand mirror, her gaze slid over herself. Crimson eyes staring back. Placing her hand over her chest, her grey lids fluttered over her eyes as she took in a breath. "I failed you, Ventar. I failed my family. But I shall fail no others. That is a promise."

Ashari and Valina found themselves before the tavern. The usual noise rattling out into the air. The same drunkards staggering out into the streets, tripping over their own feet.

The *Dead Condentai* woman was at the bar once more, the same human man leading them through the tavern and opening the little door. Lillian greeted them as she always had and down they went into the darkness, the stairs groaning beneath their feet.

And once they entered the room, all talking was silenced as Valina stepped through the doorway, Ashari trailing just behind her. The weight of hundred gazes was upon the pair as they stalked toward the table of the leaders. Shandal and Shadanar greeted them with a nod of their heads. Shadari offering a smile.

"What's the plan? When shall we avenge Ventar's death?" There was a sharpness to her tone and death in her eyes, fire roaring within her soul.

Shandal did not speak, did not offer a word of a plan. Instead, his wholly black eye drifted above her head.

Irritation simmered within her, she would not be ignored as if she were nothing. Her fists slammed down on the table, the wood groaning beneath the force, a crack sounding and forming somewhere upon it. Even the ground trembled beneath her boots. A snarl escaped her lips.

"*Do not ignore me.*" She never would have spoken to Shandal in such a way before, but now, her vengeance had tainted her sight. Her heart darkening with each life the king had stolen, each person she held close leaving behind this world – leaving her behind.

A pale had rested atop hers, "My hunter." Ashari's voice was calm, soothing the beast.

"You wound me in thinking that I could be killed so easily, my dear."

Her body stilled as that familiar voice drifted toward her ears. The butterfly stirring awake and flapping its wings.

Slowly, she turned. And a sound like a choked sob escaped her as she took in the sight of the *Blood Condentai* man.

Ventar offered a smile, "Hello, my Valina."

Her feet moved, and she dashed across the room, not caring about the watching and judging eyes. Ventar opened his arms to her and her body crashed into his. He staggered back but kept a firm hold on her, his arms tightly wrapped around her waist as he buried his face in the nape of her neck. Valina's arms were tossed around his neck, her fingers gripping tightly to his midnight hair. Tears trekked down her cheeks.

She had not lost him. Ventar was alive. Ventar was here.

Later, she would feel foolish for showing this side of her to a room full of rebels. But that was later. For now, she would soak in this moment, soak in *him.* His scent enveloped her, wrapping around her being, her senses absorbing it.

He was alive.

"I ought to stab you." Valina spoke, her voice hoarse.

A chuckle sounded from him, rumbling against her chest. "The only acceptable way I'll die." Leaning back, her arms loosened from around his neck and lowered to where her hands rested upon his chest. The look within his crimson eyes held her in place. His hands reaching and caressing both her cheeks. "I am truly sorry for the pain I put you through, my dear." His thumb gently wiped away her tear. "It shall not happen again."

"Good." Was all she could say.

His usual smirk returned to his face and it stirred that desire deep within her. She wanted him. But not on this night, there was something with more importance that needed tending to.

"There's something that I must tell Shandal."

Ventar raised a brow, "And what have you done?"

She swatted his hands from her face, "Quick to assume that I've gotten myself into trouble when you're the one that now has a target upon his back."

He shrugged his shoulders, "I am known for being a troublemaker, my dear." There was a glint within his eyes, "And a lot more so in bed."

"Bastard." She rolled her eyes as she turned on her heal and marched toward the table.

"Only the best kind." Ventar called behind her.

When she stood before the table, Ashari returned to stand beside her. Her silver eyes drifting toward the *Blood Condentai* just behind Valina, "Welcome back, hunter." She spoke.

"And hello to you as well, Ashari."

Shandal turned his attention back to Valina, "I am sorry that we had to keep the plan from you, Valina."

She raised a brow. "Plan?"

"We knew that you'd go looking for Ventar – specifically his house – where we lured the king. We needed him to believe that his death was real. And your emotions had to be real."

"So, you mean to tell me the whole thing was planned? What if the king did not take the bait and burned those children?"

A heavy sigh escaped Shandal, tiredness lurking beneath his black eye. "Then we would have prayed to the Goddess to save their souls. We are too few in number to swarm the castle. We'll all perish, and it'll do the people no good when the king unleashes his wrath upon them." His scarred hand plucked a silver figurine from the map, "There is always the choice between the worst and the hardest. And it is never easy choosing between them."

Valina could see the weight that weighed upon the *Shadow Condentai's* shoulders. All the decisions and consequences that follow behind each and every choice.

"The king said the guards spotted him entering his home."

Shandal nodded his head. "Ventar said he had a room beneath his home."

Valina turned to face him, "A secret room?"

He nodded his head. "A safe room with an exit that led into the forest. My mother had it built after guards stormed our house when I was young and drug father away. We never got the chance to use it. We weren't prepared when they returned and took my mother." There was pain within his voice, as if it physically hurt him to speak of his parents.

"Once again, I apologize, Valina." Shandal's gaze drifted back toward the map that was laid out before him. "Now, Shadanar, do you have your group ready for tonight's hunt?"

His cousin nodded his head, "We'll report back whatever information we find."

"Good. An eye for an eye."

Valina waited until the room was almost empty. When Shandal moved to step away from the table to begin his own hunt for the night, Valina called out to him.

"Shandal, there is something I must tell you. Privately."

Shadari cast a glance back at her husband, her body bound in tight, black leather. Swords sheathed across her back. And her midnight hair woven into a single braid that swept past her hips.

Their daughter stood just beside Shadari, Shallara. She was the picture image of her mother, a striking resemblance, her twin brother just as much so. All three had thin, straight noses. Pouty lips, and sharp cheekbones. The women kept their hair long, but the twin brother had his cropped short, neatly combed back from his face. He was rather handsome, the women beautiful.

"Go ahead, take Shallara and Shallor with you."

Shadari nodded her head and led their children out of the room, disappearing into the shadows.

Shandal turned his black eye upon her, "What is it you wish to speak of, Valina?"

"I have another member who wishes to join."

The *Shadow Condentai* raised a skeptical brow, "Why did this matter have to be spoken of in private?"

She straightened her back, holding his gaze, she said, "Because he is a child of Nicitis."

Shandal's eye widened, "The one who escaped?"

Valina nodded her head. "The king has been killing his people. He's come here to put an end to it."

The leader of the rebellion was quiet for a moment, his brows furrowing. "Bring him here to the next meeting. I would like to speak with him."

"But what of the others? They won't take kindly to a child of light entering our dark world and joining us."

Shandal turned his back toward Valina as he followed the trail of his family, "Then they can join the king."

With that, the leader of the rebels disappeared.

"It appears that we both had our own hidden plans." Ventar spoke.

"Then that makes us even," she turned to face him, "Do not hide something like that from me again. Not when it involves your life."

His hand reached toward her, and he trailed one finger along her cheek, "It shall not happen again, my dear."

"Good." She turned her back to him.

As their small group began to leave in search of Luzell, a man stepped forth from the shadows. Milky eyes watching only Valina as he approached them. "I wish to join you, Valina Veshanr."

Ventar narrowed his gaze upon the *Dead Condentai* that stood before them and still Diaval did not tear his eyes away from Valina.

"You may."

Ventar cast a sideward glance toward the *Dead Condentai* but still his milky eyes remained upon Valina as they traveled into the night.

The night welcomed them with silence. The shadows stirring beneath their hurried feet and gathering above their hooded heads. The forest seemed to watch them, the trees following their movement, branches seeming to move away as they dashed through. The predators of the land watched the group travel through the forest they called home, all bloodthirsty gazes hungrily eyeing each soul. But it took one glance from the *Blood Condentai* woman leading the group, one flash of her fangs, one snarl, and they knew better than to tempt fate.

The wind whispered into Valina's pointed ear as she ran though the darkness. The sound of footsteps following just behind her as three others of Severina's children trailed behind her; all searching for the son of Nicitis.

Ahead, Valina saw something within the darkness mangled between the aged, crooked bodies of the trees. A faint, golden glow. So faint that she almost missed it. It flickered as if it were a flame about to go out.

Her feet carried her further, pounding onto the earth beneath her, causing it to tremble. She soared through the air, leaping over roots and fallen bodies of trees. Shrieks of agony shattered through the silence, rattling within her ears.

The light was brighter now.

She leapt over another fallen tree – leaping into that forbidden light.

A cluster of trees surrounded her, a golden glow burning her eyes. Her arm flying up to shield her gaze. Then, she heard it – heard *them.* Howls of hunger. Snapping, hissing jaws. A shout coming from a man as a blast of light ignited within their world of night. Even the shadows seemed to shriek and recoiled back into the forest.

She lowered her arm just enough to see the child of Nicitis and she found herself in awe at the sight before her. His long, golden hair glowed and flowed along a ghostly wind. Those blue eyes of his burning brightly as if a flame was trapped behind them – as if the sun itself lived inside the man. That warm, brown skin of his had a tint of that golden glow flowing through his pores and casting itself out into the world.

Valina's crimson eyes caught movement within the shadows lurking behind the man. A sliver of movement, a body sleek as the night sky. And eyes of crimson irises with slit pupils stared back at her. Its tongue flickered out in a taunt. The serpent rose into the air, heads taller than Luzell.

The man had no idea of the predator that loomed over him.

It arched its neck back, opening its wicked mouth wide – ready to devour the man and extinguish his light.

Valina had only moments to react and she knew her power over blood would not save the man. The serpent was a creature of shadow – one Severina's darker twists on Sybil's creations.

Darkness flowed through its veins, pounding within its heart, whispering through its brain.

The daggers whispered, and her hands wrapped around their leather hilts. Then, she leapt into action.

The world slowed around them.

Valina raced toward the closest tree, jumped, and ran up its side. Twisting her foot, she pushed off the trunk and her body soared through the air. The wind whispering past her ears and tangling within her midnight locks.

The serpent's head slowly came down, jaws open and ready to swallow Luzell whole. But that would never come to pass.

Valina collided against the creature's body and it let out an ear-piercing shriek. It thrashed its head, trying to toss the *Blood Condentai* back into the air but she stabbed her dagger into its neck and held on tightly. Shadows poured out from the wound, wrapping around her hand before joining the darkness within the forest. A cold chill tingled along her spine and she imaged that was how death felt when it came for you– dark and cold.

Stabbing her other dagger into its neck, she began to make the climb to its head. The shadow serpent threw its body into a tree. A crack sounded as its massive body collided with the old wood and the tree came tumbling down. The earth trembled as it met with the ground. Valina's teeth rattled together from the force of the blow, one side of her meeting with that damned tree.

There would be a lovely bruise in the coming night.

Finally, Valina had climbed her way to the top of the serpent's head. A loud hiss sounding from it as it continued to thrash its body about. She had sheathed one dagger, holding tightly onto the creature with one hand – using all the immortal strength the Goddess gave her. In the other hand, her dagger weighed within her grip. Her eyes flickering toward that thin line of crimson etched into the blade before she rose it into the air and brought it down upon the creature's head.

A shriek erupted through the night, startling the hunters hiding within the shadows, even causing the shadows themselves to cower.

The skull gave away beneath the wicked, obsidian blade as it forced its way down until it met with its brain. Shadows wisped forth and swirled before Valina's eyes.

The serpent went still for a moment, giving the *Blood Condentai* time to rise onto her feet, standing upon its head. And down the creature fell. Its lengthy body thudding down onto the ground and Valina simply walked down its head, standing between the spot of the creature's nostrils – and she stepped down onto the earth.

The child of Nicitis stood before her, his body still glowing – but not as brightly as if he knew that the light hurt her eyes.

Ashari, Ventar, and Diaval all stood there staring at her. She dusted off her clothes, "You all were a grand help, I thank you."

"My dear, it appeared as though you were handling yourself just fine without our aid." Pride flickered within his gaze, "And I believe you would have cursed us for even thinking of helping you, am I right?"

Valina rolled her eyes and turned to face Luzell. "Are you hurt?"

He stared at her with those brilliant eyes and she could see herself getting lost within them, wishing to swim in the oceans of his irises. "I am not, thanks to you, Valina."

Her chest warmed as he spoke her name – remembered her name. "I see you have fended for yourself quite well out here." Though his clothes were dirtied, she saw no sign of blood or bruising upon the man.

Luzell ran a hand through his golden hair, taming it. "I did happen to swipe a few foods during my run, not much. Tonight, was my first trouble, I hadn't had that many creatures come at me at once before."

She cocked her head, like a predator sizing up its prey. "They sensed your weakened state, sensed that you had not eaten much and were growing weaker. That is how this side of the world works, the weak are hunted."

Luzell was meant to fear her – fear their dark world but he did not look upon her with fear. He looked upon her with pity and that was worse than fear.

"And this is how you wish it to be? Always hunted. Living under the ruling of a mad king?"

This is all she has known. True peace did not exist in their world – only the eternal darkness and shadows. She only knew of the wicked things that had tainted her. Only knew of the wicked things the king before and now have done.

But she couldn't help but wonder what peace would feel like, even just the smallest touch of it.

"The issue with the king shall be fixed soon enough, Luzell." Valina said crossing her arms over her plump chest and she did not miss when his eyes slid down there for a moment – but only a moment before returning to meet with her gaze. A smirk appeared upon her lips, "You'll be coming with us unless you wish to remain out here with the creatures of the shadows."

Luzell cast a glance behind him, "Going with you seems like the safer choice. I happen to enjoy living."

"You and I both, child of Nicitis." Ventar approached, standing beside Valina. His crimson eyes stern as he took in the man before him. Both were matched in height.

Luzell regarded him with a questioning eye, "You may call me by my name, Luzell."

Ventar inclined his head, "Ventar." He turned his gaze toward Valina with a wicked grin that held a promise of another night. A warmth blossomed between her legs. "Or bastard. Whichever you choose."

The child of Nicitis's gaze lingered upon the two *Blood Condentai* and the tension that lingered within the air between them.

Luzell tore his eyes away from them and landed upon the other two children of night before him. He offered them a smile that was warm and welcoming, "Luzell, a pleasure."

Ashari returned the smile and bowed her head to the man, "Ashari, son of Nicitis, the pleasure is likewise."

Diaval did not return the smile, his milky eyes were upon Valina. He only broke his gaze to meet with Luzell's for a moment, "Diaval."

Luzell turned his attention back toward the *Blood Condentai* that had saved him, "And where are you going to hide me? You certainly cannot take me back to your home."

Valina met Ventar's gaze once more, "Is the safe room still intact?"

He nodded his head. "It's below ground, I made sure to move some debris over the entrance, so none could find it."

"So now am I to be buried in the ground?" Luzell cast an uneasy look toward Valina.

She raised a brow and placed a hand upon her hip, "It's that or remain out here with the blood thirsty beasts. Your choice, son of Nicitis."

A sigh escaped him, "I am no fool. I shall hide wherever you wish to put me."

"So, if we wanted to stuff your body inside a barrel, you would be content in doing so?" Ventar spoke, sarcasm dripping in his voice.

Luzell's blue gaze slid down Ventar's body before returning to meet his eyes, his brows furrowing. "I am beginning to think that we won't get along, Ventar."

The *Blood Condentai* merely winked an eye, "I tend to grow on people." He turned his head toward Valina, "Isn't that right, my dear?"

"Bastard." She snarled before stalking off into the shadows.

Ventar gestured his hand toward her, "See? She adores my presence."

Luzell merely shook his head and followed the woman that had saved his life and hoped that she would not change her mind and be the one to end his.

CHAPTER TWELVE

MONSTERS AT PLAY

"When children of the night save a child of light, their worlds collide."

AFTER THEY hid the child of light away beneath the earth, Ventar slid burned debris over the metal door. Ventar showed Luzell were the food was kept – Valina noted the fresh apples, grapes, and other fruits, and the containers of water. As if he made sure to keep this place stocked in case something was to happen. And, it did. Though *Blood Condentai* did not need those foods and water, it helped when there was no blood to supply their body. But those mortal things could only fuel them so much before the need for blood drove them mad.

The group ventured toward the town where they would part ways. Once the town had come into sight, Diaval turned his attention to Valina, his milky eyes gazing into her own, the look that a young teenage boy would have toward a girl he took a liking to – shy and admiring. Gently he grasped her hand with his cold fingers and brought it up to his lips. They softly brushed against her skin and though his lips were cold, warmth stretched along her skin. "Goodnight, Valina Veshanr."

Her head cocked to the side as he let go of her hand and his milky eyes returned to hers. "Why do you always speak my last name?"

"Because I find it improper to speak a woman's first name only when I have just begun to know her. I have not earned the right."

Valina dared to allow her gaze to travel. Diaval wore a grey button-up shirt, many of the top buttons were left undone revealing a muscled chest that Valina was not expecting. She could imagine herself running her nails down his chest, marking him as hers. And she wished to do just that and much more.

She took her bottom lip between her teeth and his gaze did not miss the movement, his eyes locked upon the plumpness of her lips. She could see desire kindling within the *Dead Condentai.* And she could feel it kindling within herself as well.

"I would wish to know you more, Diaval. I do not know much about you, not even your own last name."

A small, shy smile quirked at the corner of his lips. A boyish grin and Valina could not stop herself from smiling as well.

I am supposed to be a feared monster of night. Not a blushing idiot. She thought to herself.

"Darthollow is my name of last."

She nodded her head, "Then, goodnight, Diaval Darthollow."

"When next we meet, Valina Veshanr." Then the man disappeared into the shadows.

Warm breath traced along her ear, "Setting your sight upon your next prey, my dear? Have you grown tired of me already?"

Ventar was pressed against her back and she could feel his bulge pressed against her ass, even soft it proved to be large. "Sometimes a woman wishes to have multiple lovers, dear Ventar. I do wish you do not allow your jealousy to get the better of you."

His hand traced along the length of her arm, his lips still against her ear. "As long as I am amongst your lovers, I shall never worry of the other men you bed."

"Always so cocky believing that you'll still remain within that list." But, he would. He always would.

"You wound me, my dear."

The sound of someone clearing their throat broke them apart from one another. Ashari eyed them with that haunting silver gaze of hers. "The spirits whisper to me. Guards are lurking within the shadows, their eyes watching and ears listening. I suggest we hurry home."

Valina nodded her head and turned her attention back to Ventar. "I assume you shall be needing a place to stay?"

His face hardened, "If the king learns that I am still alive and living beneath your roof, I do not wish to think of what he would do to you. I won't be placing your life in danger."

It was a rare occasion when Ventar dropped the playfulness. "I have plenty of rooms that could use a body to fill them, Ventar. My home is open to you. And if you have forgotten, we are rebels and now aiding our enemy. I believe my life is already in danger."

A smile found itself upon his lips, but no cockiness filled it – it was a smile softened by the heart. His hand reached out and stroked her cheek, "So rebellious, my Valina."

She leaned into his palm for a moment, savoring his touch and breathing in his scent. Her grey lids fluttering closed. Then, she pulled away from his touch, his warmth leaving her cheek.

"Come, let us go before the king sees you and wishes to spike us all on his fence. I have no interest in becoming his latest decoration."

During the journey back to Valina's home, Ventar continued his argument that he should not stay beneath her roof. Suggesting that he could return to the safe room and bunk with the child of Nicitis. Valina rolled her eyes, not many people could handle Ventar even during his better times. And she did not wish to force Luzell to handle him. Besides, having Ventar closer was a tempting thought. Being able to bed him whenever the pleasure arises within her.

The two *Blood Condentai* kept casting glances at one another, desire lingering within their eyes, as they journeyed through the shadows. Both of them promising the other a night filled with ravenous love making. They both needed it, needed to touch and fall into one another.

When they had finally stood before her door, she quickly withdrew the key and plunged it into the lock. Everyone scurried inside, and the door slammed behind them, the lock clicking into place.

When Valina turned away from the door, she nearly ran into Ventar. He looked down upon her with a hunger afire within his eyes. A warmth began to tingle between her legs at the promise within his gaze. Her mind began to think of all the things she wished to do to him and all the things she wished he would do to her.

Ashari stepped away from them, approaching the stairs. "I shall retire for the evening. Please do keep the noise down as the spirits and I wish for a *peaceful* night of sleep."

A smirk curled upon Ventar's lips, but he kept his gaze locked with Valina's, "No promises, Ashari. I do apologize now if we keep you awake."

A sigh escaped the *Ghost Condentai* and she walked up the stairs to her room.

Valina took a step closer to Ventar, her finger tracing down the length of his chest. Leaning closer to him, her lips traced along his pointed ear, being sure to blow gentle, warm breaths along his skin. A growl of pleasure rumbled within his chest. "Shall we take this to my room?"

"Unless you wish for me to take you right here and now, my dear Valina." And she could hear the promise within his words. And she would let him fuck her against this floor if she did not have a roommate who sometimes liked to linger out of her room.

"Room." She growled. "Now."

"Your wish is my command, My Valina." He scooped her body into his arms, her heart began to hammer within her chest.

He carried her up the stairs and she pointed to the door that led into her room. Opening it, he stepped inside and closed it behind him quietly. Though there was no point since the two of them were going to be quite vocal with their love making.

Approaching her bed, he lay her down gently. And she hoped that was the only time he would be gentle with her. He crawled atop the bed and lingered above her, the intensity in his gaze boring into her own. But it was not the intensity of desire but of a hidden pain.

"Why?" His voice rasped.

Her chest tightened at the pain sounding within his voice. She knew what he spoke of; why she left before he awoke and why she treated him as if what happened between them was nothing.

She decided that just for this night, she would allow her barriers to fall. Her grey hand reached up and caressed his cheek, he leaned into her touch, his eyes never leaving hers. "I fear allowing people close to me, fear that they would disappear or be killed by the king's hands as it has happened before." She took in a breath, suppressing the memories that began to surface, silencing the screams that rattled through her dreams whenever she slept. "And for a moment, that fear had become true. For a moment, you were dead and gone." She hated how her voice had begun to shake, hated how she felt the tears begin to form behind her eyes.

"I regretted how I treated you at the meeting, how I spoke to you as if you meant nothing to me." A tear had dared to fall, and she did not move to wipe it away, "You mean something to me, Ventar. And I do not wish for anything to happen to you because of me. I do not wish to lose you to the dark void and the welcoming arms of the Goddess. She cannot have you, not yet."

His hand formed over her own that still rested upon his cheek. "And she shall not claim my soul yet, for my soul is yours. *I am yours.*" He moved her hand so that her palm was exposed, and his lips pressed into it, "You mean more to me than you shall ever know."

"Then how about you show me." Seductiveness purred within her voice.

There was a gleam within his crimson eyes. "That, I can do, my dear Valina."

One of his hands trailed along her side, tugging at the fabric of her shirt the lower it traveled. Until it reached her tight pants. Down it slid beneath the leather. His finger brushed over her clit and a moan rose within her throat as she sank her fangs into her lips. The taste of blood coating her mouth. Slowly, he rubbed her clit in circles. Taunting her. Her fingers gripped the crimson sheets as his fingers worked down.

A breath escaped her lips as he slid a lone finger inside of her. Moisture seeped into her pants as he aroused her body. Gasping moans filled the silence as he plunged his finger inside of her again and again, slipping a second inside.

Valina gripped the back of Ventar's head, grabbing a fistful of his midnight hair, and brought his face down to hers. Her mouth devouring his with a hunger that could only be satisfied by the pleasure he brought upon her body.

Rapidly, he began to move his fingers inside of her. Her back arched and a loud, gasping moan escaped her plump lips. Ventar lowered his face to her neck and kissed upon her skin that was afire with desire and pleasure. It rippled and singed through her being, setting a fire that scorched within her soul.

Warmth exploded from her, a heavy sigh echoing through the room. Her heart rapidly thundered within her chest, threatening to explode just as she had.

A feral, smirking grin tugged at Ventar's thin lips. A wildness gleamed within his crimson eyes. "Did you find that enjoyable, my Valina?"

A growl escaped her as she forced Ventar onto his back. He lay there grinning, his hands resting behind his head. It only encouraged the beast within her as his own reflected within his gaze – calling out to her. And her beast roared back.

Her hands worked on his trousers, yanking them down his legs till they rested at his ankles. A wicked smile appeared upon her lips as she beheld Ventar's cock, erected just for her. Her fingertip began to trace along the tip of him and a groan escaped the man.

Valina's mouth lingered before his ear, blowing hot breath against his skin. "Tell me what you wish for me to do, Ventar." Her hand began to slowly work its way up and down the length of him. Her fangs nipped at the flesh of his ear, "Tell me what you want this pretty mouth to do."

A growl rumbled within his chest, his lips pulling back to reveal his sharp teeth. *"I want that pretty mouth wrapped around my cock."*

"Your desire is my command." She purred into his ear before lowering herself down.

First, she teased him. Placing kisses along the length of his erection. His crimson eyes watching her every move, a fire ablaze within his gaze. And then finally, she gave him exactly what he wanted. Her lips sealed around his cock and a heavy sigh escaped Ventar as her tongue caressed itself around him while his cock was within her mouth.

"*Valina.*" He growled her name on a moan that roared from his mouth. His hands clenched the sheets.

Control. She was in control and that was how she preferred it. Controlled what he felt and how he felt it, controlled that pleasure and stirred it awake within his being. And it was by her doing that he felt this way, that his heart raced within his chest. That growls of pleasure echoed through the room.

One of his hands found itself within her hair, fingers tangling within her midnight locks as he urged her head down lower. His cock filling her mouth and reaching her throat. Soon, he would be exploding inside her and she would swallow every drop of it.

With a loud grunt, he filled her. Warmth exploding inside her mouth. Her lips did not leave his cock until she had swallowed every bit of him. A heavy sigh escaped Ventar as his hand freed itself from her now tangled locks. His breathing heavy.

Valina smiled, pleased with herself. Her tongue gliding across her lips, taunting the man before her. "Did you find that enjoyable, dear Ventar?" Her voice purred.

A chuckled escaped him, "More than enjoyed, my dear." The bed shifted as he rose to face her. His hand trailing across her cheek and tucking a stray strand of hair behind her pointed ear. "Now, how else may I please you, my Valina?"

Just at the sound of his voice claiming her as his, caused the throb of warmth between her thighs to intensify. Leaning toward him, her teeth sank into his bottom lip, drawing forth that sweet blood. Drops of it spilling into her mouth a soft moan escaped her at the taste of it.

"Fuck me." Her voice whispered upon his lips.

Her gaze flickered up to meet with his to find an animalistic smile dancing upon his lips. There was such promise within crimson eyes that she nearly moaned. "Your desire is my command, my dear."

Within a second, he had her body pinned against the bed, his own weighing atop her. Her wrists had been trapped above her head. Ventar began to kiss upon her skin, lips grazing her neck, fangs gently nipping but being careful to not tear apart her soft flesh. To not draw forth her blood, something none has ever done before.

Valina began to wonder when she would ever trust someone enough to allow them a drink of her blood. When she would ever allow someone that close to her heart to offer them what she has offered none before.

As Ventar gazed upon her, she wondered if he would be the first to taste of her blood. Something she has kept carefully guarded all these years.

The two monsters of the night tangled their bodies with one another. Forgetting about the darkened, wicked world around them. Finding a world of their own within one another. A world where only two monsters existed, and the shadows were theirs.

CHAPTER THIRTEEN

A MONSTER CREATING ART

"If a monster is found creating art from their soul, are they truly a monster with not a shred of goodness to be found within their darkened hearts?"

WHEN VALINA AWOKE she once more found herself wrapped within Ventar's embrace. Her head resting upon his chest where his heart beat sounded within her ears, almost luring her back to sleep – begging for her to return to the land of dreams and shadows. And for once, her nightmares had allowed her to rest. Allowed her to feel what a peaceful night of sleep truly felt like. No screams had erupted through her mind, no burning bodies surfacing from the depths of her memories. It was only the darkness of her mind that had greeted her.

For a moment, Valina allowed herself to lay there enjoying the warmth of the sheets wrapped around her naked body. Enjoying the warmth that radiated from Ventar's body, her body absorbing it and the heat caressed her undead heart. Her fingers gently traced along his chest where her nails had clawed at it the night before, drawing forth his blood as she drank upon it.

Gently, she removed herself from his embrace. She needed out – out of the house. Her hands itching to create – to carve into wood and set free the woes of her mind.

Ventar did not stir as she slid from the bed and quietly dressed herself. Once she stepped into the kitchen, she was greeted by the sight of Ashari. A silver nightgown draped over her curvy body. Her white hair woven together in a thick braid that swept down her back, barley brushing the floor at her bare feet.

The scent of tea filtered through the air, steam rising from a kettle that rested upon a stove. And then, the sound of a song found its way into Valina's ears. She leaned against the doorway, enjoying the sound of Ashari's gentle and haunting voice.

"Oh, Goddess of Darkness, maker of shadows and night, creator of creatures and shadows." The song was an old one, older than Valina, rumored to come from the time when Severina herself touched feet upon this divided world. "From her soul children had birthed, blessed by the shadows that poured forth form her being and blessed this earth."

Ashari began to mix sugar into the tea, a drop of honey. Opening a cabinet door with the slightest of creaks, she grabbed a silver tin from the shelf. And Valina knew exactly what it was – a contraceptive. A smile finding itself upon her lips as she shook her head. Ashari sprinkled a pinch of the powder into the tea and returned the tin to its place upon the shelf.

"Oh, Goddess of Darkness, whose heart lay in ruin scattered throughout the shadows upon this world. Where her soul shattered and divided the *earth. The light forbidden within the darkness that was hers. Oh, Goddess of Darkness, who lingers within the night, watching over the children who vowed to love her when her lover could not."*

Sadness washed over Valina, as if a shadow itself had wrapped around her being. The song held the Goddess's heartache and it poured forth from Ashari's lips.

Though Severina preferred one lover, many of her children did not. But it was always spoken consent and never hidden within the shadows. Valina made sure that any of the lovers she bedded, knew that there would be many more.

"The hunter found herself busy within the night." She turned with a smile and the cup of tea. "One must always be prepared so no children of surprise find themselves born into this world."

With a chuckle, Valina took the offered tea. "Thank you, Ashari. I find myself not wishing for children just yet."

The *Ghost Condentai* raised a brow. "If you continue like you have been, my dear friend, you shall find a small one growing within your womb soon enough."

Valina raised the cup into the air, "And that is why I am welcomed with this every night after the fun."

Ashari simply shook her head. Then, her silver gaze traveled down the length of Valina's body. At the loose trousers that draped down from her hips, the simple grey tunic tugged over her chest, cropped a little short to show her belly. Noting the single braid that snaked over the *Blood Condentai's* shoulder.

"You are to carve." She said. "Be careful of the shadows and what lurks within them. Wandering and spying eyes, ears listening to the slightest of sounds. The spirits have warned that the king has eyes even amongst those we claim as friends."

Her voice whenever she spoke in such a way, caused a chill of unease to rush along Valina's spine.

Setting the now empty porcelain cup down upon the counter, Valina approached Ashari and placed a kiss upon her brow. "I shall return."

"Be safe, my hunter."

"Always." And then, Valina stepped out into the awaiting shadows.

A small satchel thumped against Valina's leg as she traveled through the shadows on swift feet, the wind roaring past her ears, her braid trailing through the air behind her. Creatures of the night slinking back into the darkness as the *Blood Condentai* sped past them like a whisper of wind.

They did not wish to end up like the serpent that dared cross the path of the monster that lurked within the woman of night.

Soon enough, her destination was in sight. A small cluster of trees and that was where her art was birthed into this world. As she grew closer, stumps of trees scattered themselves along the forest floor. Other trees had depictions and murals carved into their aged bark. Images of the Goddess and monsters of the night marked almost every tree nearby.

As she passed the trees, her fingers traveled along the carved bark. Over the smooth and roughness of her work. She entered the cluster of trees. Their crooked, bare hands reaching over her head, seeming to sweep low to gently brush the top of her head.

Valina approached a lone tree, its trunk thin and crooked. Seeming as though it would topple in any passing second. Reaching a grey hand into her satchel, she drew forth a silver dagger. Much thinner than the wicked daggers that weighed at her sides. It was her carving dagger, one her father had gifted her when she was a mere child and found her love for carving.

———————————

The grey skinned man that she resembled, knelt before her. A sweet and tender smile upon his face, unending love flickering within his crimson eyes. "My little, Ina." Her father voiced the pet name he had given her.

A smile appeared upon the young girl's face. "Yes, father?"

She noticed that her father held a hand behind his back, placing his free one upon her shoulder. "Your mother has told me about the dullness of her kitchen knives." Her heart sunk within her chest, the smile fading from her face, but never from her father's.

Though they thrived on blood, her mother often prepared the sweetest of treats within their kitchen. The knives she used were small since they were only used for slicing the sweet fruits she added into her pies.

"I'm sorry, father! I shall spend the day sharpening them all!" Her voice cracked as the tears had begun to form.

Her father only chuckled, "I have taken care of the sharpening. But, you, Ina, are not in trouble."

Her head cocked to the side. "I'm not?"

"No. I have something for you."

Once more, the smile returned to her face, her crimson eyes widening.
"A gift for me!"

Her father withdrew his hand and she saw an item wrapped in
midnight cloth laying within the palm of his hand. "Take it."

He did not have to tell her again. Her hands eagerly swiped the item
from his hand to find that it weighed heavily within her own. With
excitement burning within her, she tore the fabric from the item. A small
gasp escaped her lips as she blinked down upon the weapon within her
hand. A silver dagger. The handle curved to fit nicely in the palm of her
hand. And she noticed, when she gazed upon it closer, that her name had
been carved into the silver of the blade; To my Ina.

"It's beautiful, father!"

She felt the warm brush of his lips against her forehead, "For my little
wood carver. Now, there shall be no need to steal your mother's cooking
knives."

Laughter sounded around them.

As the memory faded, and the sound of her father's laughter no
longer echoed within her mind, a sadness had gripped her heart.
Her father was a kind and gentle man, a man who should have been
born in the land of light. For the darkness did not seem to call to
him as it did to her, her mother, and the other creatures that lurked
within this darkened world.

But, her father had been a rebel. And perhaps the night had
called to him, but he hid his monster away better than most.

Her hand wrapped around the curved hilt of the dagger and she stabbed the silver blade into the heart of the tree. And she could have sworn, she heard it scream.

Bits of dark, dying bark fluttered to the ground before her boots as the blade hacked away at the aged tree. She allowed herself to fall deep into the pits of her mind; where the darkest parts of her lurked within the shadows of her soul. This is where she set herself free, the only place where she felt safe enough to do so. Deep within the forest where the monsters lurked but never daring to pounce.

The shadows curled at her feet, whispering into her ears. The wind blowing its chilling breath against her neck, causing bumps to arise along her skin. But still, she carved. Unbothered by the world around her for she was lost within her own.

It was not a world of peace, she hardly knew what that felt like. She only knew what chaos and bloodshed felt like. It surrounded every aspect of her life. Even she craved the bloodshed, the monster within her pleading for it. Memories surfaced within her mind; the first man she had murdered. And felt no remorse in doing so. The man that had set her family afire by the king's order. The sound of her blades hacking away at his flesh sounded like sweet music into her ears. His cries the softest of lullabies. The warmth of his blood upon her skin was that of a hot bath.

She remembered the sound of his limbs thudding upon the ground before her feet as she sawed them from the man's body. He had died after she had begun to take his second arm. But still, she continued. To prove a point to the king; one day, that bloody pile shall be him.

And this was the part where she was glad she found solitude within the forest; when the tears had begun to fall. Repeatedly, the dagger stabbed into the tree, shadows weeping from the old wood. No longer was she creating. The memories had become too much. The emotions she spent every night suppressing forcing themselves out in the world.

With one last, shuddering cry, the dagger embedded itself in the trunk. Heavy, shaking breaths escaping Valina as she tilted her head back to gaze upon the dark sky that loomed above her.

A lone tear trekking down her grey cheek.

A snapping branch shattered through the silence. Her hands were a blur of motion as she drew forth her daggers and whirled to face the intruder that dared defile her place of solitude. A loud snarl rippling from her lips.

But, her blades lowered when she took in the sight of the *Dead Condentai* before her. His milky eyes gazing into her own and she saw as his gaze flickered down to the tear that now slid beneath her chin.

She raised a brow to the man, "How did you know where to find me?"

His hand sheepishly brushed through his grey, shaggy hair. "Your friend Ashari was shopping within the market. I asked where you were, and she told me where to find you, and to proceed with a warning."

Her daggers returned to their sheaths and she crossed her arms over her chest. "Why were you searching for me?"

Diaval remained silent as he approached Valina. And when he was close enough, his milky gaze finally broke free from her, to gaze upon the tree behind the *Blood Condentai.* "You are a carver." His voice was a hushed whisper, admiration coating his words.

She turned to face the tree, "I am."

He reached a sickly, pale hand to the bark. His fingers tracing over the smoothed image of a gruesome scene. A body lay in ruin atop a pool of their own blood. A woman looming over the man, cloaked and hidden within the shadows. Bloody daggers held by her sides that dripped onto the ground at her feet. Swirls and whirls of shadows hung above them, some slithering down from the sky to wrap themselves upon the cloaked woman, claiming her.

"You are the woman." Diaval spoke, his eyes still lingering upon the mural that marred the trunk of the old tree. "And he was your first kill."

Valina nodded her head. "The king gave the order to burn them, and he held the torch."

Flames began to blaze before her eyes in their wicked, mocking dance.

His milky eyes slid back to her face and there she found understanding within his gaze – not pity. "My own family was long dead, my mother stepping into the open arms of the Goddess once I was birthed into this world."

Dead Condentai were a rarity within their world. Though they could raise the dead, death always lingered above their shoulders.

They danced upon that thin line that separated their worlds of living and dead. And some danced too close and death swooped in and stole them away. Many died while giving birth, taking the smallest step over that dividing line.

"A family friend – a human – was the one to raise me. She died by the king's order when I reached the age of sixteen. She had stolen food so that I may eat since money was scarce."

"What was the order?"

A long moment passed before he spoke in a hushed whisper, "A public whipping."

A snarl escaped her lips as she cursed the king. A whipping was one of his lesser punishments. Many could live through them, but they would forever bare scars upon their skin, some whipped to the point where they could no longer walk. But when a human was whipped, there was rarely a chance of surviving.

"I was made to watch as a lesson," Diaval turned his back to her, "And as a reminder, I was whipped three times." Lifting his shirt, Valina could see the wicked line of scars that branded his sickly skin. Three long strikes that trailed along his back.

Valina took a step closer to the man and reached a grey hand toward him. When her fingers came into contact with his skin, Diaval took in a breath but did not speak – allowing her to travel her slender fingers along his scars. His skin was so cold against her own.

As her fingers brushed against the risen scars upon his back, she felt her rage begin to boil. Her veins turning to liquid fire. *"He shall pay."* Her voice growled from her lips.

Diaval lowered his shirt to cover his scars once more and turned to face the *Blood Condentai* before him. He raised his hand as if to touch her, to caress her cheek. But it lowered back to his side.

Her eyes had caught the movement, her gaze remaining upon his hand. "You fear touching me?"

The *Blood Condentai* turned her head toward the tree, her eyes taking in the detail of the carving. Looking upon the man's face that would forever remain in a scream of agony. The woman that symbolized her and the monster that lurked within her soul. The blades that were held within her hands that dripped with blood.

"I would fear me too."

Then, she felt the cold touch of a hand upon her cheek. When she met with Diaval's gaze once more, she found his brows furrowed. Emotions stirring within his gaze as he stared upon her.

"I do not fear you, Valina Veshanr." His eyes took in every feature of her face, every detail. His thumb stroking her cheek. "I admire you."

She raised a brow, "Admiring a monster?"

He shook his head, "We are all monsters in this world. But you, have more humanity within your heart than most. You carry such burden but do not share it. You shoulder other's burdens so that they shall not feel alone but you do not allow anyone else to shoulder yours." His hand moved down to her chin, his fingertips a ghostly whisper tracing along her skin. "You have strength within you." Then, his voice lowered to a whisper as he said, "I find myself wishing that someday, you shall allow me to shoulder some of your burdens. And if not me, then someone. There is no weakness in that."

The way he spoke to her was gentle, the way he looked upon her caused her knees to buckle. There was such a tenderness within his milky eyes as he gazed upon her – *into her* – and accepted every part of her. Even the darkest of parts and did not shy away, did not turn away. So few could do that.

And it was then that she had decided; she would allow him into her heart as well as she had Ashari and Ventar. Opened her heart bare and allowed him to gaze inside.

"I think," her voice lowered, "you have earned the right to call me by my first name."

A sweet, boyish smile caressed his lips as he lowered his head closer to hers. "Valina." His breath was cool against her mouth, lingering just before her lips.

A whisper of death trailing along her skin.

Desire clawed and screamed within her. Pleading for his mouth against hers. And, as if he could hear the pleas of desire roaring within her, his lips had met with hers. Cold but warm all at once. His hand moving to once again caress her cheek, the other finding itself upon her hip as he drew her body closer to his. Her hands trailed upon his torso, coming to rest on the back of his neck. His grey hair gently sweeping over her fingers – silky to the touch. The fire that had been kindling within her since they met, blazed to life in a great inferno.

But as soon as the kiss began, it had ended. Diaval parting his mouth from hers, leaving her wishing for so much more. For another taste of him, for a moment longer. But the moment was to not happen tonight, but there was a promise of another haunting his eyes.

His hand gently brushed her stray hair behind her ear. "I am no fool, I am aware of your lover and the fact you might have more, but I shall wish to be amongst them. Amongst the ones who know your true heart. That is all I wish."

Valina bit her bottom lip, his eyes watching the movement with a hunger hiding away in his gaze. "Then, your wish shall be granted." As would hers.

Diaval's hand fell away from her cheek, his coldness leaving her skin. He took a step closer to the tree and wrapped a hand around the curved handle of the dagger that protruded from the bark and pulled it free. Facing Valina once more, he bowed his head and offered the silver blade.

"Never stop creating." He said.

She took the dagger from his hand and returned it to the satchel by her side.

The *Dead Condentai* gently grasped her hand and placed a kiss upon her skin, "Until next we meet, Valina."

A smile found itself upon her lips, "Until next we meet, Diaval."

CHAPTER FOURTEEN

LIGHT JOINS THE DARKNESS

"When the light joins the dark, shall they become a shadow as well?"

T HE FOLLOWING NIGHT, Ashari, Ventar, and Valina traveled into the shadows to fetch the son of Nicitis. On this night, he was to meet the rebels and hopefully join their cause – if the creatures of night did not try to slaughter him first.

Valina would dare them to try and lay a finger upon the man, and they would be leaving with one finger less.

They cloaked him, hoping to conceal his golden glow. But even with the darkest cloak draped over his shoulders and his head hooded, his glow still emanated. So, the group traveled through the edge of the forest where the darkest shadows hid. Valina felt the watchful eyes of the hungry predators lurking within the darkness. All of their crimson eyes focused upon the strange new man that treaded through their home. Valina made sure to stay close by Luzell, her daggers drawn and ready.

The old tavern was in sight, the rusty chains swinging the wooden sign with groans as the wind swept past. The doors wide open allowing the music to filter through into the night. Drunken laughter and shouts could be heard from inside.

Luzell gazed upon the tavern with judging blue eyes. His brows furrowed. Turning to face Valina, he raised a brow to her. "This is the place of meeting?" Luzell made sure to keep his voice lowered to a whisper.

Valina flashed her fangs in a smile, "Welcome to the land of darkness, Luzell."

Ventar took this opportunity to slap a hand on the child of Nicitis's shoulder, "It'll grow on you." He winked a crimson eye.

Luzell said nothing, only glancing down upon the grey hand that gripped his shoulder.

On silent feet, the group approached the tavern. Once more, the *Dead Condentai* was behind the bar, mixing a drink. When the group approached, she raised her milky eyes to gaze upon them. Valina watched as the woman raised a grey brow, her gaze drifting over her shoulder to stare upon the man of light. Luzell kept his hood lowered over his face, his head bent down.

Valina spoke of the code and it took the woman a long moment before she cast her gaze toward the human man who was to lead them to the rebels. And when the man faced them, he even lingered upon his chair for a moment. Valina narrowed her eyes at the man and he finally slipped off the bar stool and led them away.

They were led into that cramped broom closet once more, the space filling from their numbered group. The man yanked the carpet back from the secret door and knocked upon the wood.

Soon, Lillian answered the call and the door swung open, revealing the young human woman. Her blue eyes sparkled as she took in the group, her brows creased together as she cocked her head to the side. Her gaze remaining upon Luzell who lingered close behind Valina. The son of Nicitis kept his gaze trained upon the floor. Never once did his own blue eyes cast up to meet with Lillian's.

"Come, come!" She waved the group down the dark flight of groaning stairs and the door slammed above their heads, encasing them beneath the tavern.

"Are you sure this shall go well?" Luzell leaned down and whispered into Valina's ear once they reached the bottom of the stairs.

Her chest tightened as his breath caressed her ear. "No."

Luzell tensed behind her. The *Blood Condentai* peered over her shoulder and flashed her fangs in a wicked smile – a promise to get him out alive if things went horribly wrong.

Lillian skipped toward the second door, retrieving the rusted silver key from her pocket, and unlocking the door that would lead them into a room full of rebels. A room full of monsters.

Once the group stepped foot inside the room, all talking had been silenced. All eyes once more turning upon them as they always had but this time it was different. Every pair of eyes trained behind Valina, curious and predatory. Her hands moved down to her daggers, fingers resting upon the hilts. Ready to draw them forth if needed.

The leader of the rebellion turned his dark eye toward the group. His brows furrowed as he pushed away from the table and approached. Valina kept her back straight, chin held high. Shandal knew who she had brought, just who stood behind her – a child of a God who was their sworn enemy. A child of light treaded into their world of darkness.

He crossed his dark, scarred arms over his muscular chest and nodded his head toward the man. "This is who you spoke of?"

Valina took a step aside, allowing Luzell to step forward. Ventar moved to his side, Ashari falling behind them. He was under their protection, none would dare lay a hand upon him.

Shandal's dark gaze watched the man before him, "Remove your hood."

Keeping his head lowered, he turned his gaze toward Valina. She simply nodded her head. Luzell raised his sun kissed hands and lowered his hood – revealing to the entire room that their enemy was amongst them. Hisses and snarls soon rippled through the air. Chairs clattered upon the floor as the monsters pounced, ready to tear into Luzell's flesh.

An *Organ Condentai* flung herself toward the child of light – ready to erupt the organs within his body and lay him in ruin from the inside out. Valina leapt in front of Luzell and took command over the blood within the woman's body. A growl sounded from the woman's lips. The blood flowed through her veins slowly, almost coming to a halt. Her body unable to move as Valina called upon the life force within her. A wicked smile appeared upon the *Blood Condentai's* mouth.

Shandal raised a dark hand, the room falling silent once more. "Valina, release Oldaa. Please."

Valina did as she was asked, Oldaa taking in a shuddering breath and another *Organ Condentai* appeared by her side. Offering her a body to lean against, the man casting a hateful gaze toward Valina, but she only winked a crimson eye at the man.

"Child of Nicitis," Shandal spoke in the tone that he had first spoken to Valina in, "Why have you come to us? What has brought a child of light into the land of dark? What has brought you to your death?"

Luzell stood straighter, meeting his gaze with Shandal's one dark eye – peering into that vast darkness. "I have come here to kill the king. To take vengeance for my people – for the ones that have died by his doing and for the ones who have suffered by his doing. He has entered into the land light bringing with him the darkness - the shadows of bloodlust."

His words should have been an insult – but they were not for they were true. The darkness was something to be feared, the monsters living within the shadows were something that would haunt nightmares until the end of time.

Shandal turned his attention upon one of the few *Mind Condentai* that lingered within the room. "Malon, come. Please."

The man stepped forth from the group of rebels. His light grey eyes focused solely upon Luzell as he approached. When he stood before them, Valina could not help but stare upon the dark tattoos that inked his bald head. And she found herself wondering what sort of story they spoke of.

Shandal focused his attention back toward the child of light, "I may believe you, but the rest of the rebels shall need proof." He nodded his head at the man that now stood beside him. "Malon is a *Mind Condentai.* He shall journey into your mind and seek the truth."

Luzell cast an uneasy glance toward the bald man that now stood before him, but he did not speak a word – only nodding his head.

The *Mind Condentai* closed his eyes as he began his search, ripping through every memory. Tearing his mind apart at the seams to search for the truth that hid itself away. The man digging deep, deeper than he probably should. Treading into memories that were not his to see, not his to gaze upon.

Valina noticed the discomfort upon Luzell's face, sadness glazing over his bright, blue eyes. His lips pressed themselves into a thin line. There was nothing she could say, if they wanted to prove his innocence, then this had to be done. Valina placed a hand upon his shoulder and glared toward the *Mind Condentai.*

"Malon, enough." Shandal ordered, a growl almost escaping him.

Relief washed over Luzell's face as the man left his mind, retreating from his memories. The *Mind Condentai* stared upon the child of light before him, fascination gleaming within his grey eyes as he studied him. Valina wondered just what the man saw within Luzell's mind to cause his hatred to flicker and die out.

And for a moment, envy nipped at her. She wished to know what lingered within his mind – and she knew it had to be something beautiful. A world of light, where no shadows lurked, no monsters prowling within the darkness for there was none. A forest that was not dead, where trees lived and thrived. Flowers blooming. And light showering itself upon the world. And perhaps a ruler that did not rule with a wicked hand but a kind one. A land where peace thrived.

And she wished so badly to step into their world if only for a moment, to allow a second of peace to touch her soul.

But only a moment, for she knew where her place was. And it was here within the darkness. Where her inner monster was free to roam, free to drink of blood.

"Did you find the proof that you needed?" Shandal did not need proof – he had trusted Valina enough to bring their enemy to them. Trusted her enough to not lead death to their door.

Malon nodded his head, "He speaks the truth."

"Show any other who has doubt what you have seen as proof."

Malon bowed his head and wandered off, many people questioning the *Mind Condentai*. Many wishing to see just what he had seen. And Valina found herself wishing to approach him, to ask him to show her what hid itself away within Luzell's mind. But, she had a feeling that he would tell her in time. So, she would wait.

"I am Shandal." He offered a dark hand to Luzell, "And welcome to the rebels."

Before, Shadanar would have lashed out. Would have spewed hatred, anger ablaze within his eyes. Before, he would have cursed his cousin for allowing their enemy amongst them, for not striking him down right then and there. But that was before, Ashari had helped the man more than anyone shall ever know. Gave him the peace that he needed to move on and accept his family's deaths – no matter how tragic they were. The hatred lifted from his heart, but his curiosity still remained, questioning lingering within his black eyes.

Shandal clasped a hand on Luzell's shoulder, "Come, allow me to introduce you to the rebels." With that, he led the child of light away.

Ventar approached Valina's side, "Since there have been no killings as of recent, there are no hunts planned on this night."

"So, what are we to do? Listen to guards useless drunken chatter again?" Valina's gaze never ventured away from Luzell.

Watching his interactions with each child of night. His blue eyes staring upon them in wonder. The woman *Organ Condentai* approached him and bowed her head in apology.

"Not tonight, my dear. What would you say to a drink in the bar?"

Valina raised a brow and cast a sideward glance toward the man, "And drink from the glasses she washes with that same dirty rag?"

Ventar tipped his head back as laughter escaped him, "I shall purchase us the bottles, if the dirty glasses bother you."

"You do remember that the entire town believes you dead? What would happen if you drank a little too much and allowed your hood to fall?"

Ventar offered his hand to her, "Many of the patrons are part of the rebels, others are too drunk to remember their own names."

Valina glanced upon his hand and finally slipped her own onto his palm, "Try not to get yourself killed – *again.*"

Ventar's only response was roaring laughter as he guided her away.

The bar was loud, the music filtering through the air and echoing within her ears. Drunken laughter shouted over the sound of instruments and their melodies. Women approached some men, their dresses low enough to almost reveal their breasts, one side of their skirts tied up to reveal a slender leg. They bent over the counter, their lips pressed against the drunken men's ears, tempting them with a night of passion – for the perfect price.

Valina herself began to wonder if she should charge her lovers. Goddess knew many of them in the past had not been worth the trouble and casting a glance toward Ventar, she knew he was trouble. But he was trouble worth keeping around. Her head tipped back as she took a swig of the bitter alcohol, washing it down her throat.

Ventar leaned against the counter beside her, refusing to take a seat. His crimson gaze drifting through the room, unease and awareness coating his features.

One human man staggered toward the bar, his body falling against it as he tried to steady himself. He was an older man, slightly on the heftier side, sweat gleaming upon his nearly bald head. The white surrounding his brown eyes were blood shot – he was too far gone. He flashed a yellow smile Valina's way and edged closer to her.

"W-What's a pretty... lady like you doing here?" His breath was wretched, her nose crinkling at the smell.

"Leave me alone." A growl escaped her lips.

But the man was persistent. "Come on, sweetie, I could show you a g-good time..."

Ventar snarled beside her. But he knew she could fend for herself quite well.

Her hand drifted down to one of her daggers, her fingers wrapping themselves around the handle and drawing it forth. Her gaze flickered down to the man's hand that rested upon the bar. Within a breath, the wicked blade flashed within the air and embedded itself into the wood of the bar between the man's pinky and ring finger.

Fear had consumed the man, his body trembling. Valina leaned toward the man, flashing her sharp fangs in a wicked smile. "And I could show you a good time as well."

The man finally took the hint and stumbled away from the bar, bumping into other patrons.

"Always so wicked, my dear." Ventar whispered into her ear.

She winked a crimson eye, "It's one of my better qualities."

Ventar began to speak, but the bar suddenly became draped in silence. All talking, and music had ceased. And fear had crawled into the bar, grasping ahold of the patrons, rooting them in place.

Valina peered over her shoulder and the doors swung open. And she could have sworn that her soul had left her body – fear trailing its cold fingers along her back.

The king had entered the bar.

His gaze had not yet fallen upon the two *Blood Condentai.* Ventar took the opportunity and vanished into the shadows, leaving Valina alone at the bar. It would appear suspicious if the two left together and there was too much a risk of the king spotting them.

Valina turned on the stool, facing her back toward the king. She prayed to the Goddess that he would not find her, but her prayers did not reach Severina in time. A presence lingered behind her, looming over her shoulder. And she knew that when she turned, she would be faced with the king.

"My dear," His voice purred into her ear. "I did not expect to find you here amongst the low lives."

The *Dead Condentai* briefly glanced up from the glass that she was cleaning, her milky eyes staring daggers toward the king. But he paid her no mind. His focus solely upon Valina.

She took another swig of that bitter alcohol and allowed it to burn its way down her throat. "I quite enjoy their company. Much nicer than the rich who seem to have every bit of their coin shoved up their asses."

Valina met with the woman's milky eyes for a second and found a small but quick smile twitching at the corner of her lips.

The king answered with a chuckle as he leaned an elbow against the bar counter. "You would find the rich to be more enjoyable company if you ever attended my balls, Valina."

She shrugged her shoulders, "I have attended them, my king. And I still find them quite annoying."

"On many nights, I find them annoying as well." And the way he spoke those words, made it seem like they did not live to see the next night.

"If you do not mind my asking, what brings you here?" Valina knew she treaded upon a dangerous line with how she has spoken to him and continued to do so.

His gaze weighed heavily upon her and she was forced to cast a glance toward him. And she cursed herself a fool as she took in his handsome face. But no amount of beauty could hide the wickedness that plagued his soul more so than others.

"There were sightings of the enemy in this area." Her stomach twisted itself into a knot, but she kept her face neutral – bored. "I came here myself to find the child of Nicitis, but he is nowhere to be found."

"Perhaps he has already returned to the land of light."

His crimson eyes studied her, searching her face as if he knew that she was hiding something. But he couldn't, she had been careful. "Perhaps, a pity. I wished to end his life myself or have you bring me his head, but it seems as though I cannot always have my way."

His eyes traveled along her body, glancing upon her perky breasts, before trailing back to her lips where his gaze remained for a long moment. "Perhaps when my birthday arrives, I shall have one thing that I truly desire."

Valina did not flinch away from his touch as his hand found itself upon her cheek. She had pushed too much, tipping over that line. So, she allowed him this – this one simple touch. And she hated how it made her feel. His skin pressed against hers, his warmth tracing along her cheek – caressing it gently. As if the king knew anything of gentleness.

And when she finally made herself peer into his eyes, she could have sworn she saw a flicker of the boy that he used to be. A glimpse of the kind soul that had been before his father poisoned him.

But he was no longer that boy, no longer kind nor gentle. No longer the boy who gazed upon her with sadness in those crimson eyes of his. And she had to remind herself that he would never be that again.

Valina turned away from his touch, tipping her head back and swallowing that bitter liquid. "Sometimes, we all cannot have what we truly desire." Her finger traced along the opening of the bottle, "I desire to have my family returned to me, but that shall never happen. I desire to know where my mother is, but I shall never know. I desire to have Ventar returned to me, but that too, shall never come to pass."

The silence seemed to become more deafening after those words left her lips and they hung heavy within the chilly air. The king should have struck her down then and there for the way she had spoken to him, for the way she had turned away from him.

But he did not.

"Goodnight, my dear Valina." The king pushed off the counter, turned his back upon her, and approached the doors. He halted at the threshold. "I do hope you shall attend my birthday ball, Valina. It shall be a dreadful night without you."

There was a threat that lingered heavy between every word he spoke. A promise to hunt her down if she did not show. And he would not be merciless. His time for waiting had come to an end.

"Goodnight, my king."

And then, he stepped into the night.

CHAPTER FIFTEEN

NIGHTMARES THAT TORMENT

"Can one ever truly find peace when the past refuses to leave them?"

*T*HIER SCREAMS ERUPTED *around her.   Shattering her hearing.   Flames danced before her eyes, tall and wicked.   They seemed to roar with cackling laughter – taunting and mocking her as she cried and pleaded.   Her family hung within the air above, tendrils of shadows wrapped around their bodies as they dangled above the pit of fire.*

"PLEASE!"   Her tiny voice shouted at the flames.   But they only answered with more laughter.   "Please! Not my family!"   Tears trickled down her cheeks as she begged for their lives.

But the fire did not listen to those pleas.   The shadows released their hold upon her family and down they plummeted into the awaiting flames.   The fire reaching and grasping for them.

"NO!"

Agony voiced itself from their lips as their screams sounded from the fire.   The smell of burning flesh soon found its way toward her.   Gag and bile rose in her throat, burning as she forced it back down. Down she fell onto her knees, caving in on herself. Then, the flames made their way toward her and she did not move. She lifted her head, eyes filled with tears, and waited to join her family as the fire embraced her.

"My hunter." A gentle and soothing voice called to her, luring her from the flames that had engulfed her being.

Slowly, Valina's eyes fluttered open, taking in the sight of the *Ghost Condentai* seated upon the edge of her bed. A cool hand gently resting upon her wetted cheek where tears had escaped during her sleep.

"The nightmare has gotten worse." Ashari tilted her head to the side, a thick strand of white hair cascading over her bare shoulder. "I heard your cries."

Valina rose onto an elbow, propping herself up. "Always coming to my rescue, I see."

Ashari offered a sweet smile, "I shall until the day comes when we are parted."

Valina rose onto her knees and placed both of her hands on either side of Ashari's beautiful face. "I hope that day never comes to pass." Her crimson eyes took in the sight of the silver eyes that stared back at her. "I would be lost without you."

A cool hand came to rest upon one of Valina's as Ashari leaned into her palm. "And I would be lost without you."

Valina inched herself closer to the *Ghost Condentai*, her face lowering until their noses were mere inches apart. She could feel Ashari's breath against her lips, her tongue flicking out and licking her own. Then, she tilted her head and placed her mouth against Ashari's. The *Ghost Condentai's* lips were cool – almost as if Ashari herself had turned into a spirit and kissed her from the world of the dead.

When Valina pulled away from the kiss, she rested her forehead against Ashari's, releasing a heavy sigh. "The king was at the tavern."

"I know, the spirits whispered to me before Ventar rushed into the room to inform everyone." She felt the soft brush of Ashari's cool fingers against her cheek. "What did the king want?"

A sad smile appeared on her lips as she said, "I do not think I can run from him any longer."

Ashari moved her head away from Valina's and placed her hands on either side of her face, "Runaway, my hunter."

Valina blinked. "No. You know I cannot do that."

"It is the only way you shall be safe from him."

She shook her head, "You know he'll search the entire world for me if he had too, he would search the ends of it until he found me. There is no escaping the king."

"The king shall meet his end soon." Within those silver eyes of hers, Valina found the promise of death afire within the *Ghost Condentai's* gaze. "He shall not have you, not while I breathe upon this world."

Valina placed a kiss upon Ashari's forehead. "I love you."

"And I love you." She whispered back.

The *Blood Condentai* leapt off the bed and began to dress herself, "Now, I must go feed."

Finding her prey had been easy on this night. Not long after Valina had ventured into the shadows, she heard the horrific cries of a terrified child. The pleas of a mother. The *Blood Condentai* followed the cries and the shouting until she came upon a dark alleyway in the lowest part of town where thieves and criminals made their living.

A hefty, human man had a woman by her hair, a fistful of auburn. She cried by his side, forced onto her knees unable to move underneath his strength. The man's other hand back handed a small boy before him and the child fell to the cobblestones, smacking his head against the hard stone.

A snarl rippled across Valina's lips.

The man moved toward the boy, leg ready to kick. But he would not get the chance to land that foot into the boy's stomach. Valina marched down the alleyway, her monster uncaged and out to play. The woman's terrified, hazel eyes widened with relief – with a plea to save her child – as she met with the monster's eyes. Valina's gaze flickered back toward the man and she called upon his blood.

His body buckled and down he fell onto his knees, the bones cracking against the cobblestones. The man unleashed a whirl of curses as he tried to move his body. But the blood came to a halt within his veins. The woman beside him was freed as his grip faltered on her hair. She scrambled over to the crying boy who had curled into himself on the ground.

Valina now stood over the man. The woman had taken the child into her arms and scooted away from the monster that had bloodlust within her eyes.

"Take your child and leave." A growl had echoed around them, "Do not look back no matter what you may hear."

The man's dark eyes widened with fear and it caused her smile to broaden. Hurried footsteps echoed down the alleyway along with a quietly whispered thank you. The woman and child had disappeared into the night, leaving the man alone with a beast.

The man's pale face had begun to redden as the blood within his body began to rise to the surface. The whites around his eyes lined with thin, crimson veins. Sweat had begun to form and bead down his head. Valina stalked around him, slowly. Her fingertip trailing across his shoulders.

"I heard what you have done," She began to say, "And though a monster I may be, I have no tolerance for those who abuse women and children."

The man struggled to form words, "Fuck... you... b-bitch..." Spit sputtered from his lips as he gasped in pain.

Valina stood before the man once more, kneeling into a crouch. Her gaze locked with his as she cocked her head to the side. "Tonight, was my night of hunt, for you see I am thirsty." Her sharp nail traced along his cheek and down to his chin. His body trembled. "And you just so happen to be my prey of choice for the evening."

She rose onto her feet once more. Her hold on his blood loosened enough to allow him to stand – to give him the illusion that he had a fighting chance. The man leapt to his feet and reached for her with grasping, sweaty hands. She simply stepped to the side and called upon his blood once more – toying with her prey.

"Your death shall be a slow one, human." Valina approached her prey once more and found hatred burning within his eyes but fear could be found lingering within those flames, turning them to ashes. "You shall feel every second of pain, so you know what your child felt as you hit him. So, you know what your wife felt as you beat her."

Valina reached for one of the daggers that hung by her side, drawing it forth. The man's dark eyes followed the movement. And fear engulfed that burning hatred and smothered it out. She traced that wicked blade upon one of her fingers. Slicing her own skin to draw forth a droplet of blood, her tongue licking at the crimson substance.

"I promise this shall hurt." She flashed her fangs in a wicked smile.

She grasped his hand and held it up before his face, so he could clearly see what she was going to do. The dagger began to trace along his fingers, taunting him. The man swallowed, his wide eyes watching the blades every movement. Then, the dagger embedded itself into his first finger. A scream ripped free from his lips and echoed within her ears.

With a quick flick of her wrist, the finger flew into the air and landed before the man's feet. Blood spurted and splattered across Valina's face. Her tongue licking at the liquid that sprayed at the corner of her mouth. She almost moaned at the taste of it – the warmth of it.

Whimpers escaped the man as he beheld the stub of a finger he had left, blood trickling down his arm. "I'll truly enjoy every second of this."

As the monster tore apart the man's body, petrified screams echoed through the night. No passersby dared to even glance down the alleyway out of fear that whatever was happening to that man, would happen to them as well. Hurried footsteps passed by, hoping to escape the monster's wrath. Even the creatures that lurked close by in the forest shrank back into the shadows.

None would dare interrupt the *Blood Condentai's* feast on this night.

Valina stepped forth from the alleyway, blood dripping down her chin. Her hunger finally satisfied. Behind her, she left the bloody remains of the man. Guards would have heard the screams by now and were possibly waiting nearby in the shadows to begin cleaning the mess she had left behind.

Killing was not illegal in their dark world, not unless you murdered one of the king's guards or servants. Of course, there were limits as to how many killings happened per night, per person. Valina only took one life every few nights and drank enough on the nights between to satisfy her thirst for a while. The guards made sure to keep a careful watch, keeping track of the killings in a single night. So, none would question or raise a brow at the scene and sounds that occurred on this night. It was simply another normal night to the people. Many of them praying their thanks to the Goddess that their souls had been saved, that they did not end up like the mutilated remains of the man in the alley.

A group of three guards made their way toward her and she flashed a bloody smile at them before vanishing into the shadows.

As she traveled through the town, she noticed many of the stores had closed. But a few remained open. Wiping her mouth with the back of her hand and pulling her hood over her head, she entered a store and began to collect food for Luzell. Once she handed the shopkeeper a few silver Ventra, she left the shop behind and hurried off into the night.

Soon she found herself before the ashy remains of Ventar's home. The burnt wood crunched and turned to dust beneath her boots as she walked across it. Bending down, she lifted a door and slid it aside – revealing a smaller door hidden beneath. It let out a groan as she lifted it and then silence met her ears.

"It's Valina." She called out as she ventured down the dark stairs.

Once she closed the door above her head, a golden light encased the room – chasing away the shadows. And there Luzell stood, in the center of the room, a golden aura pulsating around his being. As if he harnessed a piece of the sun inside of his soul.

He smiled at the sight of her, no fear to be found within his eyes. "Come to visit me?"

She slid the brown satchel from her shoulder and extended her hand, "Came to bring you food. I figured you might have run out."

Luzell approached and took the offered bag from her grasp. "Thank you, Valina."

She nodded her head. Luzell took a seat upon an old wooden bench against the far side of the wall and reached into the satchel. Luzell retrieved an apple and took a bite from it, a sigh escaping him as he savored the sweetness of it.

Valina approached a nearby wall and leaned against it, kicking a foot up behind her and crossing her arms over her chest. "What's it like?" She voiced the question she had wanted to ask him since she first lay eyes upon the child of light. "The land of light."

Valina's eyes did not venture up from the ground – remaining focused upon her boots and the specs of blood splattered across them. But, she felt the weight of his blue gaze upon her.

"It is bright." He began to say in a voice that sounded with reminiscence. "There is light to be found no matter where you turn. Plants that grow beneath the sun's blessing light. Its warmth pouring down onto us. There is no darkness – no fear. A king and queen who rule with kind hands."

Valina scoffed at that. A king who was kind? Let alone a queen who ruled beside him equally? That is something this dark world shall never see.

"And the people," He continued, "Do not thirst for blood and death but for light and life."

She wondered what it would be like to only crave light. To never once crave blood or death. But that was all she knew. And if she did not feast upon blood then her life would cease to exist. She could not survive without the blood and thus, without the death.

"What kind of *Condentai* are you, Luzell?" All of the Gods children who had been blessed with their touch of power were called; *Condentai.* No matter what side of the world they had been born upon.

"A Condentai of Light."

Valina should have guessed, the answer was obvious. Perhaps she merely wished to hear it from his lips. "What others are there?"

"There are *Condentai of Earth*; they grow and nourish the nature in our world. *Condentai of Light*; we conjure the light of the sun and call it forth – harnessing its warmth within us. *Condentai of Healing*; curing any sicknesses that may plague the people of our land – any bruises or bloody wounds. *Condentai of Emotion*; people who can sense whatever it is your feeling, not quite like reading minds but feeling the ache of one's soul and soothing that pain. *Condentai of Forms*; people who can shift their bodies into any form of animal that walks on the side of light. And *Condentai of Fire*; people who summon forth the very heat of the sun itself – bringing to life the flames that warm and bless our world."

Valina's gaze flickered up from her boots to meet with Luzell's eyes, "Are the Light and Fire *Condentai* not one in the same? Both harnessing the sun within them?"

Luzell simply shook his head, his golden locks cascading over his shoulders and she wished she could run her fingers through his silky hair. "We harness different aspects of the sun within us. *I* harness its light and the *Condentai of Fire* harnesses its fire."

"And are some of those *Condentai* immortal like some are here in the land of dark?"

A shadow seemed to cast itself over the child of light's face, his light flickering. The life within his blue eyes dimming. And then he smiled – but it was a smile of sadness. "Yes, but I am not one of those few."

Her chest ached at the truth – that his life would come to an end as old age warped his body, but she would continue to live until their world itself came to an end. Luzell did not seem as though he wished for that, he wished for a life that would never cease. So, he could bask in the sun's warmth for all eternity. To live in that luscious world of light where the plants grew and blossomed. Where there was no darkness to be found – no monster lurking within shadows.

"I have come to accept my fate. My God placed me here for as long as I was needed upon this world. This is my only life and I plan to do something great with this chance that Nicitis has given me."

Valina moved from the wall, Luzell's eyes watching her every move as she approached the bench and seated herself beside him. "Being immortal is not as great as it sounds." Her voice had turned to a whisper and her gaze was focused ahead. "Time becomes a blur. Years become minutes, but hours seem like months. Then comes the time for your mortal companions to return to the Goddess's side. Leaving this world and you behind as you watch them grow old and take their last breath while you forever remain young but forever remain dead within."

"It sounds like a great burden to bear." He spoke gently, as if afraid of shattering something within her. But there was nothing left for him to shatter.

"It is. Life continues on around you and you watch it all happen. You watch children grow and have children of their own but then you watch time take away their youth and soon you see them buried within the earth. You watch towns be built but also watch as they become abandoned – stores and homes forgotten and left behind." A sigh escaped her, "No matter how much you wish it; time shall never cease, it goes on and you have no other choice but to walk by its side."

She felt the warm brush of skin against her hand and she did not pull away as Luzell wrapped his hand over her own. His warmth seeping into her, thawing the ice that encased her heart. "You carry many burdens upon your shoulders, Valina. And I wonder if you ever allow someone to help carry that weight. But I know you would rather face them alone than allow someone to feel and carry what you do."

Diaval had said the same. But she had begun to realize that she was slowly allowing people in – but not enough so to speak of the burdens she carried. Not enough to let them carry her monsters as well.

"You are a person of light and I am a creature of dark, you could not begin to understand my burdens." Though her words held venom, Luzell did not flinch at them, did not move his hand away from hers.

His grip gently tightened. "You are right." He spoke, "I may not understand but you could help me too."

Her crimson eyes flickered toward him, she raised a brow. "Why do you care of my burdens?"

Luzell's blue eyes crashed over her like a wave. "Because I can see the pain hiding away within your soul and I wish to help somehow. You saved my life and I wish to save yours – in even the smallest of ways. Shouldering some of your burdens."

Valina found herself wanting to lean into his warmth, to feel the sun against her grey skin. But she pulled away from him, his hand falling from hers as she stood. "I shall come back for you when the next meeting of rebels takes place."

"Be safe, Valina." He spoke in a husky voice drenched in warmth behind her.

"I always am." And then she vanished.

CHAPTER SIXTEEN

A BIRTHDAY BALL APPROACHES

"A wicked king has his sights set upon a divine creature of night, but her sights are set upon the daggers that wish to pierce his heart."

THE TOWN WAS bustling. Frantic people rushing about preparing the festivities for the week of the king's birthday. There would be parades and music, dancing and food. All in the name of the wicked king – some of the people forced to praise him, others more than happy to bow before their king that they adored.

Ashari and Valina once more found themselves within the town market, more carts set up along the road. The scent of sweets and roasting meats filtering through the air. Valina used to find joy in these parades and festivities but that was long ago now. When she was a child that knew nothing of the true darkness of their world, had not been shown its true wickedness. But now she has seen it even taking part of it within her and she found it very hard to enjoy herself in the name of the king that damned her family and herself.

Once more Valina saw the old woman seated before her cart. Her figurines lined along the shelves that they were seated upon. And she saw the young boy, taking over the business for her. Handing over the figurines as people gave him the proper amount of Ventra.

The old woman's gaze met with Valina's for a moment and she offered the *Blood Condentai* a grateful and sweet smile. Valina returned the smile and carried along through the market place.

Banners and streams in shades of black, grey, and crimson hung above the cobblestone streets. Draped from one building across to the next, hanging over the people's heads. Fires roared within their steel cages that were scattered along the sides of the street. Many people roasted meats above the open flames.

Many men and women were dressed exquisitely in fabrics that shimmered and clung tightly to their bodies. The women wearing a band of fabric across their chests and underwear to match. Fingerless gloves of lace decorated their arms, coming to points atop their hands. The same lace decorated their legs and bare feet up to the highest points of their thighs. A long trail flowing down from the back of the women's underwear. A crimson, shimmery river rippling behind them.

Dark patterns had been painted upon their faces. The women wore the more intricate and delicate ones – though some of the men wore them as well. Swirls whirls of patterns that danced from their temples down to their cheekbones. The men having a dark line across the bridge of their noses and underneath their eyes. The men wore midnight shorts that stopped high above their knees. They wore the same gloves as the women but left their legs bare.

They danced through the streets, as if the shadows themselves carried their every step. Drifting them along the air. Their limbs moved with fluidity, with grace and elegance in every movement. The dancers had always been Valina's favorite part of the festival, since she was a young girl she admired them. For a moment, they allowed her to forget all her pain as she watched them dance through the street.

"Why do you not sell your carvings during the festival?" Ashari stood beside her, her silver eyes viewing every cart that surrounded them. "It seems a great opportunity to sell your work."

Valina simply shook her head. "I refuse to sell my carvings in the name of the king, during his festival."

Valina was aware of the opportunity the festival presented for sales. But she refused to push her hatred aside and work within a festival that worshipped their king.

As they walked along through the market, they passed a small group playing instruments. Flutes, harps, and violins filtering their melodies through the air, guiding the dancers movements as they glided through the crowd.

Valina gazed upon the gathered group and noticed they were all human. She almost did not see the one hiding herself away in the back of the group. A woman with her chin resting atop a violin as she dragged the bow across the strings summoning forth its music. The woman's bright blue eyes flickered up for a brief moment to meet with Valina's. Both women held one another's gaze and slightly, Lillian nodded her head in recognition toward the *Blood Condentai* before dropping her gaze once more.

She never knew of Lillian's personal life, only knew her as a rebel with blades that thirsted for blood. With revenge scorned into her being. She did not know of the talent the human had with music. Did not know what she did when she was not hunting guards within the shadows, how she made her living, how she spent her nights.

As the pair continued along through the market, Lillian's music followed after them.

After what felt like hours, Ashari and Valina finally began to make their way out of the festival. Ashari carrying a bag of trinkets and oddities she found while drifting from cart to cart, Valina watching the *Ghost Condentai's* smile and eyes widen with each new-found trinket.

"Soon you'll run out of space in your room and be forced to sleep on the couch."

A giggle escaped Ashari, "Would you truly allow me to sleep on the couch, my hunter?"

Valina placed her hand upon Ashari's cheek and leaned down to place a brief kiss upon her lips, "Never."

The *Blood Condentai* took the bag from Ashari's hand, offering to carry it for her. As they traveled along through the market, making their way out, a voice crept up behind them like a shadow lurking within the night.

"Leaving so soon, my dear?" Valina's body stiffened as the king's voice purred behind her.

She cast a glance at him over her shoulder, "Yes. We aren't ones for festivals, unfortunately." Sarcasm dripped from that last word.

The king shook his head and moved to stand before the two women, "A shame." His crimson eyes seemed to devour her as he took in her body. She did not wish to know what traveled through his mind as he thought of her. "I'm glad I found you, Valina. I have a request."

Her heart dropped. "And what might this request be?"

"I would like for you to carve a mural for my throne room. I have grown tired of the tapestry hanging above it and wish for something new."

The tapestry of the Goddess has hung over his thrown for many centuries. It is a disgrace to the Goddess to tear it down and replace it.

She straightened her back. "I did tell you before that I do not work for free and that you must pay like everyone else."

The king moved one hand from behind his back and held a large, midnight coin pouch. It dangled from its strings that hung from his fingers before her eyes. She watched it sway before her. "Five thousand gold Ventra."

Ashari took in a breath beside her. Valina has never been offered so much to carve before. People mostly ask for a little carvings of animals or the Goddess, never a mural.

"What do you want the mural to be?" She hated the look of satisfaction in his eyes, hated herself for falling into his trap because gold Ventra hung before her.

Oh, Valina had money. But more money was always welcomed. And money was such a tempting thing. A darkness that clawed at everyone, driving friends to kill one another. Breaking apart families. It was evil, but everyone craved it.

The king approached and grasped her free hand and placed the silky, heavy bag onto her palm. "A carving of me upon my throne. I'll send guards to your home with the wood I wish to be used."

Valina nodded her head.

She felt the warm brush of his hand against her cheek, "Thank you, my dear. I shall be eagerly waiting for my masterpiece." But she knew he meant more than just the mural. He wished for her as well.

Then the king turned his back upon them and vanished into the night.

Valina stood there, her crimson eyes staring upon the bag of Ventra. Feeling as though she just sold herself to the king.

Once Valina and Ashari returned home, Ventar was instructed to remain upstairs locked within the room he was staying in – no matter what he heard.

Three loud knocks sounded on her door. The guards had arrived. Ashari lingered within the kitchen while Valina approached the door and swung it open, allowing the king's men into her home. There were three, the one leading them and the two that carried a large piece of flattened wood, larger than a table top.

"Where do you wish us to put it, miss Veshanr?"

Valina blinked at the guard, none of them ever addressed her as miss. And then she realized who the guard was. One of the inside people Shandal had spoken of the day that the king was going to have children burned. This man was a *Mind Condentai.*

Valina leaned against the wall and crossed her arms over her chest, "The living room. First doorway on the right."

She watched as the guards carried the wood through her home and disappeared into the living room. A thud sounded on the floor as the guards dropped the wood. A hiss escaped her lips. They had better hope they didn't scratch her floor.

The men once more appeared and made their way toward the door. The *Mind Condentai* halted at the threshold. He bowed his head, "Goodnight, Miss Veshanr." She felt a light brush against her mind, *I hope to see you at the meeting.* And then, he stepped out of her home.

The light sound of careful footsteps found their way into Valina's ears as Ashari approached the doorway and glanced upon the large piece of wood that now covered the living room floor. "It shall be a large mural." She spoke lightly.

"Too bad it's too large to shove up the king's ass."

Ashari's ghostly laughter echoed within the room.

"Always so lovely, my dear." Ventar's voice sounded from the top of the stairs where he leaned against the wooden railing, his cocky smile upon his face.

"Isn't that why you enjoy having me in your life?"

Within a blink, Ventar appeared before her, his hand resting upon her cheek, "That and many more reasons."

Her gaze glanced upon the dark cloak draped over his shoulders, "Leaving for the meeting so soon?"

"It is never too soon to go to a meeting of rebels. Are you coming?"

Valina nodded her head and stepped away from Ventar, taking one of her own cloaks down from one of the hooks upon the wall. Her daggers hadn't left her side since she put her belt on before they went to the festival.

"Ashari are you joining us?"

The *Ghost Condentai* lingered within the doorway to the living room. "I shall be going to the Cathedral of the *Ghost Condentai.*"

Valina nodded her head, "Be safe."

Those silver eyes stared into her soul, "And you as well, my hunter."

The two hunters disappeared into the shadows.

When the two *Blood Condentai* and the *Condentai of Light* had entered the room, they were greeted by devasted faces. The air heavy with sadness, threatening to suffocate them. Shandal approached them and told them of what happened, sorrow glazing over his dark eye. There was pain within his voice as he told them that his cousin, Shadanar and a few other rebels had been killed by the hands of the king. They were caught within the tavern above speaking of the king's downfall when one of the king's guards was in the room, not in uniform.

The king was growing suspicious and planting guards in places where rebel activity would occur. Everyone would have to be more careful.

They were executed at the castle during the festival. Burned and pierced through on that damned fence as if they were nothing more than decorations. As if they weren't people.

Valina did not like Shadanar when she first arrived here but she understood why once Ashari revealed what had happened to his family and helped him to move on. Helped cure that anger that tortured him. A man that had been tortured by his heartbreak, a man who had finally found an ounce of peace in this dark world, had been murdered.

"Tonight, there shall be blood." Shandal had a look of vengeance upon his face, a fire scolding within his eyes. "Tonight, kill any guards you find. Make them suffer. *Make them pay.*"

The monster inside Valina purred at that; there would be blood. Every guard that crossed her path on this night would be devoured. Not even the Goddess could save them.

"They'll all pay." Her daggers already weighed within the palms of her hands. Facing Luzell, she said, "You remain here until we return."

Luzell had enough sense to know to remain where he was, to not venture out on this night.

Shandal held her gaze for a long moment and nodded his head.

It was time for the hunt to begin.

CHAPTER SEVENTEEN

THE HUNT BEGINS

*"When predators of the night begin their hunt of revenge,
none are safe from their wrath."*

T HE NIGHT WAS quiet but it would not remain that way for long as the rebels dispersed into the shadows beginning their hunt. Ventar and Valina traveled together, both ready to sink their fangs into flesh, to drink of blood. Ready to bring death upon those who have taken their people.

Already their first prey of the night was in sight. Two guards patrolling the outskirts of the town, unaware of the two monsters that lurked within the darkness ahead of them.

Valina flipped the daggers within her hands and cast a glance toward Ventar, "And now the fun begins." She flashed a smile, her fangs gleaming.

"Always so bloodthirsty, my dear." Ventar flashed his own fangs in a feral grin.

Valina would not use her powers on this night; her blades had been crying out for a taste of flesh. And she would answer their pleas. The first guard was unaware of what happened, the other thinking too slow to realize what was happening. Valina had launched herself at the first man, straddling his back as she plunged her wicked daggers into his shoulders. She felt bone giveaway beneath the black blades, heard the flesh tear apart. Then came the sight that drove her beast into a frenzy; blood. The man cried out in a scream of agony as the daggers tore into his body.

The other guard bellowed, raising his sword into the air. But it never had the chance to strike Valina. A shadow slammed itself into the man's side. A terrified scream escaping him as Ventar sunk his fangs into the man's neck, drinking his fill of the warm blood.

The man that Valina straddled tried to thrash about, wishing to toss her off of him. He had a fight in him, but his fight was not enough to win against her. She forced her victim down onto the earth, a heavy thud sounding as his body met with the unforgiving ground. Valina yanked her daggers free of the man's shoulders, a whimper of pain escaping his lips.

His arms would no longer be of use to him; not that it mattered. He would not live to see the next night. Bringing the wicked blade up to her mouth, her tongue flickered out and tasted the blood that dripped from it. Her eyes rolled into the back of her head as a moan escaped her.

And when her grey lids pulled back, her crimson eyes were glowing. Sometimes all it took was the smallest taste, the smallest drink, to make her eyes come alive.

"P-Please... spare me..." Tears swelled within the man's green eyes. His body trembling beneath her.

A hiss escaped Valina's lips as she lowered her face closer to his, her bloody dagger tracing down his cheek, "Did the rebels you murdered beg for their lives as well? Did they not wish to live as you do now? You took their lives and now, I shall be taking yours. *Slowly.*"

The man held her gaze, something no human ever dared to do to her when she was angered. Some even feared her when she was simply walking past them. "You are a monster."

If he meant it as an insult; she did not take it that way. She answered with a grin, "Only monsters can recognize others of their nature."

She did not allow the man to speak another word as she took her dagger and split his mouth wider. Screams rattled from the man's lungs, gurgles following after as blood filled his mouth. Valina did not stop there. Her daggers wished, and she granted their desires. Slicing at his skin until it barely clung to his bones.

"This is for every rebel you have killed. Every body that you placed on that damned fenced. Every person you have burned. This is your payment."

Valina was no longer the wood carver, no longer the lover of many, no longer that scared little girl watching her family burn. She was the monster that they all feared. She had become what all *Blood Condentai* could be; what lurked just beneath their grey flesh.

She did not stop hacking away at his flesh until she felt a warm hand grip her shoulder; bringing Valina back. Her monster caging itself once more. Slowly, she turned her head and blinked up at Ventar. Blood dripping down his chin, his crimson eyes glowing down at her.

"Come, before guards find us."

Raising from the ground, she wiped her daggers off on her pants and sheathed them once more. "Let's go."

They left the mutilated remains of their victims behind to rot within the shadows. But the other predators of the night would crawl forth from the darkness they were hidden within to feast upon the corpses.

When they returned, they found rebels drenched in blood all around them. Even Lillian was coated in it from head to toe. But tears had streaked down her cheeks, clearing a path from the crimson clinging to her skin. Though her blades had tasted revenge, it seemed as though the death she brought upon her victims wasn't enough. Their punishment wasn't enough.

Valina wondered what one of the rebels had meant to her; family, friend, or lover? But she would never ask, never intrude when the wound was too freshly open. She knew that pain too well.

But the sorrow within those once bright blue eyes told the story; *lover.* The light had been dimmed within her, leaving behind a shattered heart.

Valina approached the woman and placed a hand upon her shoulder. Lillian glanced up at the *Blood Condentai* for a moment, slightly nodding her head before casting her gaze back to the blade she cleaned of her victims' blood.

It was the only comfort Valina could offer without tearing that wound open more.

When she turned her back upon the human woman, her gaze met with eyes of striking blue. Luzell stood a few feet from her, not daring to make a step closer. His gaze slid down her form, taking in the damp clothing – the blood that dripped from her body.

She could see the fear swelling within him, she could almost taste it. She watched as he fought himself – fought the light within him that no doubt told him to flee this dark land.

Valina approached him, standing by his side, not glancing at him as she spoke, "This is what I am. This is what I shall always be." Finally, her eyes slid toward him for a moment where they met with his before they broke free of his gaze. "A monster living in the land of dark."

Then, she brushed past him.

Valina retreated into the shadows of the furthest corner within the room. Wishing to take a moment to herself. Everyone would remain here for a while, until the chaos above cleared, and it was safe enough for everyone to return to their homes.

Crossing her arms over her chest, she leaned her head back against the wall and a heavy sigh escaped her lips.

She felt the presence of another person slip beside her, quiet and watching. She did not have to open her eyes to know who stood beside her.

"Hello, Diaval." His name whispered past her lips.

"I hope I am not disturbing you, Valina."

She came to this corner to be alone but now that he was here, she did not wish for loneliness. "Not at all."

"How was your night of hunt?"

"Killed three guards." Two more had wandered across their path during their return to the tavern.

Their deaths did not come quickly either. More blood drenching Valina's already soaked body. Her thirst had been quenched for the night and many more nights after. The daggers hanging by her sides hummed with pleasure as their blades finally tasted blood and flesh.

"I killed the same." A soft sigh escaped him, "But it doesn't seem enough. It'll never seem enough."

Valina opened to her eyes then to gaze upon the *Dead Condentai* beside her. His milky eyes were cast downwards. His grey hair matted with blood.

"It was Shadanar who found me. Who brought me to the rebels. He nursed the wounds on my back and taught me how to use a blade. He became almost like a father to me. But then, he lost his family and he changed. He wasn't the same after but who wouldn't be?"

Valina had no idea, Diaval had never mentioned this. And the two never interacted whenever she joined the rebels. Shandal had seemed the more nurturing type. But Shadanar was possibly the same way before his family's demise.

"I'm sorry for your loss, Diaval." Her arms had fallen to her sides, she had half a mind to take his hand. But her hand never reached out.

He nodded his head. "We all joined knowing the risk. We all know that each of us could die tomorrow, could have died tonight. We take the risk of caring in this dark world."

Her eyes glanced about the room until they landed upon Ventar. He stood at the table talking to Shandal and his wife. Valina thought she had lost him, thought him gone from this world. And for a moment, he had taken a piece of her soul with him. She would never forget that pain or the pain of losing her family.

"We take the risk because we know it's worth it. No matter how short our time may be. No matter how monstrous we may be, we know that the coming pain is worth it."

She felt the cold brush of fingers against her own before a hand had taken hers and gently squeezed. "You are a risk worth taking, Valina Veshanr."

Warmth caressed her dead heart and she offered him a smile. She did not know how to respond, what to say to the *Dead Condentai*. That fear came crawling back and mauled at her insides.

Valina stepped away from the wall, her hand falling from his grasp, "And the same to you, Diaval Darthollow."

The night stretched on. Hours passing by slowly. Souls becoming restless. The room growing smaller, the walls closing in. the beast within Valina howled to be set free, to roam the darkness of the land.

She felt trapped, just as the other rebels felt. Shandal had promised soon that they would be allowed to leave. But soon was not coming quick enough.

Valina felt as though she would scream until finally, Shandal said it was safe enough for them to leave. Small groups spaced out over a period of time. Valina was part of the third group; Ventar, Diaval, and Luzell. They did not use the tavern above, instead Shandal showed them one of the many passageways that led out of the room.

There was a narrow, metal door in the furthest corner, hidden by shadows. Shandal opened it to reveal a tunnel, it was wide enough for one person to lead and the others file behind them.

"Safe travels, rebels." Shandal bowed his head to them before turning his back and approaching the other waiting groups.

Ventar took the lead, Luzell following just behind him and Valina behind Luzell. Diaval taking the end.

The darkness did not phase the children of the night. But Valina's ears listened to Luzell's fumbled footsteps, grunts of annoyance. She reached out a grey hand and placed it upon his shoulder. "Call upon your light, just enough to allow you to see."

Then, the faintest glow warmed the narrow tunnel. Golden light chasing the shadows back into the darkness. "Thank you." He whispered.

Once they reached the end of the long tunnel, Luzell doused his golden glow. His warmth fading. Valina took in a long, deep breath. Savoring the air and the shadows that filtered through her lungs as she breathed the world in. Her beast had finally calmed itself, no longer feeling trapped within that room.

"I'll take him back to the safe room." Ventar offered.

"Don't do anything foolish, Ventar."

The *Blood Condentai* appeared before her, his cocky smile written upon his lips. "When have I ever done anything foolish, my dear?"

Valina raised a brow. "Do not get me started."

Ventar leaned down and placed a kiss upon her lips. "I won't be long."

She watched their forms vanish into the awaiting darkness. Her stomach twisting into knots as her fear clawed at her.

"I shall walk you home, if that is alright with you, Valina." Diaval appeared by her side, a soft smile on his face.

She nodded her head, "Thank you, Diaval."

Valina was more than capable of walking herself home but she found herself wishing for the *Dead Condentai's* gentle presence.

They traveled through the darkest of shadows, allowing the darkness to engulf their beings. Many guards were still prowling about, groups of four armed men watching the smallest movements within the night.

"We lost thirty men, Jonathan." A *Mind Condentai* scolded a human guard within their group. "And you think our patrol is *unnecessary?*"

The human had a sheepish look upon his face, bowing his head. "It seems unnecessary because no one has been killed in three hours. We have found sight of no murderers."

The *Mind Condentai* scoffed at the man, shaking his head. "I do not see why the king even allows humans within his guard; foolish and weak you all are."

Valina could see the anger within the human's face. His grip tightening upon the hilt of the sword he held until veins rose upon his hand, his knuckles turning pure white. But the human spoke not a word, just following behind the man that had insulted his entire race. The group wandered along the cobblestone road, vanishing within the town.

Valina found it very tempting to unleash herself upon those men but she caged her beast. She couldn't risk being caught, there were too many guards patrolling the night. She knew she wouldn't stand a chance against multiple groups. And she wouldn't place Diaval's life in danger.

Once it was clear, they continued on. Slipping into alleyways and traveling behind stores and homes until her own was in sight. A breath of relief escaped her. Finally, she could tear these drenched clothes from her body and wash the blood and dirt of the night away from her flesh and curl into her silky sheets.

Turning to Diaval she said, "If you would like, you are more than welcome to stay the night."

He cast his milky eyes toward her home and for a moment, it seemed as though he would take the offer. But his gaze met with hers as he shook his head, "Thank you, but I shall be returning to my own home for the night."

Disappointment nipped at her heart. "Alright. Goodnight, Diaval."

The *Dead Condentai* took a step closer to her, closing the distance between them. Their chests a breath apart from one another. His hand reached for her and slipped past her cheek, cradling the back of her head, his fingers within her midnight hair. Tilting her head, he bent down and pressed his lips against hers.

Both children of the night had forgotten their blood-soaked clothes, the blood that crusted within their hair and upon their skin. They had been entranced by each other, being lost to the touch and feel of one another. The kiss causing them to lose track of the world around them.

The thrill from the night coursed through both of their veins. Adrenaline rushing through their bodies, their thoughts becoming a mess. In this moment, Valina wanted to take him inside her home and bed him. To fuck him until their bodies tired out – if they ever tired.

And Diaval wanted to do the same to her. To feel the soft skin beneath those blood-soaked clothes that clung to her every curve. He wanted to taste her, to feel her body against his. She drove him mad in every good way possible. Taking away any sense he had, pushing aside his gentleness.

"If you wish to fuck one another like animals, might I suggest not doing it where the guards may find you?"

The two broke apart from each other to find Ventar leaned against the fence, a cocky smile on his face. "Unless the thrill of being caught turns you on more."

Valina rolled her eyes. "Bastard."

Ventar winked a crimson eye and made his way toward the stairs, "Only the best kind."

Facing the *Dead Condentai* once more, she found him running his hand through his grey, blood stained hair. A blush creeping into his cheeks. "You'll have to excuse him, he is indeed a bastard."

A chuckle escaped Diaval. "No trouble at all." His hand fell away from his hair as he reached for her own and placed a kiss upon it. "Goodnight, Valina Veshanr."

Her hand fell back to her side as she watched the *Dead Condentai* disappear. "Goodnight, Diaval Darthollow."

CHAPTER EIGHTEEN

A CARVING FOR THE KING

*"A king who requests a carving shall receive something much
more than the portrait he asked for."*

W HEN VALINA AWOKE she dragged herself out of bed and gathered her clothes, slipping her limbs into them. Making her way down stairs, she stepped into the living room to find the massive piece of wood laying upon her floor – staring back at her, mocking. With a growl, she grabbed it by its sides and drug it from the room. Once she stood before the door, she grabbed her satchel from the table and walked out into the night.

Soon enough, her carving spot was in sight. The trees seeming to watch her every move as she dragged that piece of wood into the forest. She felt the eyes of every watchful creature upon her. The wood landed with a thud before her feet as she tossed it to the ground.

Valina reached into her satchel and retrieved the blade her father had given her, "You want a mural, you'll get a damned mural."

Kneeling down upon the ground, she stabbed her silver dagger into the heart of the wood. Imagining that it was the king's chest and the dagger had pierced through his damned heart.

The wood groaned and as her blade carved into it – tearing at its hardened flesh. Bits of it fell all around her, scattering across the ground. Snarls escaped Valina as she carved the king's face, wishing to carve out his eyes instead. His body began to take shape as he was seated upon his throne. A wicked grin formed upon her lips as she drove that blade back into the wood.

A figure began to form above the king's head. Long tendrils of hair fanning out across the wood. The face of the Goddess of Dark staring up at her. Severina's arms were spread out by either side of the king's head. Wisps of darkness closing in on them, spiraling in from all sides.

He wanted to tear away the tapestry that honored the Goddess, but he would not remove her from this land. And this carving would serve as a reminder; she was the true ruler, not him.

She was tempting death with this carving, but she did not care. Valina wished to see the look upon his face when the mural was unveiled to him to find not just his own face staring back, but the Goddess's as well.

Footsteps sounded behind her, grasping her silver dagger she whirled to face the intruder only to find Ventar standing there. The blade lowered, "So, this is where you disappear too."

"Let me venture a guess, Ashari told you where to find me."

He winked a crimson eye, "A bastard never reveals where he gathers his information."

Valina rolled her eyes and placed the dagger into her satchel along with the few random wooden figurines she had carved not too long ago.

Ventar approached the piece of wood that stretched across the ground, his gaze flickering across every detail. "This is the king's mural, I am assuming."

"You would be assuming correctly." She crossed her arms over her chest as she moved to stand beside him, her gaze falling upon the king's face.

"You have such a wonderful talent, it's a shame you had to use it to carve that bastard's face." His gaze fell upon her, "When shall you ever carve my handsome face?"

She rolled her eyes, "When you pay like everyone else."

Ventar faced her then, his hands falling upon her hips. His eyes staring deep into hers, "And how much would a piece of your art cost me, my dear?"

Her fingers trailed upon his chest, her nails tracing along his strong jawline. "A night that I won't soon forget."

Ventar raised his brows, "Have you already forgotten our nights together, my Valina?" Leaning down, his lips brushed against her neck, his teeth gently nipping at her skin. "Have you forgotten the things I have done to you? And the things you have done to me?"

She suppressed the moan that rose in her throat as he continued to nip at her flesh. "The memory has grown foggy."

"Well now, that simply won't do. Allow me to refresh it."

His hand fell to the lower of her back, bringing her body closer to his. Ventar leaned down toward her but she placed a finger against his lips. "You should not be wandering around so recklessly when everyone presumes you dead." Her hand fell away from his mouth and trailed down his body until it felt his hardness press against her palm, "And fucking me out in these woods would cause everyone to come searching to see the show. You of all people should know I am not a quiet lover."

"Another night then, my dear. And I promise it won't be a night easily forgotten."

Valina took his bottom lip between her teeth and tugged, her hand still grasping his cock. "I shall hold you to that promise."

There was a wild hunger within his eyes, a promise to take her body and pleasure it in every way possible. "You are a tease, my dear."

Valina winked a crimson eye at him and turned her back toward him. "Let's return home before we are caught out here. I'm not in the mood to deal with the king's guards today."

She bent down to pick up the mural and watched as Ventar lifted the other end. "I know you won't allow me to carry it, at least allow me to help."

She was already tired of carrying the damned thing around, so she didn't argue and allowed Ventar to help her carry it home.

Ashari stood before the mural, her silver eyes taking in every detail. "Lovely work as always, my hunter." She glanced over her shoulder toward Valina, "But you are aware that the king shall not take a liking to the Goddess above him."

Valina flashed a smile, "Oh, I am well aware."

Ashari shook her head and faced the carving once more. "The spirits whisper to me. They fear something that lurks within the shadows, but they do not know what it may be or when it shall strike."

Valina leaned back into the couch, her gaze drifting toward the dancing flames within the fireplace. "Once the king is dead, there won't be anything to fear from him anymore."

"His birthday is quickly approaching, are you worried?"

She hated to admit that she worried, especially when it came to the king. But truth be told, she was. "Yes."

Ashari stepped toward the couch and took a seat beside Valina, her cool hand laying atop hers. Valina could not force herself to look upon the *Ghost Condentai*, to see the worry within those silver eyes reflected back at her.

"He'll have his way with me. He refuses to wait any longer." The fire continued its wicked dance, eating away at the logs that fueled it. Crackling echoing through the room. "But I have heard that hate sex is the best kind of sex. Perhaps the night won't be so terrible." Though she tried to joke, she knew Ashari would see through it and see her pain and fear.

She always could.

"If that ever comes to pass I shall bring upon him something far worse than death. I shall send every soul that he has ever taken from this world to his doorstep." Valina looked at Ashari then to find her silver eyes burning with anger, her white hair glowing and drifting upon a phantom wind. "They shall sing their lament every day and every night until madness becomes him and he takes his own life from this world. And then he shall be my prisoner. Forced to spend the rest of his days here upon this world where only my kind can see him. Where we can control his spirit. There shall never be an end to his torment."

And it was moments like these when Valina feared Ashari; when her monster was unleashed from its cage to remind people that she was more than what she appeared to be. Beneath that sweet and gentle surface was something fierce and lethal. One of the things that Valina admired about the woman. Though she could be kind, she could also be vicious.

"And I shall enjoy knowing that every moment he'll be in pain." Valina placed her other hand atop of Ashari's that still rested atop her hand and gave it a gentle squeeze. "But I do not think that shall be necessary."

Ashari raised a brow, her hand cocking to the side. "You have a plan."

Valina nodded her head. "The king will want me to stay with him after he's done with my body. When he sleeps, I'll slice his throat."

She had been turning this plan over in her mind for the last couple days. So much could go wrong. If he found her blade strapped upon her or woven into the fabric of her dress, he would kill her then and there. Guards will no doubt be stationed outside his bedroom doors, if they so much as heard a wrong breath they'll burst into the room.

"There is much risk in that plan, my hunter."

"I know. But it's time for me to stop hiding in the shadows."

There was a sadness within her eyes then. "You know I wish for you not to place yourself in such danger, but I know you'll do what you think is best."

Valina placed a kiss upon the *Ghost Condentai's* forehead. "You should get some rest, Ashari."

She nodded her head and rose from the couch. She approached the doorway but stopped at the threshold. "You'll be up late, I assume."

"For a while."

"Do not stay up too long, my hunter. Your mind and body need rest as well."

"I won't be long."

Ashari stepped out of the living room, "Goodnight, my hunter."

Then, she ascended up the stairs. Her footsteps light and quiet against the wood. Once she heard Ashari's door close, Valina stood from the couch and left the room. Grabbing a cloak from the wall, she flung open the door and stepped out into the night.

The town was quiet, not a soul was to be found wandering the darkness. Every home and store and she passed was shrouded in silence. Remnants from the festival lingered, waiting for the next night to continue their celebrations. Drappings hung above Valina's head, swaying in the light breeze. The cold air whispered through her long hair. Soon the first snow would present itself in their dark world.

A bit of excitement stirred within Valina then. A bit of child-like happiness bursting forth from locked away memories. But she pushed them back, locking them away once more and continuing along.

Soon, the *Cathedral of the Blood Condentai* loomed before her. The vast building cloaked in darkness. Her boots sounded softly as she ascended the stairs and stood before the double doors. The carving of the Goddess etched into the wood stared back at her. Opening the doors, she entered the cathedral.

Singing had greeted her ears. But it was one lone voice echoing throughout the cathedral. A woman standing alone before The Fountain of Offering. Blood pooling in each level. Crimson droplets escaping down the sides, fresh blood had been offered here on this night. But there were no souls lingering about to reveal who had given their blood.

She walked toward the Priestess whose voice still hauntingly echoed around them. No words escaped her sweet lips, just the beautiful sounds of a melody. She had to be human, though Valina could not see her face, if the woman was one of her kind, she would have heard her approach. But she continued singing undisturbed.

Until Valina stood beside her and a light gasp escaped the human. She was beautiful, dark skin and dark hair that curled to her shoulders. Her warm auburn eyes taking in the creature before her.

She bowed her head, "*Blood Condentai*, how may I serve you on this night?" Her voice still sounded with a hint of that melody.

Her crimson gaze flickered toward the fountain. "I've come for a drink and to pray to our Goddess."

The woman bowed her head. "Allow me to fetch you a glass." Her crimson robe trailed behind her as she approached a small table where a basin of water sat, it was stained by blood from their recent offering. Behind the basin was a rack of clear glasses. The glasses were crafted with depictions of the Goddess. Her arms raised above her head holding the empty cup.

The woman plucked one of the glasses and approached Valina once more. She bowed her head and offered the glass. "Drink your fill, *Blood Condentai*. May the Goddess bless every drop."

She took the glass from her hand, "Thank you."

Approaching the fountain, she dipped the cup into the thick, warm liquid. It dripped down the sides as she raised it from the fountain. She eyed the blood, her beast eager to take its drink. Lifting the glass to her lips, she indulged in the sweetness of the blood. But it did not taste as sweet as it would have from a fresh victim that still clung to life.

Valina glanced upon the empty glass. The urge to hunt clawing at her. "Do you wish for another drink or would you like me to take the glass, *Blood Condentai?*"

Valina handed over the glass. "Thank you."

The woman bowed her head and took the glass, "When you are ready to pray to the Goddess, feel free to pray wherever you like."

She nodded her head and the human drifted away, disappearing somewhere within the cathedral.

Valina approached one of the front row benches and seated herself upon the crimson velvet. For a long while, she stared at the fountain in silence. Thinking about her plan, thinking what could go wrong. How it might possibly go wrong.

With a sigh, she bowed her head and kept her voice low, "*Goddess, hear my prayer. Hear me as I ask for your guidance – something I rarely ask for. But this, what I plan to do, I need your blessing. Goddess, I need you.*" She hated how desperate she sounded but she was. This needed to work.

And then, she felt a warm brush against her cheek. As if a hand caressed it lovingly. Her eyes snapped open but found herself alone within the cathedral. Not a single soul to be found. Her hand reached up, her fingers brushing against her skin that was still warm.

Severina had heard her prayers and answered.

"Thank you, Goddess."

CHAPTER NINETEEN

ONE LAST MEETING

"One last meeting of rebels before the ball begins. Shall the king meet his end, or shall they?"

THE ROOM WAS full of rebels. All anxiously waiting to hear their leader's plan. The king's birthday was a night away. This would be their last meeting before then. Their one and only chance to listen carefully to Shandal's plan. Valina's nerves were on edge. She would be the king's prize, his one true gift. Or so he thought. Her hands fell down to her blades, resting upon their hilts. Her nerves calmed at the feel of the daggers. Her plan would work.

All murmured conversations were silenced as Shandal stood before the largely gathered group. His wife beside him, her hand resting upon his muscular arm. "As we all know, the king's ball is the next coming night. It shall be larger than any ball we have infiltrated. There shall be more risks of being caught, our chances of many of us making it out alive are very slim. As I'm sure you all know."

Valina blinked. Shandal planned on taking their group into the ball and rebelling then and there? That was madness. There was not enough of them to fight off the king's guards – many of them human and would be the first to die. It would be a suicide mission. None of them would make it out alive. It would be a massacre, the rebels wiped from the face of their dark world.

Shandal's dark eye glanced over to his children and Valina could see the regret and heartbreak within his eye. "I know what I ask would end in our deaths, but the choice remains yours. I shall not force you to go if you do not wish it. Perhaps some of us should remain behind so that what we built here shall not be for nothing, shall not be forgotten."

One man stepped forth, one of the king's guards that had become their inside person. "There will be many guards, every single one will be at the ball." The man glanced around him, looked into the eyes of every rebel. "We won't make it out alive."

Shandal nodded his head, he knew the outcome. All of them did.

It did not take long for the rebels to step forward and pledge their lives for the cause. Laying down their existence in hopes of a chance at taking down the king. So that their children, families, and friends would be freed from his wickedness. But they would never reach him. Not like she could...

"Wait."

All heads turned toward her then. All eyes watching.

"What is it, Valina?" Shandal's brows furrowed as he watched her closely with his one eye.

She took a step forward through the crowd, people stepping aside allowing her through until she stood before the leader. "You do not have to go through with that plan. It's madness. It's suicide."

He cocked his head, "You suggest something better?"

"I do." She heard gasps behind her as she dared offer another plan. Dared defy their leader.

Shandal did not share that same distain. Only nodding his head, encouraging her to go on.

"I plan on killing the king."

There were a few scoffs behind her, but they were silenced instantly as Shandal snapped his head up and glared at them. She found it hard not to smirk at that. "How do you plan on getting close to him?"

"I'm sure it is no secret by now that the king wishes to bed me, to make me his." Her skin crawled at the thought of allowing him to touch her in such an intimate way. "I plan on slicing his throat in his sleep once he's done with my body."

There was a look of pity within the leader's eyes. This was one of the reasons why the rebellion was born. To protect those from others would abuse them in such a way. But it was the better alternative than marching the entirety of the rebellion to their deaths.

"You know that I shall not ask you to do this."

"I know. I *want* to do this. I *need* to do this."

Shandal nodded his head and placed a warm hand upon her shoulder, "You are your father. He would be proud."

Her chest tightened at the mention of her father, memories clawing at the doors they were locked behind threatened to emerge. "Thank you."

"No, Valina. Thank you."

His wife, Shadari, stepped forward. Her hands coming to rest upon her shoulders, tears watering within her eyes. "My dear, you are a brave soul. Not many would take this chance."

Everyone within the room knew that if she did not return, then she was dead and possibly the king's newest decoration upon his fence.

Shadari pulled Valina into an embrace, weeping into her hair. "You make him pay, Valina. Make him pay for all that he has done and all that he has taken from us."

Valina's arms wrapped themselves around Shandal's wife. It was not often that she embraced others. "For Shadanar, for all those we have lost."

Shadari pulled back, her hands moving to grasp either side of Valina's face. Tears trekked down the woman's dark cheeks, her black eyes gazing into hers. *"May thy Goddess watch over you, Valina Veshanr."*

Then, her hands fell from Valina's face and she drifted off into the darkness. Her children following just behind her. Shandal glanced at Valina one last time, nodded his head to her, and followed after his wife.

Other rebels approached Valina, thanking her for her sacrifice. As if they knew she would not return. She should have taken offense, should have bared her fangs at them and growled. But she did not. Only nodding her head to them and watched them leave the room.

Though they did not speak it, she knew that each rebel was relieved. Their lives would not be lost. Their children not being forced to lose a parent or both. Families remaining together. Friends no longer fearing the loss of one another.

Lillian was the last rebel that approached her. The human woman standing before her. Those bright blue eyes taking in the *Blood Condentai.* "You'll come back. I know you will. But promise me one thing."

Valina cocked her head to the side, a brow raising. "What is it?"

Lillian offered a sweet smile that dripped with venom. "Give him a few stabs just for me. Okay? Make sure he feels them."

Valina's beast purred at the thought and she flashed a wicked smile back. "I promise."

Lillian stepped forward and wrapped her arms around Valina in a brief embrace. *"May thy Goddess watch over you."* Lillian whispered into her ear before stepping away. She did not mention Sybil. Knowing that Valina did not worship the earth Goddess as Lillian did.

There were only a few people remaining within the room now, and those few made their way toward Valina. Ventar, Diaval, Ashari, and Luzell all stood before her. Anger and fear blazed through Ventar's crimson eyes. Worry showed itself within Diaval and Ashari's gazes. Luzell's was the only one Valina could not understand. Too many emotions flickering within his bright blue eyes.

"This is madness!" Ventar roared. "You know what he'll do to you if you're alone with him! You know what he'll do if figures out your plan!"

Valina furrowed her brows, matching his rage with her own. "And the other plan wasn't madness? The other plan involved *all of us* marching to his castle an getting massacred. My plan saves hundreds of lives!"

She watched as the rage began to flicker within his eyes, the fire dying out. Defeat weighing upon his shoulders as he approached her and cupped one of her cheeks within his hand. "I would rather die alongside you, than live a life without you, my Valina."

Ashari stepped forward then, "And I feel the same, my hunter. My life would be empty without your presence. A part of my soul would be missing from this world."

Valina's gaze drifted toward Diaval to find his milky eyes already upon her, "I wish to know you in this life, Valina Veshanr. But if I must, I shall find you in the next."

Then, the child of light stepped forth. His blue gaze piercing. "I told you I wished to save you, even in the smallest of ways." His hand reached for her and grasped her hand. Warmth enveloped her skin as his hand began to glow, "I wish to gift a piece of light so that not all is dark when you face the king."

Before he removed his hand, she felt the weight of something drop into her palm. When he stepped back, she found a golden necklace resting within her hand. A large pendant hung from the thin chain. Oval in shape with intricate designs carved into the gold. In the center of the pendant was a small opening covered by a thin layer of glass. And behind that glass glowed the warmest light she had ever seen. It pulsated just like his aura when he called upon the sun's light that he harbored within him.

Her fingers curled over the warm gold. "Thank you, Luzell. Thank you." She would never know light or the peace it brought. But she had a small piece of its warmth – a small piece of him to carry with her into the darkness. And that was peace enough.

She held the necklace against her chest and took in the gathered people before her. Each one had snuck their way into her heart. Each one meaning something to her and she would be more than willing to lay down her life for them. They were hers and she was theirs.

"I promise to each of you that I will bring the king down, even if I have to go down with him. His blood shall run." She allowed her walls to fall, for this moment, so that she could let them see how much they meant to her. "If I don't return, then I want to thank each of you for being a part of my life. No matter how short our time together may have been. I'll take each memory with me into the afterlife when I meet our Goddess."

But she had hope that she would make it through this. The Goddess was by her side, she could feel her now. A steady and warm presence that lingered over her shoulders with just a touch of that coldness that lived within the dark.

She would not be alone when she faced the king.

After the meeting, Diaval escorted Luzell back to his hiding place. Ashari and Ventar returning to Valina's home. But she did not go with them. The forest had called to her – but it did not call to the monster within her. Instead it called to the carver that lingered within.

She needed this. Needed to do one last carving before she marched into death's dance. The trees rushed past her, the cold wind roaring against her pointed ears. Her long, midnight locks whipping behind her.

Soon enough, her spot was before her. She burst through the trees into the small clearing. Valina had not brought her carving blade with her. But her daggers hung by her sides. This would be the first she has ever taken a blade to wood that was not what her father had gifted her those years ago.

Approaching a tree, it seemed as though the tree stared back at Valina. As if it knew what she planned on doing to it and it did not seem to mind. Withdrawing one of the wicked daggers from its sheath, she palmed it within her hand. A thousand thoughts raced through her mind. A thousand images she could carve into the dead bark of the tree.

And finally, one spoke out amongst the rest. Screaming. And so, the dagger met with the tree. Bits of bark falling around her boots as she carved into the aged wood.

A face lingered within her mind. One she has not seen since she was a child. A woman. With skin as grey as hers, eyes the color of freshly spilled blood, and long flowing hair as dark as the shadows. The dagger carved every detail of the woman's face; to her slim, short nose to her pouted lips and slightly thick brows.

Then, the blade began to carve a smaller woman – a child that resembled her. A smile of happiness upon both their faces as the woman's arms embraced the child.

Tears burned within Valina's eyes as she carved into the tree, the blade digging deep into the wood. This was a pain that she never spoke of; never whispered to another soul. Watching her family burn had gutted her – destroyed a part of her. But when her mother left behind her only child, abandoning her to this dark world it left a wound that could never be mended. A gaping hole carved into her heart, just as she carved into wood.

Valina thought that perhaps the pain of watching her husband burn, her family burn, had caused her to vanish within the shadows. But why leave behind the only family she had left? The only child she ever birthed into this world. Why?

That was a question that Valina would never have answered.

Why?

Valina returned the dagger to its sheath and stared upon the carving before. Stared into her mother's eyes. Her hand reached and trailed across her mother's hair that flowed around. The wood was smooth against her fingers.

"When I'm finished with the king, I will find you, mother. No matter if you're dead or alive. I will find you."

CHAPTER TWENTY

TRUTH SHINES IN THE DARKNESS

"The time to dance with death has come."

THE NIGHT OF the ball had arrived. The town bustling with festivities. Music could be heard all around their dark world. Laughter and cheers. Dancers performing through the streets. Sweets being sold at every cart, their enticing scents filtering through the air. Valina found herself drawn to the festivities but today was not a day of play. No matter how her mouth watered at the thought of the sweets.

The king's ball would soon begin and the dress that hung from the back of her bathroom door stared at her. Guards had arrived earlier within the night to deliver it. No sign of the rebel guard could be found and Valina hoped that the worst had not happened to him.

The dress was beautiful, and she hated to admit that. But the king knew her tastes well. As dark as the night with skirts that ruffled in layers of crimson to the floor. The neck line cut into a dangerously low V, dipping between her breasts and exposing most of them for all eyes to see. The dress was almost off the shoulder, the sleeves long and coming to points atop her hands. Sleeves crafted from the finest lace. The corset seemed to be made from a leather material, tied together in the back with crimson buttons lining down the front.

And she knew she would look divine in that dress. And a small part of her was eager to wear the damned thing.

She was standing before it, her body nude with only a black velvet choker wrapped around her neck, when there was a knock upon her door. "Come in."

The door opened to reveal Ventar. His crimson eyes trailed down her body with a hunger afire within his gaze. She flashed a smile to him. "What brings you to my room, Ventar? Hoping for a quick moment of love before I leave?"

"Though I would love nothing more than to bed you right now, my dear, I have brought you something." Within one of his hands he held her belt that her daggers rested in, the other hand hidden behind his back.

She raised a brow to him. "What is it?"

He gestured toward her bed and she seated herself upon the edge. Ventar knelt before her, so close to that spot between her legs and she found herself wishing he would fuck her here and now. And she could see him wishing the same.

"Though I cannot be with you, I want you to be armed. Though I know you probably had the idea already."

"I was going to take one of my daggers with me, but I find myself in need of a thigh peace." She had two once before but couldn't find the damned things when she needed them most.

It was then that Ventar's cocky smile appeared. "Then I have brought the perfect gift." Ventar moved the hand he had been hiding behind his back to reveal a leather thigh peace. And she noticed that the initials V.V. were embroidered into the leather in the color of blood. "I had this made for your birthday, but I thought now would be the best time to gift it to you."

Valina's birthday would come in two months, when winter hit the world at full force and plunged them into coldness.

"May I?"

Valina offered her bare leg to him, "If you insist."

Once his hand touched her skin, warmth flared within her. His fingers lazily trailing up her leg until they reached her thigh. "Continue tempting me, Ventar, and you'll find yourself missing a hand."

"Apologies, my dear Valina."

The smooth leather wrapped around Valina's thigh and Ventar clasped the buckle, locking it in place. Then, taking one of her daggers from her belt, he slipped the wicked dark blade into the sheath that rested against her bare thigh. "It fits you beautifully." His finger traced over the embroidered initials.

Valina leaned toward him, her two fingers placing themselves beneath his chin to tilt his head back. His crimson gaze locked with hers. "I see it in your eyes, Ventar."

He did not question her. Did ask what she saw, for he knew. "Is it truly such a bad thing that I worry?"

Leaning her head down, her lips sealed over his. "You need to learn to have more faith in me. Or have you forgotten that I am capable of defending myself?"

Ventar's hand grasped hers, moving it away from his chin. His thumb tracing lines back and forth within her palm. "When you unleash yourself upon him, make sure that he knows exactly what he's paying for."

Valina flashed her fangs, "Trust me, dear Ventar. He shall be begging for mercy before I'm done with him. Blood shall stain those castle walls and it shall not be mine."

Ventar smiled, "How truly wicked you are, my dear."

Light footsteps entered the room and Valina glanced toward the door to find Ashari standing there. The *Ghost Condentai's* silver eyes took in the two before her. "I came to help you dress for the ball, am I interrupting something?"

Ventar stood back on his feet, "Not all." He glanced back at Valina for a moment before excusing himself from the room.

"Is it that time already?"

Ashari approached the dress and took it down from its hanger. "I'm afraid so, my hunter."

Valina rose from the bed and Ashari held the dress low so that she could step into it. The fabric brushed against her legs like soft silk. Ashari pulled it up Valina's body and she slipped her arms into the long sleeves. Another perfect fit. The king knew her body well.

Ashari stepped behind her to begin tying the corset. She pulled until Valina could hardly breathe – one of the reasons Valina hated corsets. They were too constricting. But they flattered her body, cinching her waist and complimenting her curves.

Once the dress was on, Valina followed Ashari into the bathroom where the *Ghost Condentai* would help fix her hair and makeup. "You know you don't have to do this."

Ashari's cool fingers began to brush through her midnight hair. "I know. I enjoy doing this."

Ashari pulled all of Valina's hair to one side – the left. Leaving one wisp of dark hair falling before one pointed ear on the other side. The rest had been smoothed and pinned back with a ruby clasp. A dark wisp of bang fell across her face, almost covering her left eye. Then Ashari's fingers began to work, weaving thick strands of hair together in one long braid that swept down to Valina's waist. Small clips with rubies atop them were placed throughout the braid. Like small droplets of glistening blood.

Once she was finished with the hair, Ashari pulled open one of the drawers in the bathroom counter and retrieved the makeup. When she faced Valina once more, she saw a dark stick held within the woman's pale hand. "Close your eyes, my hunter."

So, she did. She felt the pressure of the stick press against her eye and smear that darkness onto her grey lid. "Now, open them and look up." Then the stick moved to the bottom of her eye. "Look down for me." Ashari changed from the dark stick to another with a brush at the end. Lowering her lids, Ashari began to coat her lashes.

Ashari took a step back to admire her work, "One more thing."

She returned the makeup to the drawer and took out one last stick, the shade of blood. "We can't forget the lips."

With a steady hand, Ashari lined the outside of Valina's lips first before coloring them the shade of crimson. The *Ghost Condentai* smiled, "Always beautiful, my hunter. You shall turn heads at the ball."

"All thanks to you, Ashari." When Valina caught a glimpse of herself in the mirror, she found a beautiful reflection staring back. Valina had always thought herself beautiful but dressed like this she admitted that she was stunning.

"I simply did your hair and makeup. You have always been beautiful, my hunter."

Valina rested a hand upon the *Ghost Condentai's* cheek, her skin cool and soft. "I would kiss you, but I'd rather not ruin the lipstick you just put on me."

A giggle escaped Ashari's lips. But their moment together had been ruined by a pounding on the door. A sigh escaped Valina. The guards had arrived to escort her to the ball and take with them the mural for the king.

Ashari raised onto the tip of her toes and placed her cool lips against Valina's cheek. "I love you, my hunter. *May thy Goddess watch over you.*"

"And I love you, Ashari."

Before she left the room, she eyed the golden necklace that rested upon a small table beside her bed. The golden light pulsated from it like a beating heart. Her hand snatched it from the table and slipped it into one of the hidden pockets in her dress. She felt the warmth from it radiating against her side.

When Valina opened the door, she found four guards standing there. Still no sign of the hidden rebel amongst them. She took a step aside, allowing two men in to gather the mural. They marched into the living room and lingered in there a breath too long. Valina forced away the smirk that twitched at the corner of her lips as they stared upon the Goddess carved into the wood above their king.

When they finally appeared in the hall carrying the large piece of wood, they eyed her as if she were crazy. She supposed it did not help when she flashed a smile to them revealing her fangs.

The town was still awake. The festival surrounding them. Fires roaring, people laughing and singing drunkenly through the streets. The dancers drifting along the wind as the air carried them. Their bodies moving with grace, each move fluid like a shadow.

The aroma of candied apples found her, and her mouth began to water. She wished for nothing more in this moment than to be sinking her teeth into a juicy apple coated in caramel.

The guards on either side of her kept their gazes straight ahead, as if they were scared to even be caught catching a glimpse of her. Not a single one of them even dared to look her in the eyes except for the first two who questioned her carving. Since then, their gazes have been kept away from wandering to her.

When they finally reached the castle, she noticed not many people had arrived. Her ears only caught the sound of a few voices coming from within the castle, the doors wide open and inviting. As they approached the gate, Valina's gaze dared to drift toward the fence. And it was there that she found Shadanar and the other rebels. Their eyes had already been plucked from their sockets by other monsters who roamed the night. The great crows of shadow feasting upon the rotting corpses.

One of the creatures still lingered. The bird the size of a small child. It feasted upon one of the corpses of a woman. It lifted its head from its meal and its glowing red eyes met with Valina's. Blood and flesh clung to the creature's beak. The crow stretched out its wings, wisps of shadows dancing on the ends of each feather and let out a *caw* that echoed through the night.

She did not allow the creature to bother her, still holding its gaze until it cocked its head and returned to its meal.

Valina averted her gaze from the bodies of the rebels. The blood within her veins began to boil, the dagger that hung at her thigh cried out to her and she had to resist the urge to unleash her beast upon the guards that escorted her.

When they reached the stairs, that was when the king decided to reveal himself. He stood at the top, dressed in the finest clothes he owned. The fabric so dark he could have blended in with the night. And she noticed the hints of crimson upon his clothes. On the cuffs of his sleeves, were embroidered designs. The collar of his tunic trimmed in crimson. They would be the perfect match at the ball.

And that was why he had chosen this dress.

That damned crown rested atop his head, his dark hair neatly combed back. Her rage began to claw at her until she met with his gaze. For a moment, she faltered in her steps. For when she looked into his eyes, there was something different to be found there.

A look of affection. But not of the wicked kind – not the kind where his thoughts danced with her naked body. It was the soft and gentle kind. And then, came the sadness she found there.

Valina shook her head. No. The king knew nothing of gentleness and sadness. Did not know pain. It was an act to fool her and she would not dance into his trap.

The two guards ahead of them held the mural she had carved. The king glanced down at them, "Aw, the mural. Reveal it to me."

The guards flipped the wood so that the image could face him. Her heart leapt with excitement. Waiting to see his reaction – his anger. His crimson gaze stared upon the carving, taking in every detail. And there was no trace of rage to be found, not even the slightest hint of annoyance.

Finally, his gaze had met with hers and she found a smile upon his face. "Wonderful work, Valina. Though I knew it would be beautiful." His attention returned to the guards, "Hang it above my throne, now."

The two men hurriedly made their way up the stairs and passed the king, disappearing into the castle.

Valina blinked at the king before her. Confusion causing her feet to become rooted in place. Was this a dream? Had she really wakened and dressed for his ball or was this all in her mind and she still lay sound asleep within her bed?

One of the guards beside her nudged her with his elbow. "Well go on then. Don't keep your king waiting." Annoyance echoed within the man's voice.

Valina whirled on him, fangs barred and snarls escaping her. *"Do not touch me unless you wish to have your arm torn from your body."*

Footsteps sounded down the stairs, "Though it would be a lovely sight, I do prefer to keep my guards intact."

"If he touches me again, I cannot promise I'll behave."

The king smiled at her and offered his hand, his gaze drifting down her body in admiration. "I knew that dress would suit you, my dear. You look ravishing."

She glanced down at his hand before slipping hers into his palm, allowing him to lead her into his castle. "Thank you." Valina could push him so much before she had to act somewhat decent toward the man who murdered people for even looking at him.

Behind her, she heard the sound of more people arriving to the king's birthday ball. Giggled laughter echoing through the night. Before their laughter was swallowed by the sound of music once Valina stepped foot inside the ballroom.

Black lanterns hung low from the grand ceiling, casting a warm glow about the room as fire danced within them. Black ribbons wound around the pillars that circled the room. Crimson drappings sweeping above the dance floor. In the center of the room was a circular stage with a small band atop it, playing their instruments. Flutes, harps, and violins. Each person dressed in the color of blood.

The women wearing dresses that clung to their bodies and pooled at their feet, their sleeves long. Their hair kept up atop their head with wisps of hair framing their faces. The men wore crimson tunics with black trousers. Their hair kept neatly combed to the side.

Then, ahead of them, Valina saw the king's throne and the mural that now hung above it. A perfect carving of him in all his glory with the Goddess watching over him.

Voices filtered into the room as groups flooded into the castle behind them. Many of them approaching the servants that scurried about, requesting a drink. Valina noticed one *Blood Condentai* woman, she approached a young human girl with a wicked smile. The girl cowered beneath the woman's gaze.

"My sweet, I find myself in need of a drink. May I?" The woman knew the girl feared her and she thrived off that fear – Valina did as well when it came to her victims. It drove the beast inside of her wild.

The servant did not offer the knife she held within her hand, for she knew the *Blood Condentai* wished to fetch the blood herself. Wishing to sink her teeth into that soft flesh. So, the servant obeyed and exposed her neck to the monster. The woman ran her tongue over her lips before she plunged her fangs into the girl's skin. A gasp of pain escaped her lips as the monster began to feast.

Watching the woman drink, caused Valina's own thirst to begin. She found herself wishing for a taste of blood. She had not hunted before the ball, had not drank before waltzing into the castle.

A human boy approached then, as if he could sense her growing thirst. He held a tray of clear glasses filled to the brim with fresh blood. He bowed his head, "Miss Valina, may I offer you a drink?"

She flashed a smile before swiping one of the glasses from the tray, "Thank you."

The human bowed once more before walking away. Though he hid it well, she could still sense his fear.

Tipping her head back, she downed the glass. The blood flowing into her mouth and cascading down her throat like a waterfall of the sweetest pleasures. A moan escaped her as she savored the taste, as the monster within her drank its fill. Flicking out her tongue, she licked at the blood that dripped from the corner of her lips.

A moment later, another servant – a girl – appeared carrying a tray of empty glasses. "Miss Valina, may I take your glass?"

Valina set the glass upon the girl's tray and she scurried off to gather others.

All around them, the people gathered in the center of the room to dance. Surrounding the stage that the band played upon. A sea of dresses twirling about in shades of grey, black, and crimson. Music guiding the dancing partners movements. A steady rhythm that flowed through the room, drifting along the air. A haunting melody whispering into their ears.

The king faced her then and offered his hand, "May I have this dance, Valina?"

She raised a brow to him. Never was he this polite, rarely did he say her name without a hint of flirtation. Her hand fell into his. "You may."

And the King of Ventaria led her into the dance of death.

King Valnar spun Valina, her midnight dress fanning out around her in ripples of crimson. Then she found herself in the arms of the king once more as he pulled her back but gently. His touch affectionate but caring, his hands never daring to venture further than her hips. There was a softness about him – within his crimson eyes she could see it reflected back at her but also something else. Pain. As if his very soul ached. Something dark edged within his heart and nothing could cure it.

His touch did not sicken her. Did not cause her skin to crawl. And she felt like a traitor. To her family, to the rebels. To everyone. To herself. For she found that she enjoyed this moment with him. And she could not understand why.

The blade strapped to her thigh did not sing out to her, did not plea to eat into the king's flesh. It remained silent and listening.

"Valina." The king's voice was whispered and soothing, "there is something you must know."

"What is it?" Fear nipped at her then.

Had he found out of her plan? Did he know of the blade strapped to her thigh? Or had he found out that she was a rebel, a traitor to the throne?

They danced around the room, passing other partners who laughed and stared lovingly into one another's eyes.

The king kept his voice low, "I am a prisoner within my own skin."

She blinked at him. Confusion forcing her brows to furrow. "What do you mean?"

King Valnar's gaze flickered about the room and she noticed that he was taking note of the guards, how all of their eyes were upon him. Their hands resting upon their swords as if to threaten him – to scare him.

But, why?

He dipped his head low, his lips brushing against the skin of her ear. His breath warm. "My father is alive."

Valina felt her heart sink into her stomach. That wasn't possible. He couldn't be. "How?"

"He survived the poisoning, but his body was left paralyzed." His answers were quick, and his voice kept low, so none could hear.

The former king was rumored to be poisoned by an assassin, killing him. None knew how the person broke into the castle, who they were. They had poisoned the king and vanished without a trace.

They had never been found.

"But what does that have to do with you?" Her brows furrowed.

A heavy sigh escaped Valnar as his gaze met with hers once more. There was a heavy sadness to be found within his eyes, as if she could see his soul shattering. His hand came to rest upon her cheek, his thumb brushing against her skin. Her body warmed at his touch and she leaned into his palm.

I am such a damned fool. She thought. *A traitor to my heart. A traitor to my family and the rebels.*

She should not trust this so easily, it could be his way to fool her. To trick her into his arms. But when she gazed into his eyes and truly saw him, she saw the truth shouting back at her.

"He is *Condentai* of all. He controls my mind and body, using it as if it were his own. I am his vessel, his weapon, *his body.*"

Valina could hardly believe what she was hearing. Her mind was a whirlwind. The king was one of the rarest of *Condentai.* A kind that was supposed to be ones of legend for none have been heard of in years, hundreds. Even when he reigned, none had known.

Valina felt her blood boil within her veins, her monster clawing at its cage to be set free. To devour his father and drink its fill of his blood. "How can I free you?" Her voice dripped with the promise of death.

Valnar said nothing, only gazing upon her with heartbreak in his eyes as his hand moved beneath her chin and tilted her head back. Lowering his head, his mouth lingered before her own and she felt her heart roar within her chest. His breath traced along her lips, sending a wave of heat crashing over her. Valina pressed herself against him, molding her body against his and his hand moved to the lower of her back, the other remained beneath her chin.

Then his lips had met with hers. His mouth sealing over her own. The kiss had begun sweet and gentle, leaving Valina wishing for more. Her hand slid up his chest and found itself tangling within his midnight locks, his hair soft to the touch as she curled her fingers into it. She nearly moaned as Valnar slipped his tongue into her mouth, exploring until it met with hers.

She felt as his fingers clawed at her back, at the dress, wishing to feel the skin beneath. And she found herself wanting nothing more than to vanish somewhere within the castle and fuck him until the darkness claimed them. As her body pressed itself more against Valnar, she felt his hardness against her and it ignited that warmth between her thighs. A small whimper escaped her as his mouth left hers, leaving her wishing for much more.

There was a smile to be found upon his face. A true one that had not been seen on him in many years. "All I wished for my birthday was to dance with you, Valina. I never would have imagined I would have been blessed with the opportunity. Perhaps the Goddess heard my prayers after all."

Valina's heart ached. So long she has hated him, plotting his death, imagining his blood upon her hands. And guilt tore its way through her. Ripping her apart, shredding her insides. She presumed the boy he once was had died but he had been there this whole time, covered by a wicked mask placed there by his father.

"How can I free you, Valnar?" She hated how desperate her voice sounded. How lost and defeated she must look.

She was a *Blood Condentai*, a monster to be feared.

But even monsters could be defeated. Could have a heart.

Gently, he brushed a strand of hair behind her ear. "Tonight, you saved me, Valina."

Tears threatened to fall, burning behind her eyes. She hated this. Hated how helpless Valnar looked, accepting his fate at the hands of his father. Hated how she could not help him.

"Tell me."

"Only death shall save me."

She shook her head. "No there must be another way. We can find it. I swear to you that I shall free you."

Valnar glanced around them once more, the guards watching them closely. "You should leave, Valina. Now. Before my father decides he wishes to take control of me once more."

"No. I won't leave you. Not now." Not when she had learned the truth. She couldn't leave him here.

Valina cast a glance over her shoulder, noting all the guards. There were too many for her to fight, too many for her to control their blood. They would not escape here alive.

Her gaze slid back to Valnar's. "Take me to your room, Valnar."

He raised a brow at her.

"Everyone knows the king wishes to bed me. But no one knows it's truly you, the guards won't think that I know the truth. They'll think I finally have fallen into the king's arms. They won't bat an eye."

His gaze flickered toward the guards once more. Slowly, he nodded his head. "I shall have to act like my father, please forgive me for whatever I say and however I act."

She nodded her head and allowed him to lead her away from the dance floor. His hand rested low on her back, where his father would have placed it. His face morphing into the mask it knew well. Wickedness showing itself within his eyes but only Valina would notice the pain within them too.

He approached a set of double doors on the far side of the room, walking up the four stairs that led to them. Two guards were stationed on either side. Valnar flashed a grin, showing his pointed teeth.

"It appears as though my night here shall end early." He drew Valina close to him, "I have finally persuaded Valina into bedding me." His hand traced along her cheek, "I knew it was only a matter of time before I claimed you as mine, my dear."

The guards cast suspicious glances at one another. "Please hurry, a woman does not like to wait." Valina snapped, baring her own fangs at the men.

The men bowed their heads and opened the doors, "Enjoy your night, my king." The guards eyes traveled along her body, taking in her form. Seeming to undress her with their minds, wishing to bed her just as their king would.

Not a word was spoken as Valnar led her through the doors and into the darkened hallway. Toward his bedroom where the night would truly begin.

CHARACTER GLOSSARY

VALINA VESHANR: A *Blood Condentai*, 300 years old, grey skinned, long black hair, crimson eyes, fangs, tall, and immortal.

HER STORY: Family was burned when she was a child, forced to watch. Her mother and herself were the only exceptions to the burning. After her family was killed her mother disappeared and hasn't been seen since. Valina joins the rebels years later after witnessing another burning. When she is not hunting for blood and killing those responsible for the deaths of innocents, you can find her within her home she made with her own hands, carving intricate designs in wood or crafting figurines.

VENTAR VANNAR: (Part of Valina's Harem) A *Blood Condentai*, 200 years old, grey skinned, half shaven head other half long black hair, crimson eyes, fangs, tall, and immortal.

HIS STORY: He was forced to watch his mother get ran through on the wicked fence around the king's castle after she had been wrongfully named a traitor to the crown. Ever since that day, Ventar has kept a deep seeded hatred within his heart, seeking the blood of the king to avenge his lost mother. He spends his nights just as any other of his kind, hunting for blood. Or, hunting for Valina, the only woman he has eyes for.

ASHARI ASHLAMA: (Part of Valina's Harem) A *Ghost Condentai*, 120 years old, pale skinned, long white hair, silver eyes, short, and immortal.

HER STORY: Valina and Ashari's paths crossed a hundred years ago. A day where rebels were brutally ran through on that wicked fence and Ashari dared do what no other of her kind did, release the dead rebels spirits to the Goddess. It was years after the king's son had taken the throne as his and when he had sent guards after Ashari, Valina stood before the woman. The king had matched gazes with Valina and he knew that she would slaughter any guard who meant harm upon the *Ghost Condentai*. After that day, Ashari moved in with Valina, securing her safety and to this day, she still lives with the *Blood Condentai*.

KING VALNAR VENTARA: (Part of Valina's Harem) A *Blood Condentai*, 300 years old, grey skinned, short cut black hair kept combed to the side, crimson eyes, fangs, tall, and immortal.

HIS STORY: A young boy born into a cruel fate, raised by a wicked man whose wickedness plagued him. Years of witnessing the cruel punishments his father dealt to his people had warped his mind, breeding another wicked king. To this day, he rules just as his father had before him with punishments just as wicked. (Or so everyone believed until the truth had revealed itself.) And Valina mourns for that little boy she first saw all those years ago. A boy who had looked upon her with pity when her family burned.

DIAVAL DARTHOLLOW: (Part of Valina's Harem) A *Dead Condentai*, 100 years old, sickly pale skin, short grey hair that falls into his eyes, milky eyes, purple/grey hollowness beneath eyes, medium height, and immortal.

HIS STORY: Family was long dead before he was birthed into this world, his own mother dying while birthing him. A family friend took him beneath her care – a human. But she suffered a cruel punishment not long after, a public whipping that stole her life away for stealing food so that the child may eat. Diaval himself whipped to serve as a reminder. Three lashes forever marking his back.

SHANDAL SHANDORAL: A *Shadow Condentai*, 500 years old, black skin, both sides of head shaved save for a single black braid down the center of his head down toward his back, wholly black eyes, patch over one eye for it is lost, crooked nose, scars scattered across his body, leader of the rebellion, and immortal.

LUZELL LINOW: (Part of Valina's Harem) A *Light Condentai*, 20 years old, brown skin, golden hair, blue eyes, tall.

HIS STORY: Luzell traveled into the land of dark, to kill the king. Assassins were sent into the land of light, murdering whoever stepped into their line of sight and his brother was one of the king's victims. Many of the merchants were killed during trades if they dared to look the king in his eyes. Luzell was caught, made a prisoner, and beaten. Then, the king was ready to execute him in front of all his people. Until he escaped. And his paths crossed with Valina and it was then that he joined the rebels, ready to help bring down the king.

THE SERIES WILL CONTINUE IN

BOOK TWO:

BLOOD AND NIGHT

MY OTHER BOOKS:

THE FORGOTTEN KINGDOMS TRILOGY

FORGOTTEN KINGDOMS STORIES

THE NIGHTWALKERS DUOLOGY

A TALE OF TWO PACKS

THREE YEAR WINTER

Made in the USA
Middletown, DE
30 July 2019